THE GOLLYWHOPPER GAMES

Friend or Foe

By Jody Feldman

Illustrations by Victoria Jamieson

Greenwillow Books
An Imprint of HarperCollins Publishers

The Gollywhopper Games: Friend or Foe
Text copyright © 2015 by Jody Feldman
Illustrations copyright © 2015 by Victoria Jamieson

Library of Congress Cataloging-in-Publication Data
Feldman, Jody.
The Gollywhopper Games : friend or foe / by Jody Feldman ;
illustrations by Victoria Jamieson.
pages cm.
"Greenwillow Books."
Summary: Zane thinks about little but football until after his second concussion,
when his parents say he must take a year off, so when he gets a chance to compete in
the Gollywhopper Games he is excited about applying many of the skills that help
him excel on the football field to a different kind of competition.
ISBN 978-0-06-221128-6 (hardback)
[1. Contests—Fiction. 2. Games—Fiction. 3. Puzzles—Fiction.
4. Coaching (Athletics)—Fiction. 5. Conduct of life—Fiction.]
I. Title. II. Title: Friend or foe.
PZ7.F3357752Gom 2014 [Fic]—dc23 2014035850
First Edition

15 16 17 18 19 CG/RRDH 10 9 8 7 6 5 4 3 2 1

 Greenwillow Books

In memory of my dad,
the original Bill,
who guides me even still.

To hear his friends describe it, it had been a thing of beauty: Zane Braycott soaring sideways—in slow motion, they swore—to make an epic catch. Honestly? It was stupidity. When the baseball shot the gap between second and third, Zane should have let it go. This was gym class, and this was *not* football. But his instincts had taken over, which caused his chin to hit the ground, and his teeth to clank together.

Now at lunch, it was like his dizziness had teamed with the combo-smell of peanut butter, tuna fish, and french fries to create some superscent. It weaseled up his nose and made the lights a little too bright; his turkey wrap, a little too salty; his friends, especially, a little too loud. It was like he could feel his brain and not in a good way.

His core group was deep in joke mode with the doofus managers of their football team, Thing 1 and Thing 2, who were sitting at their table today. Zane was spacing out on the conversation, but he knew the JZs—Jamaal, Jerome, Julio, and Zack—were using the Things to set up another inside gag. The Things deserved it. They always bragged how they were the heart of the team, but they pretty much stood around laughing at their own lame jokes until Coach yelled at them to do their jobs. Right now, though, none of it was amusing. Zane wanted to find a bed and rest his brain.

At least these symptoms felt different from last November's, and now he could name the months of the year backwards. Even so, he needed to prove to himself that the headache and the overly bright lights were born from fear, just fear, because Zane could not afford another concussion.

He zeroed in on the conversation and stayed with it for the rest of lunch. He nailed the vocab quiz in comm arts. He *habla*'ed *espanol* when he was asked. But his head was still clouding as Mr. Longley droned on about the freezing point in Celsius. Zane propped his chin with his hand, willing the steady pressure to get him through this last half hour. Then he'd go home, rest—

Bzzz! Bzzz!

Thirty minutes already? Had he passed out? No one was rushing the door, everyone was asking about the buzzer, and the clock, itself, had barely moved. Zane breathed.

"And now we come to what promises to be an unfortunate waste of time." Mr. Longley held up a thick, yellow envelope. "I have no idea what this is nor its purpose, but when I hand out these sheets"—he paused to read the writing on the envelope—"'You will have ten minutes to turn them over and complete as many questions as you can. Please put your answers in the blanks provided. You may use the margins of the paper as work space. If you can't figure out an answer, skip the question. This will not be graded; this will not go on your permanent record.'"

He looked up from the envelope, over his glasses. "This will, however, take valuable time from the seventh-grade curriculum." He slapped a paper on each desk. "Put your name on the side where it says 'Name.' You'd think, by now, we wouldn't need to tell you that. When I say go, turn the paper over and begin."

Zane would go. He would answer these questions. All of them. That would prove his brain wasn't bleeding, that he could play spring football, that he wouldn't be sidelined forever.

"Go!"

Zane turned over his paper. Math!

Question #1
* * * * * * * * * *

Bob ordered a pizza with 48 pieces of pepperoni at 10 cents apiece, 30 pieces of sausage at 14 cents apiece, 26 pieces of green pepper at 6 cents apiece, 3 different types of cheese at $1.28 per type, and the $3.89 medium crust. The sauce was free.

Zane stopped to calculate the cost of the pepperoni and sausage. If he could do that in his head, he was probably fine. Okay. Four dollars and eighty cents in pepperoni. Then thirty times fourteen, which—

His eye caught the last sentence of the question.

Write an A, if Bob is an omnivore; B, if he's an herbivore; or C, if he's a carnivore. _____

A. $18.19

B. $18.39

C. $17.19

D. $18.29

Since when had Zane forgotten to read the entire thing? Since the dive? He wrote *A*.

Question #2
✳ ✳ ✳ ✳ ✳ ✳ ✳ ✳ ✳ ✳

If you eliminate one letter from each name below, the remaining letters, in order, will spell a common word. Rearrange the eliminated letters to spell another common word.

_____

Alice
Peter
Clement
Dewey
Albert

Rearrange letters with a rearranged brain?

He'd try. If he got rid of the *A* in "Alice" . . .

Okay. That was a word. Next. If he dropped the *P* in "Peter," it'd be "eter." No. The *E*? "Pter" sounded like someone spitting. The *T*! Next. "Clement." Not the *C*. Not the *L*. Yes, the *L*. Not so hard, at least so far. Next. "Dewey." Either "ewey," "dwey," "deey," "dewy," or "dewe." "Dewy?" Filled with dew? That was the only one that seemed remotely right.

So far, the dropped letters could spell "late," but he still needed one more. Not the *A* in "Albert." Not the *L*. The *B*! L-A-T-E plus a *B*. "Blate"? "Bleat"? Was that what sheep did? Or was that spelled with two *E*s? "Belat." "Betal," like "petal"? Maybe it started with a *T*. A lot of words did. And a lot of words ended in –L-E. Or –B-L-E? That was it! "Table."

Question #3
✳ ✳ ✳ ✳ ✳ ✳ ✳ ✳ ✳ ✳

Which number can you put in place of the question mark if:

• you need to fit all numbers one through nine in the squares below; and,

• no square that touches another square—even at the corners—has a number that comes next in order (before or after); and,

• we've given you the following head start.

	8	?	9	
		1	4	

If he eliminated the numbers already filled in, the question mark could only be 2, 3, 5, 6, or 7. And it couldn't be 7 because the 8 was right next to it. Two, either, because 1 was directly underneath. That left him with 3, 5, and 6. The 4, though, was touching at the corner, so the question mark couldn't be 3 or 5 either. He wrote *6* in the blank.

Question #4
✼ ✼ ✼ ✼ ✼ ✼ ✼ ✼ ✼ ✼

How many Fs are in the following sentence?
The Office of Tariffs failed to offer all
of the officers full information of their
official duties. _____

Easy. "Office," "Tariffs," "failed," "offer." Seven *F*s in the first row. In the second, "officers," "full," "information," "of." Five. And just two in the third line. Fourteen total. Or was that too easy?

Zane glanced at the clock. He still had almost five minutes for two more questions, enough time to count again. This time, though, he'd start backwards, with the *s* in "duties." Two *F*s in the bottom row. Up a line. First letter, another *F.* Then one, two, three, four, five more for a total of six in row two. He'd skipped one of the "ofs" the first time. And they sneaked another "of" in the top row, too. He changed his answer to sixteen.

Question #5
✱ ✱ ✱ ✱ ✱ ✱ ✱ ✱ ✱ ✱ ✱

The names of four cities are below, but each has been broken into two parts. Reconstruct the names of the cities. In any order, write the country where you'd find each city.

Age
Par

At
Mad
Anchor
Rid
Is
Hens

_____

_____

_____

_____

At least these were hunks of words, not individual letters. And they'd all be cities. Fastest method? Trial and error.

"Age-par." No. "Age-at." "Age-mad." "Age-anchor." Wait. In Alaska. Anchorage! He wrote *Alaska* in the first blank. Next. "Par-at." "Par-mad." "Par-rid." Paris! He scribbled down *France.* Just two pairs left. "At-mad." "At-rid." "At-hens." No, no, and no. He skipped to the next one. "Mad-at." "Mad-rid." Madrid! So "At" went with "Hens." "Hensat"? "Athens"? Athens! Why didn't he see "Athens" in the first place? Didn't matter. He added Spain and Greece to France and Alaska—

Stop! His brain was working enough to catch his mistake. Alaska wasn't a country. He erased it and wrote *United States*.

Question #6
* * * * * * * * * *

Adam, Bella, and Chris each brought a gift to the party.

The gifts were: a jigsaw puzzle, a soccer ball, and a video game.

Each gift was wrapped in one of three colors: red, yellow, or blue.

The person who brought the puzzle did not wrap it in red.

Bella's gift, in the yellow wrapping, did not have 1,000 pieces.

Adam did not bring the video game, but he wrapped his gift in red.

Which present did Chris bring and what color wrapping paper did he use?

_____ and

_____

If Bella wrapped hers in yellow and Adam wrapped his in red, then Chris's had to be blue. Zane wrote that in the second blank. So which present was blue? First clue: The puzzle was not red. Second clue: The "1,000 pieces" was not yellow. Of the three, only a puzzle would have one thousand pieces. So if the puzzle wasn't red or wasn't yellow, it had to be blue.

If Zane figured that out in his head, no way he had a concussion. He wrote *puzzle*, put his pencil on the desk, and let his head follow fast.

CHAPTER 2

"**P**encils down! Eyes up!" Why did Mr. Longley need to bark? "I am supposed to grade these, but I cannot see it as a good use of my time. I trust you will be honest, especially because who knows why this matters. Please take out your red pens, then switch papers."

Zane leaned over to unzip his backpack. Note to self: no leaning. He rubbed his temples.

"I know," said Zack, sitting next to him. "It's hard to think at the end of the day."

"It's hard for you to think, period." The words vibrated around Zane's ears, along with Zack's laughter.

Mr. Longley looked directly at Zane. "The rest of you, exchange papers with your neighbors. Mr. Braycott, as we will accomplish nothing more today, please come center stage and entertain us all. You will read the answers. I'll grade your little sheet."

Funny on command? Not going to happen. Not that Mr. Longley actually wanted him to be. Zane traded his sheet for the answers. "Okay if I lean against your desk?"

"If it will entertain us."

At least it would be comfortable. But he pretended to plant his hand on the desk and purposefully missed. Big mistake. He got a laugh, though. Then he backed up to the desk for support and read the answer sheet. "'One is *A*. Two is either 'table' or 'bleat,' B-L-E-A-T. Count either right. Three is the number six. Four is the number sixteen. Five is, in any order, 'France, Greece, Spain, and the United States,' also correct, written as 'U.S.,' 'U.S.A.,' or 'America.'"

"Though, technically," said Mr. Longley, "we all know America would be incorrect."

"'And the answer to number six is 'puzzle' and 'blue,' in that order.'"

Zane held out the answer sheet, but Mr. Longley waved it away. "Stay here for a moment, Mr. Braycott. And I invite you each to claim your own paper and stand."

Was it always this noisy when everyone stood?

"Now," said Mr. Longley. "Please take a seat if you have two or fewer answers right."

About six people sat.

"Three or fewer?" Five more, down.

"Four or fewer?" Eight people were left.

"If you have fewer than all six right, please sit."

Should Zane sit?

Mr. Longley didn't say. He was nodding at Kelly. "Bring your paper up here. For what it's worth, Kelly, you and Zane got all six correct. You may both take your seats."

Zane sat to the murmurs and the back pats, and the smile he couldn't hide. That proved it. No concussion. And absolutely no more diving in gym class. He'd gotten away with it this time, but he couldn't risk it again. The fact was, if he couldn't play football, he might as well shrivel up in a corner and rot.

CHAPTER 3

For the first time, Zane understood what it meant to dodge a bullet. He went home from school, pretended he had tons of homework, lay in his dark room until dinner, then rested his brain all night, just in case. One more concussion meant no football for at least a year. On that, his parents had agreed, and they never agreed.

When he got to gym today, he'd sideline his instincts, if that was even possible. Better, he'd persuade Coach to make him a designated hitter; lie about a pulled muscle if absolutely necessary.

Right before gym, though, he and some other kids were randomly called to the media center. He'd barely made it inside the library area when Kelly, that girl in his class who'd also answered the six questions right, raced up to him. "I'm hoping it's that quiz," she said. "Regardless, it has to be something good."

"Cupcakes would be good."

She giggled. "I'm thinking bigger. Maybe National Quiz Bowl or MENSA tryouts."

"Men-what?"

"You know, the club for geniuses?"

Zane nodded, but he didn't know. And he wouldn't be trying out for any genius club. He had better things to do. The NFL was calling.

So was Ms. Mendoza. "Gather around, take a seat." She gestured to two pushed-together tables at the edge of the media center.

Kelly giggled and sat right next to Zane, as if they had somehow bonded.

"You may have heard from friends and family around the country that you were not the only ones to take that quiz yesterday."

Kelly leaned over to Zane. "My cousin in Syracuse got all six right, and she's only in fifth grade."

"So genius runs in the family?"

Kelly nodded and giggled again.

He wanted to say, "Let's alert the Genius Fairy about you and your uglier cousin," but he wasn't on the football field where players let insults fly.

Ms. Mendoza stepped up and waved a yellow envelope. "I'm supposed to read what's printed on the outside first. Then you'll need to fill out some forms. After that, you'll get more information."

"National Quiz Bowl," Kelly said again.

If she were really a genius, she'd know he'd heard her the first time.

"I can't explain it," she said, "but something here has me so excited."

He smiled, but didn't want to encourage her. Maybe Kelly was okay, but Zane had the JZs plus the girls who fit in with them—their own easy group within school. Kelly probably did, too, but their orbits never met. Even if she didn't have her own people, it wasn't his problem.

Zane filled out his name, address, email, and other basics. Then he tackled the questions.

A. Name three occupations you might want to try.

He wrote:

1. NFL corner
2. NFL linebacker
3. NFL receiver

Too bad if they wanted more variation.

B. If you could win anything in the world, what would it be?

Easy.

Super Bowl MVP

Most people would say a million dollars or maybe a billion, but if he was named Super Bowl MVP, that meant: (A) his team won the Super Bowl; (B) that he, as a defensive player, had performed out of his mind, and (C) the money would come.

C. What's the best advice anyone ever gave you?

It's what he did every time he was on the football field and had started to do off it, too.

Watch your opponent's eyes.

One glance revealed so much about another person.

He looked into Ms. Mendoza's eyes. Something was making her happy.

She snapped to and waved a smaller yellow envelope. "I'm supposed to open this envelope in exactly three minutes. But if no one needs more time . . ."

No one did.

"We can either wait two and a half minutes or open it now and see if the Envelope Police come to arrest me."

That was funny.

She didn't wait for an answer. Ms. Mendoza broke the seal on the envelope and looked around. "No police? Good. Let's see what's inside this supersecret envelope." She pulled out a card and gave a little gasp. "Well, this is fun."

"What?" said several voices.

"Let me read it verbatim." She cleared her throat. "'The Gollywhopper Games has—'"

Even Zane gasped and high-fived everyone near him.

"Even better than National Quiz Bowl," said Kelly. "No trophy, but money's good!"

"If you win, I'll buy you a trophy." Why'd Zane say that? She giggled—why did girls do that?—and looked at him like they were best friends now.

"So we're all in the Gollywhopper Games?" a sixth grader said.

"We can't all be in it," said an eighth grader. "There are, what? Fifteen of us here? And if each school in the country sent fifteen, there'd be, I don't know. Too many."

Someone threw a wad of paper at him.

"What?"

"Spoil our fun, why don't you?"

The kid pointed at Ms. Mendoza. "She's going to, anyway."

Ms. Mendoza nodded. "Ahem. 'The Gollywhopper Games has, in the past, always used a combination of skill and luck to identify contestants. This year is no exception.

"'Yesterday, more than five million students in schools and in homeschool networks across the country took the first qualifying test of the Games. Those of you hearing this made a perfect score in the first round.

"'To get into the next round, however, involves no skill. It's all luck. Your names will be entered into a nationwide drawing where thirty thousand fortunate contestants will find out firsthand what happens next. Good luck!'

"That's it," said Ms. Mendoza, "except that they're sending you a half-off coupon for any Golly toy or game."

"That's it?" said Kelly. "When do we find out? What happens next? This'll kill me."

"One less person to compete with," said another guy. "If it kills you, that is."

She rolled her eyes. "Very funny."

Ms. Mendoza shrugged. "There's nothing else, Kelly. But feel free to stay here until next period and nose around online. I'm sure you're not the only one in the world with questions."

Kelly tugged on Zane's shirt, and he followed her to

a computer. He'd normally race out to gym class, but he'd take this gift to protect his brain one more day.

"How cool to be in the actual Games! Would we do another round at school? Would they send us to Orchard Heights? That's where Golly headquarters is. What do you think? I mean, you've seen the Gollywhopper Games."

"Sort of."

"Sort of? How can you sort of watch them? They're the best!"

"They're during two-a-days."

"Two-uh-whats?"

"Right before football season starts, Coach kills us in practice two times a day, so every night I'm pretty much a zombie in front of the TV," said Zane. "I mean, if I get picked but the Games are during two-a-days, I'd probably stick to football."

"You'd turn down the Gollywhopper Games?"

"I'd tell them to pick you instead."

She giggled. "You think they would?"

Zane shrugged.

"No, you're right. I'm sure they have rules for that. They're pretty strict about their rules." She logged on to the computer and typed *Gollywhopper Games 3* into the search engine.

Zane rested his brain just a little more.

The Day After
THE SCHOOL ANNOUNCEMENTS

Bert Golliwop took a lap around his huge office, waiting for the five members of his executive team to settle around his enormous desk. Danny King, his intern, was already seated in the near corner.

"Reports!" Bert Golliwop said.

Everyone scrambled to their spots.

"The good news is," said Tawkler from Marketing, "the School Round went off without a hitch. Until we announced it yesterday, no one really connected the quiz with the Games."

"No one, really?" said Bert. "What does that mean?"

"For every person who speculated, there were

dozens, it seemed, who pooh-poohed that notion. Said it wasn't how we did things."

Bert leaned back in his chair. "So we surprised them?"

"Oh yeah," she said. "Since yesterday, hits on the Gollywhopper Games website are already topping two million. And *Gollywhopper Games Three* has been trending ever since."

"What are they saying?"

"Why don't you take that, Danny?" said Tawkler.

He moved forward and stood beside Bert. "Gil and I have been monitoring all the social media outlets. The buzz pretty much falls into five categories. First, the 'How Cool Is That' category—people excited they tried out for the Games. Or that their kids did. Doesn't matter if they made it or not, they can't wait to see how it turns out.

"Two, the 'It Wasn't Fair' category. The quiz was too hard, or they were absent from school, or we should've told them so they wouldn't have faked being sick.

"Three is the 'Curiosity' category. How will they notify us? When will we find out? What will they have us do next?"

"Good, good." Bert Golliwop turned to his head of Human Resources. "And that, Jenkins, is why we didn't give them too much information. We want them to be curious, to talk. We want them to be all over social media. Ooh. Listen to me. Social media. I sound all twenty-first century. Finally." He chuckled. "And the fourth category?"

"You'll like this one," said Danny. "I call it 'What About the Rest of Us?' Kids upset that they didn't make the cut. Or that their schools didn't participate—"

"Those schools are idiots. We guaranteed full anonymity for their students until the parents signed off. We offered them education software just for participating. And each school that produces a finalist? They'll receive a twenty-five-thousand-dollar grant. The twelve percent who turned us down are idiots."

"The kids know that," said Danny. "They're mad at their schools, not at us. But they will be mad at us if we totally leave them out in the cold."

"We're not leaving them out in the cold," Bert said. "We've left one hundred slots open for kids like them. Didn't you get the memo?"

"No, sir."

"I want Danny on those memos. Anything else, Danny?"

"Well, there's that fifth category."

"You said there were four."

"There are, but you always need to consider the Yawners."

"The Yawners?"

"People who didn't notice or don't care."

Tawkler from Marketing leaned forward. "But the people who do notice and do care? It's unprecedented," she said.

"Plus," said Jenkins, "we should congratulate ourselves that nothing went wrong."

Why did she bring that up? He'd worked so hard to clear his mind of those issues for a few hours. But now, thoughts of sabotage during last year's Games came flooding back. And he couldn't stop picturing Harvey Flummox of Flummox Corporation chortling about what other mayhem he and his traitor, someone inside Golly Toy and Game Company, could conjure next.

"Let's never expect anything to go wrong," said

Bert. "Let's work to make it all right, to create the best Gollywhopper Games ever. Let's work to keep our knowledge secure and build excitement throughout the spring and deep into summer. And those Yawners? Let them buy from Flummox because at this moment, we have an unprecedented amount of attention focused right here where it belongs."

When Zane rolled out of bed this morning, at least he remembered what day it was. Tuesday, late June. He didn't know the exact date, but he didn't need to. What he needed was a do-over. He needed to rewind last Friday evening with a duct-taped mouth to stop from calling out to his sister, Zoe. "Emily and her sleepover can wait five seconds," he'd said. "Just throw me one more!"

Not only could Zoe kick a mean football, but she had an arm on her, and that arm helped him practice catching and deflecting balls. Now that he'd been cleared to play, Zane wanted to work on his skills every single second.

"And make it tough!" he'd yelled. She did, and he'd gone back, back, back, barely missing the trunk of the old tree, but tripping over one of its roots and, she'd told him later, hitting his head on the neighbors' patio.

The next thing he knew, Zoe was sitting beside him, crying, and their dad was asking him to name the months of the year backwards. When he couldn't do it, Zane cried, too.

He really appreciated Zoe waiting on him hand and foot for a week. And he really, really appreciated his dad calling in a thousand favors to get Zane this year's edition of Football Frenzy, which had been sold out forever and which caused his mom and dad to argue about how expensive it was and how he should be resting his brain instead. Truth was, even though Football Frenzy's graphics were amazing and its play selection nearly limitless, Zane would've been happier playing GollyFarmyard with his little cousin. It hurt to remember that he himself wouldn't be doling out the hits and leaping to block passes and actually getting the school district's interception record this year. Or possibly any year if his brain didn't heal.

He played the video game just enough to fake out his parents that he loved it. He did love renaming some of the players Concussion, HeadInjury, Blow2theHead, Headache, Dizziness, and Nausea. Also adjusting pattern angles and conceiving strategies to get them knocked off harder than he'd ever seen on "Hit of the Week" highlights.

Now that no one was home, though, he was lying in bed. It was quiet. No yelling, no parents arguing. They were at Zoe's first summer football game, and she was the only girl in the league to play first string. Zane had healed enough to watch her, but it would've been too tempting to swipe a uniform and figure out a way to get onto the adjacent field where he himself should've been playing.

The phone rang. Zane rolled off his bed, ambled into the other room, and answered just before the person had to leave a message.

". . . on our way," said his mom. "Want anything?"

My brain intact, he wanted to say for the billionth time, but he'd decided to drop that line a week after the last doctor's appointment.

He said he was fine, hung up the phone, and

booted up Football Frenzy. When the car pulled into the driveway, he grabbed the controls and ran a play.

"At it again, huh, kiddo?" His mom breezed into the room and stood behind him, watching him run another play. "Well, they won, but Zoe's cleats are way too small, she finally told us, so your dad took her to get new ones. You know he'll spend too much on them."

Zane didn't need to hear either of his parents jab the other, so he pretended not to hear.

"Zane. Zane!"

"Yeah, Mom?"

"You know you don't have to sit in the house and rot."

What else was there? "I'm good."

"Maybe this will make you better." She dropped an envelope into his lap. "Not sure what it is, but the return address is intriguing."

He kept playing.

"You're not going to look? Not even when it says 'Golly Toy and Game Company'?"

"It's probably that discount coupon I won."

"What if it isn't?"

What if it wasn't? Would he even want to play in the Games? Doubtful. How much fun could he have doing quizzes in the middle of summer when he should be running football drills? He opened it so his mom might stop hovering.

Before he finished reading, she was already jumping around and hugging him.

"Careful of the brain," he said.

She eased up.

Not that she'd damage it, but maybe he needed it to read the letter again. On second thought, even quizzes could be more entertaining than moping around during two-a-days.

Dear Zane!

First, a few statistics: 98,189 schools and homeschool organizations participated in the Gollywhopper Games quizzes.

Of the 1,583,332 students who passed the School Round . . .

Only 30,000 contestants have been selected to move forward; fewer than 2%.

AND YOU HAVE BEEN CHOSEN!!!

His mom hugged him again. "Aren't you excited?"

"That I'm one of thirty thousand? Yeah, it's cool."

"Cool? Not everyone gets to go to the Mall Round."

What happened to the stadium? "A mall?"

His mom laughed. "I doubt they'll make you shop." She pointed to the letter. "Read it. I'm going to figure out what's for dinner."

Zane took the letter back to his room and eased himself onto his bed.

Just when you thought you had the Gollywhopper Games all figured out, along comes Season 3.

Big! Brave! Bold! like before . . . but so much more.

Get ready for anything!

Then it gave the date, time, and shopping mall where they expected him. That he had to be between the ages of eleven to fifteen on some day in August. And how he needed to register online within a week or forfeit his spot. Then blah, blah, blah, no guarantees about winning anything. Blah, blah, blah, the company wasn't responsible for injuries or earthquakes or nuclear wars, probably. Blah, blah, blah . . .

Great. What if he fell in a freak accident during the Games, and his brain concussed for life? Maybe he shouldn't do it. But how much fun was he having now?

Zane went into the living room to use the computer and found the contestants' website. If he could make it to the finals, he might be on some sort of team, even for a day or two. And if he won some money, it might stop his parents from arguing. He went to the kitchen. "When you have a chance, Mom, there's stuff you need to sign. Oh. And can I order the DVDs of the last two Games?"

At least he could study game film, even if it wasn't football.

The Day Before
THE MALL ROUND

Bert Golliwop tried not to squirm in his chair, but the hives that had popped up the past few nights had him itching today, worse than ever. He tried to forget those ugly pink welts, but there was no ignoring them.

Danny was sitting behind him, connecting some pens with duct tape. Bert doubted that this second makeshift back scratcher would work better than the first, but even the first was better than nothing. Still, he wouldn't use it until he was alone.

Right now, his five-member executive team sat around his desk in deep discussion. They'd gone through the security checklist for tomorrow's Mall

Round and had moved on to the placement of security cameras for the stadium challenge in August. Cameras in each concession area? Yes. One near the electrical center where that generator had blown last year? Definitely. Inside each bathroom? Absolutely no agreement. Privacy issues versus safety and all that.

Bert couldn't take it anymore. It'd be normal for him to get up and walk around the room. Maybe they wouldn't notice if he eased against the wall to scratch his back, like a bear against a tree trunk. He took half a lap, stopped and scratched, got to the next corner, stopped and scratched, and returned to his seat.

You okay, Bert? mouthed Tawkler.

Maybe he hadn't been as discreet as he'd thought.

He leaned over to her and spoke softly. "Just a few hives. Food allergy or something."

The discussion continued like he'd never gotten up, but they'd gone on about this issue too long. Bert leaned forward. "One, no matter how much we try to control the situation, the stadium will be ripe for an infiltrator like Flummox. Two, while we can station cameras outside the bathrooms, there will be no, I repeat, no cameras inside. Now, go. Travel to your mall sites." Then, under his breath, he muttered, "While I try to find a real back scratcher."

CHAPTER 5

Even before his shoes hit parking-lot pavement, Zane was in game-day mode. His hands and feet tingled. His hearing was on alert. And now, inside the main level of the mall, his eyes scanned his competition.

Several dozen kids were buzzing around the Macy's end with more energy than he'd summoned every day of the past month, combined. Zane, though, wasn't giddy like that girl jumping all over her mom. Instead, he was on task. Go in through the east entrance. Register at Table 7. Receive challenge packet. Find starting location. Do not open envelope until instructed. On the whistle, go!

That's all that letter had told him. Even though he'd watched each Gollywhopper Games DVD four times, he felt totally unprepared. Unlike football, the rules of the Games had changed between the two seasons.

His dad pointed to the bank of ten registration tables. "I can't figure you out," he said. "You're intense like game day, but it's different. Do you even want to be here?"

"It's a competition," said Zane. "I want to win."

His dad nodded. "But not this."

"This is fine."

"This is not football."

"This is not football."

His dad knew. For his dad, "not football" was every day, ever since he'd gotten cut by the New England Patriots and couldn't latch on to another team.

As they walked to the registration table, Zane kept an eye open for that Kelly and other kids from school. None of them yet, but the mall was a big place. Zane passed his confirmation page to an older man at Table 7. The guy was smiling too big, like a mascot trying to amp up the crowd toward the end of a hopeless game. Did Zane look that hopeless? "Don't worry," the guy said. "Just read carefully, think hard, and move quickly."

That already was his plan. "Thanks."

The man fastened bar-coded wristbands around Zane's and his dad's arms. Then he slid a gold envelope with a matching bar code toward Zane, but kept his fingers firmly planted on it. "Do not open this until you hear the whistle. Everything you need to know is here." He turned the envelope over to show a lot of writing.

Zane led his dad away from the table and past three stores. He slid his back down a wall and sat near the entrance of The Children's Shop.

His dad sat down next to him. "Where are we supposed to go?"

"Right here." Zane tilted the envelope so his dad could see.

"What's going on, Zane?"

"I'm waiting."

"No," said his dad. "You're acting like the doctor's about to deliver bad news. What bad could come of this?"

"It's me," said Zane. "It's mental."

"Just tell me," said his dad. "You will, eventually."

He would. "What if it gets physical? What if I run and trip?" Zane knocked on the shiny floor. "What if I hit my head down here or against these bricks? Football's already history."

"For now. Just for now."

"But I want a brain that works forever."

"You heard the doctor. You're fine. The football hiatus is a precaution, and we'll reevaluate next year. That's the good news."

"The bad news?"

His dad pointed to a tree near a coffee store. "You could be standing underneath there, and it could randomly fall over and crush you."

"What are the chances of that?"

"Exactly. What are the chances of you cracking your head in a mall?"

"They exist."

"So do heart attacks and suicide bombers and poison stinging toads, but you don't walk around worried about them all the time. Unless you do?"

Zane shook his head.

"You need to take a deep breath and jump back into your life."

Zane looked at him.

"At least most of it."

"Understood," he said, but could he, really? Would his life be there for him after his friends found out he was off the team? It was no big deal that he'd sat out for summer league. Between camps and family vacations, lots of kids did. But no one who mattered sat out during fall. Would he still matter? Would he still be a JZ? Or would he be a Daryl?

Daryl had been one of them, a real pal, a real buddy who broke his leg and fell off-grid for the season, then forever.

Or even worse than a Daryl, would Zane become as annoying as Thing 1 and Thing 2? He waved his hand, as if to swat that image away.

Three more kids and their parents moved past him. Zane leaned toward his dad. "When we hear two whistle blasts, you need to report to the parents' area inside Macy's. Ten minutes later, when the whistle blasts three times, I open this and do whatever it says. See?" He handed his dad the envelope.

It was closing in on go time. Voices had reached a higher pitch. Two kids jogged in place. Several parents had begun their good-byes; others were already waiting by Macy's.

"What time is it?"

His dad handed him back the envelope. "Two minutes until my whistle."

Twelve minutes until Zane's. Too early to gear up. He straightened his legs to stretch his muscles.

Seriously? He couldn't touch his toes without his knees bending. What else couldn't he do now? How fast had his body turned into the Blob? Maybe he *was* wasting his life.

Shree! Shreeee!

His dad bounded to his feet. He reached out a hand and pulled Zane up, not carefully, not at all. Zane got the point. "I'm good, Dad."

"You are. Now go for it." He patted Zane on the back, walked off, looked back once, and smiled.

Zane leaned over to try and touch his toes, standing this time. No good. He couldn't do anything about that now, but he could—

The old Zane would have studied the mall. He

would have gone online and memorized the stores because Golly hadn't brought them here by accident. In about five minutes they'd have him running all over this place.

And over there, not too far away, that had to be a mall directory. Did he have time?

He paced seven steps toward the directory. The last few adults were racing into Macy's.

He took seven steps back. Then seven toward it, seven back. There, back; there, back. In a rhythm. Seeing blurs, only blurs. Not concussion blurs, but focusing blurs. Focusing his mind and body to do whatever they needed to do today. The other kids might think he was crazy, but his dad would know. His dad would smile. Anyone who knew him would leave him alone, let him get psyched up. He was ready to perform.

Shree! Shreee! Shreeeee!

Go time!

Chapter 6

Zane broke the seal on the envelope and dumped out its contents: mall map, pen, five blank envelopes, and a sheet of instructions.

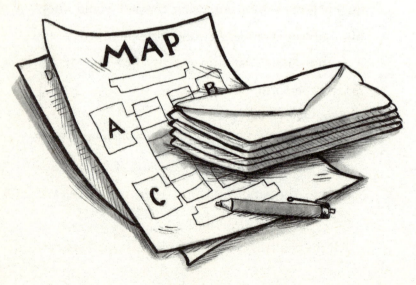

Welcome to the Gollywhopper Games
Mall Challenge!

The Rules:

The 5 white envelopes each hold a challenge. Complete these in any order.

Don't bother to follow anyone. There are 30 different challenges, which means there are 142,506 possible challenge combinations.

You must work alone. Do not speak to fellow contestants. You may ask questions of any Golly official stationed around the mall.

If you are quick enough, you will have the chance to find a winning ticket to Orchard Heights.

Good luck!

Zane sank to the floor. He slid the instructions back into the large envelope, then pulled out the cards from the five white ones.

All the challenges started with the same line: *Find*

the store indicated by the puzzle below. Once there, collect the card with your personal number.

Someone zoomed past in front of him. Then another. Were they speed-reading masterminds?

It didn't matter. Maybe he wasn't a genius, but he was smart, and he had off-the-chart instincts that had helped him earn straight As, even when he didn't study. His strategy now: solve all five puzzles, then use the map to plot out the fastest route to the stores. First card:

Imagine you're playing Golly WordScramble.
You've randomly selected 7 tiles.
The letters on these tiles
can spell, among other words:
"peer," "free," "fur" and "mere."
Figure out which tiles you have,
and use all 7 to spell a single word.

Huh? There were fifteen letters in those four words. Not seven. How was he—

Oh! To spell "peer," he'd need four tiles—two *E*s, one *P*, and one *R*. Then he'd need to add only three others—an *F* tile for "free," a *U* for "fur," and an *M* for "mere." Seven total!

Zane tore one of the blank envelopes into seven odd-shaped pieces, making his own tiles. He lined them up on the floor: *E, E, P, R, F, U, M.*

Didn't lots of words end in E-R? He moved those to the end. Now, just five to rearrange.

M-U-F-E-P-E-R

F-U-M-P-E-E-R

E-M-P-U-F-E-R

Not even close. Scrap the E-R.

Now what? He could always look over the list of one hundred fifty-eight stores making this the biggest multiple-choice test ever.

Zane shuffled the letters, but stopped from dealing them out randomly. He needed logic. Like, what if they'd given him those words in a particular order? He laid out the scraps in the order he'd discovered the letters: *P, E, E, R, F, U, M.*

Why hadn't he done that first? Just one letter out of place.

The list of stores on his mall map was alphabetized within categories: Accessories, Apparel for

Children, Apparel for Men, blah-blah-blah. Health and Beauty? Zane scanned that section, but didn't see "Perfume." He looked at each store name. Heaven Scents. That had to mean perfume. Store 778.

He circled it on the map. Second floor, not too far.

Zane resisted the urge to run with the crowd, find the store, and grab his card. He already had his strategy. Plus, if he waited, there'd be fewer cards to root through.

He shoved the perfume puzzle and letter pieces into the large envelope. Next card:

Get rid of all traces of slime.

S	A	L	SLIME
SLIME	U	SLIME	L
T	I	M	SLIME
L	E	SLIME	O

Zane could do that. He crossed out the "SLIME"s and was left with "SAL" on the top line, then "UL," "TIM," and "LEO" on the next three. Was there a store with four guys' names? Was UI even a name? Or did they want him to rearrange *twelve* letters now? He'd be here all day.

He looked at the puzzle again. *Get rid of all traces of slime,* it said above the grid. Not just the "SLIME"s. If he crossed out all the *S*s, *L*s, *I*s, *M*s, and *E*s—

Better! The letters were in order from top to bottom.

Map time. Vroom Auto! First floor, but at the other end of the mall. He circled it. Next card:

_____ in your shirt tail!

A B _____ D

_____nut hole. Yum!

Was it a shirt place? A learning center? And what type of hole was yummy? Only one he could think of, doughnut hole.

There couldn't be a single store that dressed, tutored, and fed you. He needed to fill in the blanks, and he could do that without the pen. Tuck, C, Dough. Tuck-C-Dough.

Zane heard the full word in his head. He scanned

the listings for Apparel for Men. Mr. Penguin Tuxedo Shop. Middle of the mall, floor two, close to the auto place. He circled it.

Card number four. Already? There had to be something harder ahead because it all seemed too easy.

$$10,475,832$$
$$3,701,664$$
$$+\quad 13,723$$

Zane did the math. Lots of numbers, but it was just addition. He did it once. Did it twice, but now what? There was no Numbers store. He looked at the puzzle card again. Turned it over. There on the back, in the lower right-hand corner, in tiny print, it read *A=1, B=2*, etc.

Okay! He could translate 14191219 into A-D-A-I-A-B-A-I, or not. Some of the Apparel for Women's stores had weird names, but none that resembled the capital of Ethiopia.

Why couldn't simple be simple? Then again a running play wasn't just a running play. You had to account for the blocking scheme and the—

He had to focus. What if 1 and 4 didn't translate into AD? What if the first number was 14? Then 19, then 12, then 19 again? But N-S-L-S didn't spell anything. It had to be some combination of single numbers and double numbers. If the first letter was *A*, the second had to be *D*, because the next two numbers after the first number were 4 and 1, and there was no forty-first letter of the alphabet. He clicked open the pen and wrote the possibilities for the first four numbers. He'd ruled out N-S and A-D-A-I, so it was either A-D-S or N-A-I.

Zane liked where N-A-I was going. Next two numbers? 1 then 2, or 12. So it was either N-A-I-A-B or N-A-I-L. And if 1 and 9 were 19, he had N-A-I-L-S. Was there a hardware store on the list?

Nothing under Home Furnishings. Nothing under Professional Services. Maybe the hardware department in Sears? No. The instructions said to find the store, not the department.

What was he missing? He scanned the directory again, focusing just on that word. Where are you? Where . . .

Belle Nails? In Health and Beauty.

The girls probably got that one fast. The nail salon was down an entrance hall, about a dozen stores from where he was sitting.

Last card:

You'll see me run, but never walk;
I have a face, but never talk.
I have a band that doesn't play.
My hands are moving night or day.

Zane had seen riddles like that before. The fastest way to solve them was to focus on the important words. So this thing had a face, a band, and hands, and it ran, which probably meant it was mechanical. And the hands moved night and day, around the clock. Clock. Right? He couldn't throw out the band, and if it had a band, it was a watch.

There, on the map: Watch that Time.

His game plan was obvious. Start at this end of the mall and work his way to the other end. Perfume, nails, tuxedo, watches, then auto.

He took off and became another kid running through the mall with no one warning him to slow down. Running, feeling the breeze he himself was making. Feeling his heart pump and his muscles stretch and his skin start to break a sweat. If the rest of the Games made him feel even 10 percent of this, he wanted in.

He ran even faster. Upstairs to Heaven Scents. There, to his left!

Just inside the door was a large bulletin board that still had about thirty numbered cards tacked to it. Two other kids were looking for theirs. Where was his? Number, what? Wristband: 44-173.

All the cards started with 44, but weren't in any particular order. He quick-scanned them, looking for the nice, round, easy-to-see number three. There it was! He pulled off the thumbtack, unskewered the card, and jammed the tack back into the board.

Zane turned the card over, but it was just a bar code and a number. Nothing else. He started to run out of the store, but a woman stopped him. "We need to scan you," she said. "Envelope, card, and wrist."

Zane got scanned, checked his map, and bolted

down some stairs in a side hall. Belle Nails should've been close, very close. He looked to his right, to his left, but it wasn't here. He looked at the map again. Across! Another side hall.

Inside the fingernail salon, Zane ignored the disgusting chemical smell, grabbed his card, got scanned, then headed for stop three. Tuxedos, upstairs.

This time, the escalator in the middle of the mall would be quickest. He ran up the moving stairs as fast as the kids in front of him would go.

At the top, he juked around them and sprinted past eight stores to the tuxedo shop. Found his card; got scanned. But this time the scanner emitted a long beep.

"Congratulations!" said the scanner guy. "This was your third stop." He reached into a pouch and pulled out a green envelope. "Open this before you continue."

Zane would rather ride his momentum, but he'd also rather not get penalized. He turned himself in the direction of the watch store, started walking, and tore open the envelope.

The Choice Is Yours

The Shortcut

Go directly to the food court.

No need to solve more puzzles.

No need to pick up more cards.

If you choose to take this shortcut,
   you should have

one chance to find a winning ticket to
   Orchard Heights.

The Full Game

Continue with the puzzles.

Continue collecting cards.

When you have all 5, go to the food court,

where you may receive multiple chances

to find a winning ticket to Orchard Heights . . .

if you've been fast enough.

Warning: There are a limited number of
   chances.

When those run out, this game ends.

Zane turned a quick three-sixty. A few kids were still running; a couple more, concentrating on puzzles. Were the rest already in the food court? He'd gone fast, but fast enough? With three hundred kids spread over two floors of a large mall, it was impossible to tell. He'd already done the hard work, but go directly to the food court or take his chances?

There'd been more than ten cards at the tuxedo store. He'd take his chances. Watch store. Scan. Pull. Run. Auto store. Scan. Pull. Run. Two flights down. Food court.

This didn't look like any food court Zane had ever seen. There were no tables, no chairs, and no reason, it seemed, for the haphazard placement of pieces of chain-link and picket fencing, each the size of double doors. The fence blockades were interwoven with strands and strands of string, tangling and winding its way everywhere. Among the mess, about two dozen kids were somehow progressing through the webs.

"That way, son." A man behind him was pointing toward a long table. "Check-in for the String Web is that way."

Zane got in a line behind two other kids. Where was everyone? Come and gone, or not here yet? It only took a minute until a Golly worker scanned his wristband. "We have a Five!"

A horn sounded. Lights flashed. Several Golly workers cheered.

"We haven't had many yet," said the man.

"Really?"

The man tapped the GollyReader in front of him. "One hundred fourteen kids have been through, but you are only the fourth Five-Carder." He came around the table and led Zane away. "See all that string?"

"I couldn't miss it if I wanted to."

The man chuckled. "You'll choose one piece of string at the spool station. Each string leads to a Golly toy or game. Eventually. Nine of those Golly products contain winning tickets that will send you to the Stadium Round in Orchard Heights. The rest of the toys and games contain our thanks for playing. The Threes have qualified to follow only one string. But as a Five, you'll keep going until you win or until we run out of string."

Zane nodded but really wanted to know why the man was wasting time and leading him away from the spool stations.

"For collecting five cards, you also get a hint each time you take a turn through the web." He handed Zane a tiny envelope. "Open it."

Empty? Or not. Three words were written on the inside of the envelope itself. *Don't choose blue.*

"What does that mean?" Zane said.

"Off to the spool station. You'll understand." The man took the envelope from Zane. "Want to make sure only Fives see this. Good luck, Zane!"

The spool station had taken over the restaurant counters of the food court. Massive amounts of bundled string streamed from above and fell in a semiorganized way to the sides of four different counters.

Zane stepped up to one, and the woman manning it almost seemed caught between webs. She scanned his wristband. "A Five! Pick a spool, any spool."

Each shelving unit back there was stacked five high, two deep, and about ten wide with plastic spools in red, pink, blue, yellow, orange, purple, green, black, brown, and white. His hint now made sense. Zane would have chosen blue, his team's color. "I'll take . . ."

Strategy. He needed strategy. Mostly girls would choose pink or purple, and Golly had to want boys, too. So yellow? Green? No. He'd go with the less obvious. "I'll take the white one on the second shelf from the bottom; the one there in front, on the left."

The woman lifted his spool high, unlatched his string from a hook above, carried it back to the counter, and handed it to him without it catching on any other string. Either she'd nailed the system, or it was a miracle. "I'm going to make this sound simple. Follow your string and keep it wound around your spool. Good luck, and don't trip!"

Did she have to say that?

He wound the first bit of loose string around his spool and followed it to the left, where it got nuts. The string was woven in, around, and through all sorts of random barricades and banisters along with so many other strands. The last person doing this would have it easy, but for now, it'd take more than a few minutes.

He needed to untangle his string from a massive fence web. He climbed over a low, string-filled barrier and ducked underneath another one on poles. It was like he was an action-movie spy who had to dodge the red lasers of alarm systems.

He should have been bumping into all sorts of bodies doing the same thing, but some genius had found a way to have them work in different spaces. Over a low ledge, under a higher one. Around and around, and don't trip, don't trip. Don't trip like that kid over there just did, who fell backwards, her head caught by a nest of string that miraculously didn't cause the whole rest of the String Web to cave in around her.

Aha! That's why. The string was masking hundreds of clear rods, zigzagging around the room, keeping every strand where it was supposed to be.

Not that it mattered how it worked; it mattered that Zane get through this fast enough to try again and again if he didn't get a ticket the first time.

He crawled under a crisscrossing of rods, slid his spool through three different fence walls. Dodging, ducking, climbing—which would make a great football drill. If he were playing. He was playing this now, though.

Over, under, around, his spool half an inch thick with string. And now a long straightaway. Maybe it was the end! Maybe he'd find—

Another tangle of string. But just a short one. He looped his spool through the gap in the fence, fetched it on the other side, wound it back toward him as he neared the escalators, then the movie theater, toward that large wall of Golly toys and games. He wound faster and faster and faster and nearly bumped into a man who stopped him with a hand on his shoulder.

"Whoa, Nelly!" The man took the spool from him. "Let's fetch you your prize." He tugged at the string, which dislodged a box from the shelf. Ironic. It was the GollyFarmyard video game, the one his cousin had. He hoped the cow in the picture was smiling for a reason.

The man brought him the box. "Not exactly what you'd pick for yourself, but hey! You got something. Open it!"

Why did they make the plastic wrapper so tough to open? Zane looked at the man.

"Sorry, son. I'm not allowed to help."

Zane scratched at the plastic with the little bits of fingernails he had. He wanted to run to Belle Nails and borrow scissors, but instead he sank the point of his canine tooth into the side. It bent, it bent some more, then *pop!* He opened the case. No ticket to Orchard Heights; just a note: *Thank You for Playing!*

"Sorry," said the man. He scanned Zane's wrist. "But you're a Five." He hit a button on his scanner, and it printed out a label, which he slapped onto GollyFarmyard. "I'll keep it safe for you at this table. Meanwhile, here"—the man reached into a pouch and handed Zane an envelope—"take a look, then hand it back."

Two clues this time. *Don't choose red. No winners on the top shelf.*

He rushed back to the spool station. Not blue, not red, not purple, not pink. The green, yellow, and orange were calling to him, but what about the brown ones? Would they hide a ticket behind a less-popular color? "I'll take a brown one on the fourth shelf, all the way on the right."

"First or second one in?" the woman said.

"First," said Zane. "Always."

He started winding his spool the moment she handed it to him. This time would be easier. He knew what he was doing. He climbed through the first string tunnel, winding and winding as fast as he could, but his legs strode longer and faster than his hands could move. He rolled up the slack, pushed around a half wall, sent the spool three times around a post to unwind the string, then jogged through a straightaway that took him to the other side of the room. His string, though, dragged behind. He paused to wind it up.

There were more kids than there had been before. Why were they showing up just now? These puzzles weren't any harder than the school ones. Maybe the pressure got to them, or maybe he was smarter than he thought. Whatever the reason, more chances for him.

The string took him around three half walls, then to the staircase where it wound around the banister. Zane went up five steps to a landing, unwinding the string, then back down and unwound it more.

The string wasn't done with him until he made it past a tall wall with softball-sized holes in random Swiss cheese fashion. Then straight to the prize wall, which was looking emptier, but with the number of kids out there, he had no clue if he'd get a third chance. Ticket or no ticket? Odds were, no ticket. But anything was possible. That comeback victory against Greenway had seemed impossible, and yet Zane's team had outscored them twenty-eight to nothing in the fourth quarter to win by four.

Ticket or no ticket?

No ticket.

Zane bolted back to the spool station. From a distance the prize shelves looked bare. No one was stopping him to give him another clue. Good reason. There were only three spools left: one white, one purple one on the top shelf, and one orange. If there was a ticket left, it wouldn't be on the top shelf, according to the hint. White or orange?

Zane sucked in a breath. "Orange."

This time it was easy. There was no going through other webs of string. It was just a matter of going around and through walls and fences. It was just a matter of winding and winding. There was no rushing. No fourth chance.

Zane made his way to the prize wall and tugged off the new Diamond Valley Demons video game before the Golly person could reach it for him. "How many of the tickets are gone?"

The Golly guy shook his head. "We haven't kept track."

Zane smiled at the guy, looking into his eyes.

The man looked just over Zane's head.

"So there is one left," Zane said, "and it's in here."

The man whisked him behind the prize wall.

CHAPTER 7

The man shifted his glance back and forth. "I've always been a bad liar. Go on. Open it."

Zane didn't know what the ticket would look like or what it would say, but he knew it was in there. He unwrapped the Diamond Valley Demons game, got past the ultrasticky seal, and opened the case. Inside, lying on top of a DVD, was a slip of paper that had an embossed Gollywhopper Games seal and six words:

We'll see you in Orchard Heights!

Zane pumped his

fist. He turned, out of habit, to jump onto his team-mates. Instead, he hugged the man, who laughed and laughed.

The man clamped him on the shoulder, then handed him a shiny, gold envelope. "I may be looking at the next superstar."

"Absolutely!"

It wasn't football, but a win was a win. Still, he couldn't help wonder why the Gollywhopper Games kept follow-ing him. He didn't want to use his fifteen minutes of fame on the Games and have nothing left for the NFL. Then again, Alex Karras and Jim Brown made it huge in the NFL before they became actors. They'd been famous twice. William Howard Taft was president *and* chief justice of the Supreme Court. Also . . .

Who? Zane was out of examples, but he couldn't know everyone who had been struck by superstar lightning twice.

He was getting ahead of himself. He may have made it to Orchard Heights, but once he was there, he'd still need to beat 999 other kids, 899 from these mall competitions and 100 more who'd won Orchard Heights tickets online.

This was the first time in months Zane had felt the slightest bit of hope. When he neared his dad, he kept his eyes down, shrugged his shoulders, and held up the three Golly boxes with one hand. Then he thrust the gold envelope out with the other.

His dad grabbed him. "I knew you'd do it! You've always been smart, smarter than me!"

Zane didn't stop to explain about the luck part. Instead, he danced around with his dad, got the last bit of energy out with a dozen fist pumps, then stopped to let it all sink in. "I did it," Zane whispered like he always did hours after a game he'd killed.

His dad nodded. He understood the jumping and shouting were over for now. His dad gave him one last bear hug and thumped him on the back. "This is good. No, this is great. You needed something, you know?"

He did know. He could focus on the Gollywhopper Games. He could take a break from worrying about his head every minute of every day. And his friends.

It wasn't that they'd send him off into some wasteland, but being on the outside would be different. He'd miss the horseplay after practice, the recaps after games. He'd miss deciding where the JZs were going to hang out. Could he just show up at Jamaal's house or at Jerome's dad's restaurant? Would he be in on the jokes? Would he still be a JZ?

He couldn't be. Not completely, not as long as he was shut out of football. But for now, at least he had something of his own.

Minutes After
THE MALL ROUND

The limo whisked Bert Golliwop and his intern, Danny, from the Orchard Heights Mall, back to Golly Headquarters. By the time they strode into his office, the five faces of his executive team were large as life on the big screen, each one videoconferencing from a different mall location. They were already discussing some minor glitches. Several pull cards went missing in the mall in Little Rock, but they were traced to a kid who thought stealing extras would give her an advantage; it got her kicked out. The String Web had provided expected mishaps, but no notable injuries. There was also an issue with a screaming parent in Seattle and a fight over a certain spool in Sarasota, but in each instance, the problem was cleared within minutes.

"Good thing my staff implemented all those checks and balances," said Morrison from Legal.

"And that they worked," said Larraine from Finance. "As did the cameras catching a kid conferring with a father who'd never made it to the parent area."

"Seriously?" said Bert. He noticed a long, thin mailing box on his desk. "What's this?"

"In the end it was not an issue," Morrison said, "but it put people on notice not to mess with us."

Bert pulled out scissors to cut the tape on the box. The package was addressed to him. Then he caught the return address. "Harvey Flummox? What's he sending me? If there's poison in here, you're all witnesses. Get ready to call nine-one-one."

In Atlanta, Jenkins from Human Resources whipped out her cell phone. If he'd asked for a bowl of bouillabaisse, she'd probably have a chef in his office before he could blink.

Bert opened the box. On top was a small white card:

Heard through the grapevine that this might come in handy.

—Harvey

Bert turned around to Danny. "I'll give that lunkhead credit for one thing: It's a better back scratcher than yours."

Danny laughed, but the others looked confused.

Except Tawkler from Marketing. "Your hives still acting up?"

"Not so much anymore," Bert said, "but my curiosity is. How'd Flummox know about them?"

"That was my next question," Tawkler said. "What goes on your office is supposed to stay in your office."

"Of course," said Morrison, "it does. But what went on in the office? Was I there?"

Had Bert been wrong about Morrison? Was he playing too innocent?

"Should I know what you're talking about?" asked Jenkins.

Was she?

"Not really." Bert needed to sound casual. "I had a case of hives the other day, and word must have spread. I suppose this is Flummox's idea of rubbing it in. Let's carry on with the agenda."

Bert let them carry on. Word of this *couldn't* have spread that easily. He hadn't told his wife about his hives. She would have worried. No reason to alert his kids. He hadn't mentioned it to his assistant, and he'd only scratched in the privacy of this office. Danny had guessed, but that wasn't surprising. Danny had seen him with hives at Bert's daughter's wedding.

He tried to convince himself that this was a big bunch of nothing, that one of his five execs simply had loose lips. Bert's stomach churned, though. This was a huge bunch of something. One of them had a direct pipeline to Flummox and was using it for sabotage.

When they concluded their business, Bert had Danny stay. He looked into Danny's eyes for several seconds. Danny kept steady contact.

"It wasn't you. I didn't think you told Flummox about the hives."

"Why would I do that?"

"Exactly. But someone did," said Bert. "Someone who was inside this room."

Danny's eyes went wide. "Who?"

Bert shook his head. "I need you to find out. No, I need you to figure out how to *catch* the person in cahoots with Flummox. Goodness knows, I haven't been able to. Make it your top priority. But think, and think fast; the Games are in two weeks. And hold this in the strictest of confidence."

Danny headed for the office door but doubled back. "About that. You should know I'm infinitely more creative when I bounce ideas off someone else."

Bert nodded. "Who'd you have in mind?"

"He's been guiding the younger kids through the toy testing and is extraordinarily on target and creative with his comments and suggestions."

"It's not who I think it is."

Danny smiled. "You're the one who put me in charge of him."

Bert stared into his office, not really seeing anything. Could he trust that other kid? The only thing he could trust, 100 percent right now, was these hives would keep driving him crazy.

"Swear him to secrecy."

"I don't have to," said Danny. "Gil Goodson might be the most loyal person you know."

CHAPTER 8

In their district, school gyms opened for voluntary workouts four weeks before fall sports season started. The JZs had talked about storming theirs at nine sharp. Zane conveniently skipped the fact that he would be at the mall at that time and convinced them to run in the morning, instead, when it was cooler. They'd meet up later at the gym at around noon, which was now. It was time to come clean, tell them he was out for the year and let his official exile begin.

His dad had just dropped him there after the mall, and he was standing outside the workout-room doors taking small bites from the burrito they'd picked up on the way.

Jamaal came flying out the door and nearly knocked the burrito from his hand.

"Forget your water bottle again?" Zane asked.

"Where were you this morning?" Jamaal tore off a hunk of the burrito and shoved it into his mouth. "Had to run without you. Thought, maybe, you did a Daryl."

Zane tried to ignore the sinking feeling in his stomach and took a small bite. "Don't you know it's bad to eat before a workout?"

"You're eating."

"It's a snack. Snacks are allowed." He didn't mention this was his third burrito in ten minutes.

"Good." Jamaal reached for another piece, but Zane gave him the rest. It was suddenly hard to swallow with the ghost of Daryl filling his gut.

Jamaal shoved the last bit of burrito into his mouth.

This was Zane's opening. He could do it, tell Jamaal he wouldn't be on the field, but he also wouldn't desert them like Daryl had.

"Got something to tell you."

Jamaal swallowed. "What?"

But what if Daryl hadn't deserted them? What if they'd deserted Daryl? Zane could barely get a breath.

"If you keep forgetting your water bottle, we're gonna buy you one with unicorns and rainbows."

Jamaal leaned in for more water, and Zane slipped into the workout room, spied an unoccupied treadmill, and moved toward it as invisibly as possible. Who was he kidding?

Within seconds, Zack and Jerome and Julio were all over him.

"It's a ghost!" said Zack.

"He's not a ghost," Jerome said. "You can't disappear if you weren't running with us in the first place. He's just a slacker."

"Who you calling a slacker? Me, missing one morning's run? Weren't you the one sitting out June practice with a little broken toe?"

"That's a yes," said Jerome, "but I'm not slacking now. While my toe was healing, I was doing bicep curls. Look at these." Jerome flexed his arms.

"You put me to shame," said Zane. "While my brain was healing, I turned into the Great Blob of the Midwest."

"But two-a-days are in two weeks, man," said Julio. "You gonna be ready?"

"About that." This was his chance. "I'm gonna miss a few of them."

"Coach has rules," said Julio. "Your excuse better be off the charts."

"Him?" said Jerome. "Coach'd let Zane play if he showed up like a diva, demanding only blue M&M's."

Zane started to shake his head, but he reached into his pocket instead and pulled out the slip of paper from the Diamond Valley Demons box.

"What's this?" asked Zack. "A note from your mommy?"

Jamaal grabbed it. "Yeah, right. When'd you print this out?"

Jerome took it away from him. "You are such a liar."

Zane set the treadmill into motion, feeling the weeks of inactivity, as they passed around the paper.

Julio got it last. "Hey, man. I think this is for real. He's not a dumb jock like the rest of us, you know?"

"Speak for yourself," said Jamaal.

"Think about it," said Julio. "This is Zane Braycott. Why would he waste valuable time and brainpower— especially when he has so little these days—writing some lame note with an official seal and everything?

If I had Football Frenzy, I'd be spending all my time with that."

"Unless you also had Diamond Valley Demons," Zane said.

Zack did a double take. "When'd you get that?"

"Won it this morning when I got that." He snatched the paper back from Jamaal, who had it for the second time. "I swear I'm telling the truth." And he launched into a play-by-play, starting with that school quiz. When he finished, he looked into each of their wide-eyed, slack-jawed faces.

He couldn't let them down. Not now. Maybe something would change over the next few weeks. If he survived the Games, maybe his parents would give him the okay to play football after all. The bad news could wait.

"You? The Gollywhopper Games?" said Jamaal. "I still don't believe you."

"Then come over tomorrow when they email my flight info."

"How will we know you didn't make that up?" Jerome laughed.

Zane did too. "Go study the playbook, Jerome. Then watch for me on TV."

Ten Days Before
THE STADIUM ROUND

The last time Gil Goodson had set foot in Bert's office had been the day he won the Games. After that, Gil had become so popular, Tawkler from Marketing—or was it Plago from Toy and Game Creation?—suggested they invite him and the other contestants to work in the testing lab. Bert had never expected Gil to agree and had been avoiding him ever since.

The instant Gil shadowed Danny through the door, Bert walked right up and made eye contact. Gil didn't look away. It was a good start. "Danny tells me you've put together some sort of plan."

Gil nodded.

Danny turned to Bert. "We were brainstorming ways to do this, then Gil mentioned, and I agreed— Well, you tell him."

If Bert was reading this right, Gil gave Danny a "Do I have to?" look.

"Your idea," said Danny. "You take the credit."

"It goes back to your father, huh?" Bert said.

Gil took a deep breath. "Sometimes my dad kicked himself for being so blind about the Incident. Said if you'd confronted him about the five million dollars, Bert, he could've trapped the person who actually did rig the computer system. Then he would have been your hero instead of your suspect." He looked Bert in the eye and shrugged.

Danny nodded for him to go on.

"So I thought if we set a trap for the final challenge, the rat might take the bait."

"Why focus on the final challenge?"

"That's when the rat hit you hardest last time, where it could've caused the most chaos," Danny said. "And because Ratso ultimately failed—"

"Ratso?"

"It's what Gil and I started calling the person."

"I like it."

"Well, Ratso might have an itch to succeed where he failed last time. You know, to prove something." Danny popped a pretzel into his mouth and looked at Gil.

"At least that's what we thought. So we came up with all these complicated traps that might've worked," Gil said, "but sometimes simple is better."

"And it doesn't get much simpler than this." Danny handed Bert a pen.

"I ask Ratso to write out a confession?"

Danny laughed. "Nope. Here's what you'll do. As a casual point of information, you'll inform your people that the security cameras will be turned off for an hour."

"And?"

Danny took the pen back from Bert, pulled it apart, and plugged the bottom half into a USB port on Bert's computer. It replayed every movement and word of their whole conversation.

Bert smiled.

"These spy cams come in a variety of disguises," said Gil. "So we can set up whichever one blends in best around the final challenge area."

"Areas," Bert corrected. "One for each contestant. Then each area will have several different final challenges ready to go, just in case." Bert stared silently at the pen for most of a minute before he looked up. "Would you two please step out of my office. I'll call you back in a few minutes."

Once Danny and Gil closed the door behind them, Bert made sure the surveillance system in his office was turned off—it was never supposed to be on when he was in there—then opened the safe hidden behind a sliding wall panel.

He pulled out the site plans for the Games and turned to the page with the two identical final challenge areas. There, on each side of a low wall, were the three final challenges they'd settled on: Sink or Swim, Flamethrowers, or Extreme Machines.

Danny and Gil had been right. Those would be the most likely targets for Ratso. So Bert would need six spy cams. He stared at the plans again. No. Make that eight.

Bert put away the plans, called Danny back in, then sent him on a mission.

By the end of the day, just minutes after Bert

himself had planted all the spy cams, he gathered his executive team to their seats around his desk. "There's an issue with the surveillance system in the final challenge areas. To put the fix in place, they'll need to shut down all the cameras next Wednesday at exactly seven p.m. They'll be off for one to two hours."

"Shall I get extra security detail on that?" Jenkins asked.

Bert knew someone would bring that up, but he couldn't have extra security in place *and* expect the rat to make a fatal move. "Those of us in this room— We are the only ones who know exactly when this will happen. Just us and Walt Rusk, who will be doing the work from a control room on the eighth floor. I will be with him during the entire process. Better to not call attention to this. I just wanted to keep you informed." Bert stood. "I need to leave for a personal matter, but you all stay and finalize which challenge we'll use to end the Games. I'm fine with any of the three."

Bert went out of the office, with hopes that someone would take the bait.

CHAPTER 9

Watch for me on TV? Had Zane really said that the other day? Now he'd need to be one of the last men standing, because he wasn't about to make a fool of himself for the blooper reel. Besides, winning might buy him some fame and, more important, prevent him from becoming a Daryl. A million dollars could do that.

So on top of running with the guys every morning, working out with them in the afternoons, and per- petuating the lie that he was going to play football, Zane spent his time studying Gollywhopper DVDs like game film; memorizing Gil's online guide, as if it were a playbook; reading as many Gollywhopper websites as he could stand; and having Zoe quiz him in return for shagging her punts. He wouldn't be nearly as prepared as the hardcore G-Gamers, but he could play smart, and that always counted for something.

When Zoe found out that Golly Toy and Game Company had invited their whole family to Orchard Heights, she turned girl on him, moping that she couldn't clone herself to be both there and at two-a-days. Thankfully, she snapped out of it after an hour. Thankfully, too, their mom couldn't take time off from her new job, so he'd be spared the presence of the Arguing Parent Show. It would be just Zane and his dad. And a whole new competition he couldn't fully prepare for.

Zane should have been pumped. Tomorrow was Games day, but he couldn't generate that game-day rush, not even after he and his dad landed in Orchard Heights. They worked out at the hotel, ordered room service for dinner, hydrated, and got plenty of sleep. The next morning, they took a jog around the hotel grounds before they got dressed and went down to breakfast.

Zane made a beeline for the buffet and loaded his plate with mostly protein—eggs, bacon, sausage—along with a little fruit and one pancake, no syrup. He didn't need a sugar spike to mess with any quickness, strategy, and overall smarts he'd need today.

They took the last two spots at a table with a red-headed boy whose redheaded parents swore he was the next Einstein until the girl next to him quietly mentioned she'd met some eleven-year-old who was already a senior in high school. That shut the Einsteins up until they started asking questions to gauge Zane's smarts. He wasn't playing. Neither was his dad. Instead, they smiled and gave short, direct answers. Everyone here was competition. If it ever came time for team building, though, Zane would team-build like the Games had never seen.

He kept his energy brewing at a low level for the rest of breakfast and through the bus ride to University Stadium. It moved to a simmer as they were whisked off the buses and into tents for registration and bar-coded wristbands.

Zane looked at his. In big numbers it said *798*.

"You were hoping for twenty-one?" said his dad.

"Always."

The number twenty-one wasn't lucky to most people unless it was their birthday or they liked triple sevens. It was the number, though, of both Eric Wright and Deion Sanders, Zane's football idols, and it was the number Zane wore on his jersey.

He did some quick math, and his energy ramped up to slow boil. "Dad." He pointed to the 798. "It's twenty-one times thirty-eight."

"You got this, Zane," he said, like he did before every game.

Within seconds, the Golly people ushered all the kids out of the family tents and into the stadium itself.

Even in the stands, Zane itched to put on pads and run the length of the field. His lungs craved to suck in wind that could push him faster than he'd ever gone before, but there he sat, in row twenty-one, at about the twenty-one-yard line in his assigned section D.

This year Golly had marked off ten distinct sections, from the top of the stands to the middle of the turf. Word spread that no kid from the same mall was in the same section, which meant less chance of anyone having a buddy in the next seat.

Even though the sectioning was similar to the past two Games, it felt different. There were no hot-air balloons, no confetti, no banners blazing. And the music that suddenly blasted over the speakers was just a recording—no live bands.

Um. No, it wasn't. One verse into the Mercy Neptune song, Mercy herself, surrounded by a chorus of backup singers, bounded onto the field and up onto a stage. By the end of the first song, the crowd was rocking. When the second song started, at least a hundred dancers surrounded her, then climbed into the stands, pulling groups of kids around them.

All one thousand contestants, no matter their abilities—and there were some really awkward people—were dancing with ultrahigh energy. This type of moving and jumping and stretching wasn't in Zane's pregame warm-up routine, but it could've been. It was hitting all the right muscles in all the right ways.

With the start of the fourth song, one dancer

pulled Zane to a more open space. Then she pointed to the video board. There he was, bigger than life. He found the camera that was on them, pointed to it, then looked up just in time to catch himself. Who knew? He could actually dance. The cameraman moved, but the dancing continued. And suddenly it got a little more crowded around him. He almost forgot this party was about to turn into competition. So he stepped aside with the start of the fifth song to get his mind back in the Games. Also to wipe the sweat off his face. After the sixth song, Mercy's whole troupe raced off to screams of "Encore!" Mercy ran back only to take a bow.

Workers ran on the field and removed the stage. More workers pulled off tarps from large wagon wheels that studded the field's perimeter. And then came a buzzing. Dozens—hundreds?—of bright cylinders zoomed into the airspace above the stands and the field, moving along wires Zane hadn't noticed before. At once, they unfurled to create a magical ceiling of banners that amped him up for whatever these Games would throw at him.

The banners were riddled with motivational

sayings. EXPECT MAJOR SUCCESS! YOU HAVE WHAT IT TAKES TO WIN! JUST GO FOR IT! And others.

He needed to forget football. This was the game he was playing today. This was the time. This was the place. He expected success. He had what it took. He was going for it.

CHAPTER 10

"Welcome, contestants!" The voice ricocheted around the stadium. "This isn't Gil's Gollywhopper Games. This isn't Clio's Gollywhopper Games. This is *your* Gollywhopper Games!"

With only one thousand people cheering, the gut-rumbling roar was missing. So Zane cheered louder and made his own gut rumble.

"I'm Randy Wright, the voice of your Gollywhopper Games, and as they say, the game has changed. Right now, our Golly guides are handing you each a packet. Do *not* open the packet until we say 'go.' Which leads to the one supreme rule here: follow all our rules exactly. You will face elimination if you choose to make up your own. Got it?" He laughed. "We're really not all that mean. We just don't tolerate cheaters."

A guide handed Zane a white envelope with the Gollywhopper Games logo and the warning on both sides: "Do not open until instructed."

Within seconds, a slight buzz filtered through the stands. The scoreboard clock pulsed on and off at three minutes, then started counting down: *2:59, 2:58, 2:57.*

"When the clock reaches zero, you may open your packets. Meanwhile, more instructions. These same instructions are inside your packet, but if you listen now, you'll save yourself valuable time."

Randy Wright continued. "Your packets contain six challenges. You're to solve four on your own, from anywhere within your section, except for the top ten rows."

Those appeared to be cordoned off.

"Now for something completely different. For challenge number five, you will need to choose a partner from anywhere within your section. For number six, you will need to work with three others to complete the task. You may not partner with any of the same people twice. When you have finished all six challenges—and you will be timed on these—find a Golly guide. Wave, Golly guides."

A bunch of adults in bright yellow shirts waved wildly.

"Request a GollyReader from them and then enter your answers. That's it. It might sound confusing, but it's easy as pie, which you'll discover in one minute."

On cue, the clock hit *1:00, :59, :58.*

"One more thing," said Randy Wright. "This stadium is wired for sound and pictures. You may not discuss the solo challenges with anyone. No whispers, no note passing, no nothing. We will catch you, and you will be eliminated. Otherwise, good luck, and have fun!"

Zane skipped the cheering. He had twenty seconds to strategize. First step: grab three people for challenge six, while everyone was available. The right three, though; ones who might bring different skills to the challenge. He'd worry about finding a partner for the fifth challenge later.

He turned to the faces behind him. There was an

older girl one row up, standing as confident as Zoe. Her. He made eye contact, hoped she understood. A few rows above her was a kid who seemed shy and scared. Totally different from Zane. Him. And that scrawny guy who looked like he was about four years old. He had to be really, really smart, unless he'd been an instant winner. Regardless, he was on Team Zane, too.

Three. Two. One.

Zane didn't open his packet. He reached the girl first. "Group?" he asked.

"Sure."

"Stay there."

Zane raced up three more bleacher rows to the shy kid. "You wanna be on our team?"

"Me?"

Zane nodded. "Go down to the girl with the red shirt." He ran up to the scrawny kid who had some intensity in his eyes. "There're three of us. You're our fourth, okay?"

He didn't wait for the kid to answer, but his footsteps followed. The four of them gathered where the girl had been sitting.

"I'm Zane." He pointed to the girl.

"Cherise."

The scrawny kid. "Elijah."

The shy kid. "Braden."

"We're gonna move fast," said Zane, "so no talking unless it's about what we need to do."

Elijah was holding up the instruction card marked 4-PERSON CHALLENGE. "Yours may all give the same directions, but you can't assume anything here."

Zane already liked this kid's thinking. They compared cards, and they did all match.

Your challenge: Find the word on the wagon wheel.

Why it takes four of you: You need two Wheel Runners, one Line Watcher, and one Letter Reader.

Wheel Runners: You will thread the rope and its already-attached stabilizing rod through the center of the wheel. Clamp eight bars onto the rod. Holding only the rope, you will propel the wheel forward. You may not go backwards. You may not touch the rod NOR the wheel once the rope is clamped in.

Line Watcher: Occasional red lines mark the outside of the wheel. Each time a red line appears at the apex of the wheel, alert the Letter Reader.

Letter Reader: As the wheel turns, letters will reveal themselves. Note only those letters that are revealed when the Line Watcher alerts you. The letters, in order, will spell a common word that will be your solution for this challenge.

When you are finished: Signal a Golly guide by raising all eight of your arms in the air. Good luck!

"Let's go!" Zane raced down the bleachers. By the size of the wagon wheels lining the perimeter of the field, he already knew he'd be a Wheel Runner. So would Cherise. She was closest to his height. Whichever of the other two claimed to have decent eyesight and the best memory would be the Letter Reader.

Before he got on the field, a Golly guide stopped him to scan all four of their wristbands. "You can store your packets in cubby number two if you want," the man said.

Zane shoved his packet into the back waistband of his jeans—it'd be faster than fetching it afterward—then pulled the nearest wheel away from the wall, resisting the urge to see how many others were doing this same challenge first. Except . . . "Anything in the rules about not doing the four-person first?"

"Any order we want," said Braden. "I already looked."

"Great," Zane said. "Okay, Cherise, help me with the rope. We're going to be the Wheel Runners. You guys decide which of the other two jobs you're doing."

The wheel was tall, almost to Zane's hip, but its base was wide enough to hold itself upright. Cherise fed one end of the rope through the wheel's center hole. Zane grabbed it from the other side and pulled the attached stabilizing rod to the exact middle.

"You need to secure the rod with these." Elijah pointed to the slim metal clamps, four on each side, lying flat against the wheel.

"Good eyes," Zane said, hoping they'd chosen Elijah to read the letters.

Within seconds, Cherise had snapped all four clamps from her side into place. Zane clamped only three.

"You missed one," Elijah said.

"We can't touch the wheel once the rope is in place." Zane positioned it so the wheel was pointing straight into the open field, then he clamped his fourth. "You guys know what you're doing?"

"If it works like we think," said Elijah, "Braden will walk in front of you to keep you from going too fast, Zane. He'll watch for lines. I'll crawl behind and call out letters."

"Great strategy," Zane said.

"I can crawl pretty fast," said Elijah, "but I'll say 'whoa' if you need to slow down."

"Let's do this!" said Zane.

Zane and Cherise started the wheel forward. It wobbled at first, but if they held the rope as taut and as close to the rod as possible, it stayed fairly steady. As the wheel moved, flaps on the inside-top of the wheel opened to reveal letters. There must have been fifty of those flaps. No wonder they needed a Line Watcher.

Braden moved into position in front of Zane. "A red line is coming up," he said. "And now!"

"*U*," said Elijah.

"Another, right . . . now!"

"*R*."

"Right . . . now!"

"*S*."

"Right . . . now!"

"*C*." Elijah sounded a little winded.

"We going too fast?" asked Zane.

"Keep going. *U. R. S. C.* Remember those, Braden."

He hoped Braden remembered. Zane didn't.

"And . . . now!" said Braden.

"*O.*"

"Now!"

"*R.*"

It was hard enough to keep the wheel on course.

"Now!"

"*E.*"

Cherise, though, was holding up her end.

"Now!"

"*F.*"

"Now!"

"*O.*"

"Now!"

"*U.*"

"Now!"

"*R.*"

"Now!"

"*S,*" puffed Elijah. "And whoa!"

"Too fast?" said Cherise.

"No," Elijah said. "We're back at the beginning. We're starting to repeat." He rolled over from his knees to a sitting position, then pulled the smashed packet from the back of his own jeans. Elijah took out a pen. "Your letters were *U, R, S, C*, right, Braden?"

"Right."

"Then *O, R, E, F, O*," Elijah said, writing all this down.

"That's what I remember," said Cherise.

"Then *U, R, S* again," said Elijah.

Zane had chosen his team well.

Braden was sitting next to Elijah, looking at the letters. Zane and Cherise were leaning over them.

From Zane's perspective, the letters didn't seem to spell a real word. U-R-S-C-O-R-E-F-O-U-R-S. "Did we get it wrong? Do we need to do it over?"

Of course they didn't. They needed to—

"No," said Elijah. "The word doesn't start with *U*."

"Yeah," Zane said. "I just realized that."

"Scorefour?" said Cherise.

"That's what it looks like," said Braden, "once you delete the repeat letters."

"No," said Elijah. "It's—"

"Not so loud," said Zane.

Elijah pointed to the *F*. "Start here."

"You guys are great, but hurry," Zane said. "Stand

and put your arms in the air. And just so we're all on the same page"—he lowered his voice—"the answer is 'fourscore,' right?"

The Golly guy rushed to them and scanned their bracelets again.

"Right," said Elijah. "Like Lincoln's 'fourscore and seven years ago,' where he's talking about—"

Before Elijah could say anything else, Zane turned to run off.

CHAPTER 11

Zane stopped. He didn't want to give away his strategy, but these had been perfect teammates. "We can't work together for the two-person challenge, so if you're smart, grab a good partner now."

Then he bolted up four rows of bleachers to a girl who seemed focused on a puzzle and, at the same time, aware of her surroundings. "Have you done your two-person yet?"

"I haven't finished the solo pack. Randy Wright said—"

"The instructions say any order. Work with me or not?"

"Sure, but we need to go in there." She pointed behind her.

"In where?"

Instead of answering, she climbed the bleachers. Zane didn't know where she was going, but she was going there fast. She headed through the tunnel and into the concession area, where they came face-to-face with a sign. PAIRS CHALLENGE. Arrows pointed left.

"I'm Zane, by the way," he said, jogging with the arrows, the challenge area in sight.

"Grace," she said, her eyes smiling and her black ponytail bobbing like crazy.

"So, Grace," Zane said, "what else do you know about this pairs challenge?"

"That I'm suddenly stupid for not realizing I could have already—" She gasped.

"What?"

"That wheel thing. I should've done that first. I have to find three people!"

He couldn't let her bolt on him now. Before he could convince her to stay, Grace grabbed three people coming back into the stadium from the pairs and told them where to wait for her.

"Promise you won't move. I'll be fast." They

agreed. If only she were managing their football team instead of Thing 1 and Thing 2.

He and Grace raced to the pairs line.

A Golly guide came up. "Welcome! Two sections share five pairs stations, so with six pairs already waiting, it'll be a few minutes. Feel free to use this time well, but from here on out, no talking in line and no sharing of papers."

Zane sat, reached into his packet, and pulled out an envelope marked "Solo Pack." In it, four note cards were paper clipped together. The top one said:

Solo Challenge #1
✳ ✳ ✳ ✳ ✳ ✳ ✳ ✳ ✳ ✳

The banners that descended over the field aren't there for show. Collectively, these banners contain all the letters of the alphabet. There are, however, three consonants that appear only once. Find those three consonants, then combine them with an Є and an O to spell a common-word answer. All the banners you need are within your section.

✳ ✳ ✳ ✳ ✳ ✳ ✳ ✳ ✳ ✳

He couldn't do that now. He flipped to the next card.

Solo Challenge #2
* * * * * * * * * *

If you spent \$2.20 buying a notebook and a pencil, and if the notebook cost two dollars more than the pencil, how much did the pencil cost?

Easy! The pencil cost twenty cents.

Zane started flipping to the next card, but stopped. They wouldn't ask a question he could've answered in first grade. He butt-scooted up the line—two pairs had just gone in—and looked again at Solo Challenge #2.

If the pencil cost twenty cents, the notebook cost two dollars, but the notebook needed to cost two dollars *more*. His answer had it costing only \$1.80 more. If it cost \$2.05, the pencil would need to be 5 cents, meaning he'd spent only \$2.10. Five cents more . . .

Yes! The pencil was 10 cents and the notebook was \$2.10. Together, \$2.20.

He started an answer sheet on the back of the Solo #2 card:

4-person-fourscore
2-person-
Solo 1-
Solo 2-10 cents
Solo 3-
Solo 4-

Zane and Grace moved up in line. Next card!

Solo Challenge #3
★ ★ ★ ★ ★ ★ ★ ★ ★ ★
1970s Golly Game: Hello, Good___
1980s Golly Game: Plop, Plop, ___clops
1960s Golly Game: Phony Phone ___

Games from ancient history? Zane should have studied the Golly list of toys and games, but there'd been hundreds of them. Maybe thousands. And it had seemed like a waste of time. At least it did then. He couldn't quit now. He looked at the first one. *Hello, Good_____.*

Logic would tell him it's Hello, Good-bye. He wrote -*bye* in the space.

They scooted up one more pair, and he glanced behind them. The line had grown past where they had started. And not everyone was working on puzzles. Had they finished already? He needed to get busy.

Second game. *Plop, Plop, ___clops.* He had no clue.

Next. *Phony Phone ___ .* Were his parents even alive in the 1960s? He should probably know. Now, though, it would be better to know the game. Phony Phone Phone? Phony Phone Number? Phony Phone Call? Phony Cell Phone? They probably didn't have cell phones then, and the blank came after "phone," anyway.

He tapped Grace, who was working on her own puzzles, and they scooted forward again. If he could solve this before they went in, he'd have only two left. Zane stared at the card and— Oh!

Was that a clue? That space between "Phone" and its blank? "Good" didn't have a space; "clops" either. Maybe those answers were each part of one word, but the phone answer was a separate word.

And "clops" wasn't capitalized. What single

word ended in "clops"? Cyclops! Was that it? Wait. "Bye" and "cy" rhymed. Was there a rhyming word that went with "phone"? Phony Phone Cry? Phony Phone Pie? Phony Phone Sky? He cruised through the alphabet: "by," "bly," "bry," "chi" . . . And this was ridiculous. This was not the answer.

Maybe the three blanks were supposed to merge, like "tuxedo" in the Mall Round. If the first was "bye" and the second was "cy" and the third was "phone" or "number" or—

He'd had it all along. "Bye," "cy," "call." "Bye-cy-call." Bicycle! Yes? No? If only there was a way to check his answers.

He and Grace scooted up one more spot, but before he could turn to his next card, the Golly people were ready for them.

"Hi, there." The woman scanned their bracelets. "Grace and Zane?"

"Right."

"Good. You haven't worked together yet. You're in Pairs Booth Four. Good luck!" She pointed toward the floor. A series of arrows blinked a path for them around a maze of curtains. When they got to Pairs Booth #4, the arrows divided, directing each of them to different sides of a partition that shielded them from each other.

On Zane's side was a computer monitor that instructed him to put on a pair of headphones, then touch the screen.

"You there?" he said into the headset's microphone.

"That's a yes," she said, exactly the same way Jerome of the JZs would. "Do you see the welcome screen?"

"Yep."

WELCOME TO AMAZING MAZE MANIA, GOLLY'S NEWEST VIDEO GAME!

WHO WILL GIVE DIRECTIONS AND WHO WILL FOLLOW THEM?

GIVE DIRECTIONS (CONTESTANT NUMBER):

FOLLOW DIRECTIONS (CONTESTANT NUMBER):

"Two questions," said Zane. "How are you at video games? And how are you at giving directions?"

"Fair at video games, good at directions."

"Then we have it," said Zane.

Zane typed his number next to "Follow Directions." The screen showed Grace doing the same next to "Give Directions." How had he managed to pick someone so focused so fast? It must have been her eyes. It was always the eyes.

Zane's screen flashed with a bunch of words. "You have instructions, too?"

"That's another yes." Just like Jerome again. No doubt she'd fit right in with the JZs and company. "Let me know when you're finished reading."

"You, too."

WELCOME TO AMAZING MAZE MANIA!

YOU WILL EACH HAVE A DIFFERENT VIEW OF YOUR MAZE. (THERE ARE MANY MAZES IN THE VIDEO GAME, BUT TODAY, YOU'LL RANDOMLY RECEIVE THE FOREST MAZE, THE GLACIER MAZE, THE CORNFIELD MAZE, OR THE ELECTRONICS STORE MAZE.)

TO THE CONTESTANT WHO WILL GIVE DIRECTIONS: YOU WILL SEE A VIEW FROM ABOVE,

ONE THAT MORE CLEARLY SHOWS HOW TO NAVI-
GATE FROM THE ENTRY OF THE MAZE TO THE EXIT.
IT IS YOUR JOB TO GUIDE YOUR PARTNER THROUGH
THE MAZE.

**TO THE CONTESTANT WHO WILL FOLLOW
DIRECTIONS:** YOU WILL SEE THE MAZE AS IF YOU
WERE IN IT YOURSELF. IT IS YOUR JOB TO USE
THE ARROW KEYS TO SUCCESSFULLY NAVIGATE
THROUGH THE MAZE BY FOLLOWING YOUR PART-
NER'S INSTRUCTIONS. AS YOU GO THROUGH THE
MAZE, IT WILL REVEAL A SERIES OF LETTERS THAT
WILL SPELL THE ANSWER TO THIS CHALLENGE. IF AT
THE END OF THE MAZE YOU HAVE NOT COLLECTED
LETTERS THAT, IN ORDER, SPELL A COMMON WORD,
HIT RESET AND TRY AGAIN. GOOD LUCK!

TO THE CONTESTANT WHO WILL GIVE DIRECTIONS:
COMMUNICATION WITH YOUR PARTNER MAY CONSIST
ONLY OF INSTRUCTIONS (TURN LEFT, TURN RIGHT,
NEXT PATH, OR ANYTHING TO HELP YOUR PARTNER
NAVIGATE). ANY OTHER TYPE OF COMMUNICATION
WILL CAUSE YOU BOTH TO INCUR PENALTY SECONDS.

**TO THE CONTESTANT WHO WILL FOLLOW
DIRECTIONS:** COMMUNICATION WITH YOUR PARTNER

MAY CONSIST ONLY OF "PLEASE REPEAT" OR "SAY THAT AGAIN" OR OTHER PHRASES THAT INDICATE YOU DID NOT HEAR THE INSTRUCTIONS. YOU MAY ALSO ANNOUNCE THE LETTERS REVEALED TO YOU. **TO BOTH CONTESTANTS:** WHEN YOU ARE BOTH SATISFIED YOU HAVE DISCOVERED THE COMMON-WORD ANSWER, HIT FINISH. MAKE SURE, HOWEVER, YOU ARE SATISFIED. YOUR MONITORS WILL SHUT DOWN, AND YOU WILL NOT BE ABLE TO RETURN TO THE PAIRS AREA. PLEASE REMOVE YOUR EARPHONES AND EXIT THE AREA. IF YOU CANNOT COME TO A CONSENSUS, HIT DISPUTE, AND A GOLLY ATTENDANT WILL ASSIST YOU.

"That's not gonna happen," said Zane.

"What?"

"We are going to agree. No disputes."

"Not at all," said Grace. "Ready?"

"I just hit Continue."

She must have, too, because cornstalks covered every millimeter of Zane's screen. Even the path's floor looked like trampled cornstalks. Glaciers would have been cooler, but corn was tasty.

"Forward," Grace said, "but not too fast. You'll take the second path on the left."

Zane inched forward and, almost immediately, a crow flew at him from a path on the right. He reeled back but stayed focused and turned left at the second path. An ear of corn opened and showed him a letter. "First letter, *C*," Zane said.

"Got it," said Grace. "You can go faster if you want, but you'll be turning right, then left, then right in fast succession."

Turn when? Zane couldn't ask, so he pushed the forward arrow more slowly than he wanted and waited for her signal. Forward. Forward. Forward. "Next letter, *E*."

"Great," said Grace. "There's an opening to the left, but don't take that. Do take the next one on the right."

Okay. Good. He moved a little faster, passed the left path, then turned right.

"Now left."

He did.

"Now right. Then straight."

He made the turns, then went faster, but an ear of corn opened and closed before he was sure of the letter.

"Either letter *M*, *N*, or *W*." Zane wanted to explain why he didn't know for sure, but if she was smart, she'd understand why he'd slowed down.

"Okay. So you'll take the next fork to the right, then I will lose you for a minute when you pass under some sort of cornstalk ceiling. When you're under there, you'll need to take a right. It won't be a sharp right. You'll probably just veer. More instructions when you come out."

He ducked under the cornstalk ceiling and ran into a flock of crows.

"Boo!" A scarecrow popped from the stalks, and the birds flew away.

Zane tried not to laugh. He didn't want to risk

Grace asking him why and triggering a penalty. Just as his voice was about to crack, an ear of corn gave him another letter. "*T*," he said.

But now he had choices. There were three openings coming up on the right. He slowed considerably near the first. If he turned there, he'd pick up the letter *A*, but that path appeared to double back behind him. That wasn't how she'd described it. The second choice had the letter *I*, but it looked like a ninety-degree turn. He passed that up, too. The third went off at a forty-five-degree angle. He turned that way. "*U*," he said. "The letter *U*," he clarified, so she wouldn't think he was calling out, "Hey, you!"

"Good," said Grace. "And you're back out. You're on the right track. Take the left fork, then an immediate left, like you're going backwards."

He hated not talking, not being able to say "okay" or "got it" or "thank you." But he could give her the next letter. "*R*." And why hadn't he been writing the letters down? Oh, man. He hoped she was. And he couldn't even ask. The last three had been *T*, *U*, and *R*. Immediately before that was the one he really didn't see.

"Turn right."

He did.

"Now left."

He was racing through the maze, but he was barely touching the controls.

"Right! Left! Slow down!"

He took his hands off the controls, but it acted like he was still running. Zane pressed the backwards key, and he stopped.

"Okay, next right. Then another immediate right."

He was walking again. He breathed.

She sighed. "Go straight for a while. Then one last left, and you're out."

If he was almost out, she'd done great, but what about him? Had he gotten all the letters when the maze went nuts? Would they need to do it again? He'd picked well with her, but would she curse the day he'd chosen her?

He needed another letter. He couldn't think of any word that ended in –T-U-R.

"Left turn coming . . . now."

And yes! "The letter Y," he said.

"Straight, and you're out."

Zane pushed the forward arrow as fast as he could,

exited the maze, and watched the screen dissolve to pure white with three choices: "Finish, Reset, or Dispute." Underneath it said, *You may now discuss your answer.*

The moment of truth. "You have what I have?" Zane asked, nearly holding his breath that she'd noted those first few letters.

"C-E, then it has to be an *N* and not the *M* or *W* for 'century.'"

"Great!" Zane said, exhaling maybe too audibly. "Hit Finish!" He did.

She must have, too, because the screen said, *Please exit the pairs area.*

She gave him a quick hug. "Gotta find my people. Thanks!"

"You were great. Catch you later!"

Maybe he would, maybe he wouldn't. Zane couldn't worry about that, though. He had two more puzzles to solve.

Zane sat in the first bleacher row he came to and added "century" to his list of answers. He turned to the only challenge he hadn't looked at yet.

Solo Challenge #4

✳ ✳ ✳ ✳ ✳ ✳ ✳ ✳ ✳ ✳ ✳

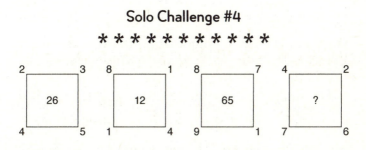

Math! He'd know when he was right. Time to decode the system.

Zane added the numbers surrounding the

first box. Only 14; 12 less than the 26 inside. And the number in the second box was 12! So—

No. If he applied the same method—if he subtracted the 14 surrounding box two from the 12 inside—there'd need to be a −2 inside box three, not 65. But here was the real question: If the numbers around box one and box two each added to 14, why were their inside numbers so different?

It had to be multiplication. There were two 1s around box two. That would automatically make that product less than if he multiplied the numbers around box one.

Hmm—8 times 1 was 8; 4 times 1 was 4. Added together, 12! But would that work with the other boxes?

He multiplied the numbers at the top of box one, then added them to the multiplied numbers on the bottom: 2 times 3 plus 4 times 5—26! And for box three: 8 times 7 plus 9 times 1? Oh yeah!

Now the answer that mattered: 4 times 2? Eight.

Plus 6 times 7? Forty-two. Zane added *50* to his master answer list.

Last card.

Solo Challenge #1
＊ ＊ ＊ ＊ ＊ ＊ ＊ ＊ ＊ ＊

The banners that descended over the field aren't there for show. Collectively, these banners contain all the letters of the alphabet. There are, however, three consonants that appear only once. Find those three consonants, then combine them with an Є and an O to spell a common word. All the banners you need are within your section.

He started copying the banners onto the back of his instruction sheet.

you have what it takes to win!
just go for it!
play fast, play smart, play quick . . . excel!
the gollywhopper games—bigger! braver! bolder!
expect major success!

All those banners, and just five sayings? Maybe so. He could always hunt for more.

Underneath the sayings, he wrote the consonants he'd need to eliminate.

B   C   D   F   G   H   J   K   L   M
N   P   Q   R   S   T   V   W   X   Y   Z

Easiest to see were the *P*s and *L*s in "Gollywhopper." He Xed through those. And there were two *X*s, in "Excel" and "Expect." He Xed through the *X*. And he could do this faster if he went through the letters in order.

B. "Bigger! Braver!" He didn't need "Bolder!" Zane Xed through the *B*.

C. In "Excel" and in "success." He Xed through that, too.

D. Either it was one of the three letters he needed or he'd missed seeing a banner. For now, Zane circled it.

When he'd gotten through all the letters, he had four left.

X X Ⓓ X X X X X X
Ⓝ X Ⓠ X X X X X X Z

He hadn't seen even one *Z*. There had to be another banner, but if this was a common word and if the only vowels were *E* and *O*, there couldn't be a *Q*; otherwise, they'd have given him a *U*.

He'd look for more banners if necessary, but right now, he'd play with the letters he had: *D, N, Z, E, O*. And if the word ended with a common suffix, if it ended in –E-D. "Zoned"!

He totally hadn't zoned out on that one.

Now what? Now he needed to find a Golly guide. There! At the base of the bleachers. He bolted down. "Got it!" he said, as out of breath as if he'd just played the last down of an overtime game. He held out his wristband.

She scanned it, pulled a GollyReader from a gear bag, scanned its label, tapped its screen to life, and handed it to Zane. "This will tell you what to do."

CONGRATULATIONS! IF YOU'RE HERE, IT MEANS YOU'VE SOLVED SIX PUZZLES! EACH ANSWER WAS EITHER A NUMBER OR A WORD THAT SUGGESTED A NUMBER. ADD THOSE NUMBERS AND ENTER THE SUM. (TOUCH INSIDE THE BOX BELOW TO ACCESS THE KEYBOARD. TYPE YOUR FINAL ANSWER. HIT ENTER.) THAT SUM, BY THE WAY, EQUALS THE NUMBER OF TOYS AND GAMES OUR FOUNDER THADDEUS G. GOLLIWOP DEVELOPED ON HIS OWN. IMPORTANT! TO COMPLETE THE STADIUM CHALLENGE, YOU MUST RETURN THIS DEVICE TO A GOLLY GUIDE.

Zane pulled out his answer sheet and finished filling it in.

4-person-fourscore
2-person-century
Solo 1-zoned
Solo 2-10 cents
Solo 3-bicycle
Solo 4-50

* * *

Now add them up. Man. If only he'd stayed to hear Elijah's explanation, he'd probably know all about Abraham Lincoln's "fourscore and seven years ago." But he could figure it out.

Lincoln wrote the Gettysburg Address sometime during the Civil War, the 1860s. And "fourscore and seven years ago" something had happened, something important. Where was Mrs. Connors when he needed her?

Zane took a deep breath. What happened before the Civil War? The War of 1812? Or wait. The American Revolution. And if they signed the Declaration of Independence in 1776 . . .

He did the math in his head. The 1861 of the Civil War minus the 1776 of the American Revolution equaled 85. So if Lincoln delivered the Gettysburg Address just two years later, then "fourscore and seven" should equal 87, which meant . . .

Zane wrote *80* next to "fourscore." Underneath that, *100* for "century."

But "zoned"? That wasn't a number word. Should he have found that last banner?

Maybe not. Maybe he'd unscrambled it wrong.

Maybe his -ED suffix should've been a DE- prefix instead. "Denoz." No. "Dezon." And then it was like the letters magically rearranged themselves in his mind. "Dozen." He jotted down *12*. The rest were easy. He marked *10* for the "cents," *2* for the "bicycle," and *50* was already there.

Eighty plus 100—180. Plus 12—192. And 10 cents was 202. Plus 2 for the bicycles—204. And 50 more. That old guy invented 254 games all on his own? Wow!

Zane rechecked his math. He touched the 2, the 5, and the 4. Enter!

The GollyReader went black. Nothing. C'mon. C'mon! And then it lit with big, colorful exclamation points.

Zane raced to a Golly guide, who checked him in, collected his GollyReader, and pointed to the cordoned-off rows at the top of the bleachers. "Report to Connie. She's expecting you."

"How'd I do?" Zane asked.

"I have no clue," said the man.

"How many people have you checked in?"

"It wouldn't mean anything if I told you."

"Did the exclamation points mean anything?"

"What exclamation points?" The man reached around Zane for another kid's GollyReader.

At least Zane had beaten her. He climbed the bleachers to the cordoned-off section. "Are you Connie?"

"I am." She scanned his wristband and let him past the ropes. "And you are Zane." She pressed a button on her scanner.

"What's this scan for?"

"We're nosy," Connie said. "We like to know who's where at all times."

That was as close to a real answer as he'd gotten.

The scanner spit out a receipt. Connie pointed to the large *151* printed above a bar code with a string of numbers and letters. "This means you were the one hundred fifty-first person to check in. You'll find out soon if that was fast enough. And if you got the correct answer. That's all I can tell you."

One hundred fifty-first out of a thousand? If the first 15 percent moved on, he'd be out. By one. If he wasn't in, he wished they'd send him home now. Maybe let him shower in the team locker room, which would be totally cool, but he needed to stop thinking about football. Better to focus on the Games. This whole morning, for the first time in forever, he hadn't thought about concussions.

Zane took his 151 receipt and a bottle of water to a seat in the bleachers under the canopy of banners.

About ten other people were scattered in his section, including that short, scrawny kid from their four-person challenge, the one who had intensity in his eyes. That Elijah.

Zane downed most of his water and stared at all those groups still on the field, rolling their wheels, trying not to bump into one another. If the Games kept going until that one incompetent group finished, he'd be there all week. He needed a diversion, something less nerve-racking than waiting for the results.

Zane moved over and sat a few feet away from Elijah. "How long have you been here?"

Elijah didn't seem to notice Zane's existence. He sat there, staring forward. Zombie?

Zane smiled and leaned way back, barely able to rest his elbows on the bleacher bench behind him. He noticed a banner he hadn't seen, the one with second the Q and the one Z. QUIT? ARE YOU CRAZY?

That could be his motto.

"How many individual fiber filaments are in each banner, do you think?" Elijah asked out of the blue. "I know there're a couple hundred thousand fibers per square inch of a microfiber towel, but this is different material."

"Are you talking to me?"

"Yeah." Elijah stuck his elbows behind him to sit like Zane, but his elbows missed and his head thwacked the seat.

"You okay?" Zane asked.

"If awkward's okay." Elijah wriggled back. If he wanted to match Zane's position, he'd need to grow another foot. Or not. He scooched his butt back, so it was sitting on the concrete. His calves lopped onto the bench in front and his elbows barely reached the seat in back.

"To answer your question from before," Elijah said, "I got here about four minutes before you checked in with the Golly guide."

Zane laughed.

"What'd I say?"

"It's not what you said." Zane shook his head. "It's when you said it."

Elijah stared at the banners. "As long as I'm being awkward, I'll wonder out loud if there's some sort of additive you can combine with unwanted cloth to generate a small yet significant alternative energy source."

"How do you even think of that?"

"It's the outside-the-box cliché. Most people trash old banners or old clothes because that's the norm. I try to ignore how things"—and he made air quotes with his fingers—"are supposed to be and think about what might be possible."

This kid was the true opposite of Zane's friends, but in a strange sort of way, it'd be okay to hang out with him. Never at school, though. That would be just weird. Then again, once football season started, everything would turn weird. Zane could find himself on the outside of the JZs' inside jokes, which might grow so depressing, he'd need to choose to be either a loner or find other people to hang out with. Was there even anyone else worth hanging out with? That Grace, but she didn't go to his school. Maybe he should've kept track of Daryl.

"So let's say," said Elijah, "there are about six billion

fibers in all these banners." He turned to Zane. "How many polyesters were killed to make them?"

Polyesters? What?

Elijah's whole face lit up in a big smile. "You know polyester isn't a living thing, right?" Then he laughed.

Zane couldn't help but laugh with him. "Sure."

"Then again, the banners are probably made of nylon, and I have no clue how many fibers are in a square inch of nylon."

"And that matters because . . ." Zane didn't mean to sound snarky but still . . .

"Doesn't matter. It's just how my brain is wired."

"Are you some sort of genius?" Zane asked.

"Yeah."

"How old are you? What grade are you in?"

"I turned eleven yesterday. In a couple weeks I'll be a senior in high school. I could handle college now, but my parents want me to slow down and enjoy life."

"So you're the one."

"Which one?" Elijah's eyes twinkled like he knew all the secrets of the world and he was willing to share with the right people.

They sat in silence, Zane finally feeling the summer

heat now that his adrenaline levels were coming down. But Elijah kept him entertained. It was like the movements of his fingers and the twitchiness of his head were overflow from the furious whirring in his brain. And the best part, Elijah probably didn't care if it looked weird. He knew he was weird, and he wore it as well as Zane would have worn the captain's *C* on his jersey this coming season.

The captain's *C*. Would his team have one less captain or would another guy prove himself worthy? How would someone do that? How had Zane done that? And what if—

He tried to shake the thought he'd been dodging all summer, but it was coming on stronger than ever, like a bullet train he couldn't derail. Zane started upright from his laid-back position on the bleachers, but resisted the instinct to curl forward in a ball. He could take this. Here it came.

What if—

What if his football ban lasted more than a year? No. That wasn't the real question. This was: What if he could never play football again?

More than once, the doctor had said Zane "should

be all right," which always brought a rush of relief, but one that fizzled fast. The doctor's optimism came with no guarantees. Even so, Zane kept holding on to the "should be" like a "will be," but he couldn't delude himself anymore. And the thought of never wearing his captain *C*? That hurt. No, it ached.

He couldn't imagine going through life as another body in a crowd, another fan in the stands, being ushered from some stadium, today's stadium even, into oblivion. He needed to be in the heart of the action. He needed to run, tackle, deny, intercept—to use his "mad skills," Coach had called them.

Were those skills the only reasons Zane had earned his captain's *C*? Or was there something more, some instinct, some other qualities? There had to be. And more important, could he find those here and prove there was more game to him than football?

Zane finished his water and turned to Elijah. "I'll be right back, buddy." Zane would have explained where he was going, but Elijah seemed to know and notice everything.

Zane waved his empty water bottle as he approached Connie, the Golly person.

She grabbed another for him.

"I'm pretty thirsty," he said. "Should I take two or won't we be here that long?"

She looked at her watch. "It appears, number one fifty-one, you're fishing for information at exactly the right time." She handed him one bottle and smiled.

"That's all you can give me?"

"Yep," she said. "Water and my best wishes for your patience."

Zane shrugged his shoulders and turned.

"Oh, and one more thing." She looked at her watch again. "You'll just need to be patient for five minutes, and four, three . . ." She pointed to the scoreboard.

"You have five minutes. Five minutes to finish," said Randy Wright's voice.

The scoreboard clock began a five-minute countdown. The contestants who had already finished, cheered. The ones on the field and the lower bleachers seemed to hunker down and work faster.

Zane headed back up to Elijah. He should have

gotten another water for the kid. He held out his unopened bottle. "Need this?"

"Thanks, no." He held up his own bottle with barely a quarter of the water gone.

"Are you part camel?"

"I hydrated earlier just in case." Elijah looked away then leaned back over. "But truthfully, I'm more afraid I'll need to pee, and they won't let me find a restroom."

"If they don't let you find a restroom, you find me. You'll get your restroom."

"So you're the enforcer type? You're big enough."

Zane shook his head. "Honestly, I'm not that tough, but I can make things happen."

"That works, too."

Time to move the subject off himself. He downed half his water and pointed the bottle at the scoreboard. "Two-minute warning."

"So you're a football guy."

"You like football?"

"I like the strategy."

"Yes!" said Zane. "Strategy! Like when you look into the tackle's eyes and realize he and the guard are gonna double-team your center, so you freelance to fill that gap, and the running back can't even make it to the line of scrimmage. Stuff like that you learn, but you also just feel."

"I don't know about that, but I was thinking more along the lines of sacrificing a few downs, perhaps throwing a bomb or two in order to stretch the field and allow your team longer gains with higher-percentage plays."

"You? You know about football?"

Elijah didn't answer him. Instead he blended in with the growing group chanting, "Ten, nine, eight . . ."

". . . seven, six, five. . ." Zane joined in.

"Four, three, two, one!"

A horn blew.

"Stop!" said Randy Wright's voice. "If you are sitting in the stands, please remain where you are. If you are on the field or anywhere outside the stands, please find a seat in your designated section. You have two minutes to get there."

Two minutes until the referees came in with a ruling.

Chapter 14

Elijah pointed to the field. "At least two hundred kids didn't finish, or so it appears."

"But I might be outta here, too," said Zane.

Elijah took Zane's ticket and studied it for a few seconds before he gave it back. "Seriously? That many checked in during those four minutes?"

"Why? What number are you?"

"Three."

"Three?" said Zane. "If it were me, I'd wonder who numbers one and two were."

"Just number two. Number one got sick all over the place—yech!—and had to leave. Couldn't handle the pressure."

"Maybe number two couldn't handle it either, and I'm looking at number one."

"I hope not. I'd love finally having someone to catch up with."

Elijah? Competitive, like Zane? How could two people so different be so similar?

"So wait," said Zane. "If number one really did leave, and even if everyone else got the right answer, I'm suddenly number one fifty."

"True, but that's important because . . . ?"

"If one fifty is their cutoff point—"

"Fifteen percent, a solid number."

"But ten percent would be more solid."

"Odds are, though," said Elijah, "not everyone got the right answer."

"You did, I assume."

"Yeah."

That wasn't bragging. That just was. "So can—"

"The answer's two fifty-four," said Elijah.

"Yes!" Zane leaned back again, not able to hide his smile. At least there was that.

The buzzer sounded again, and a man ran to the center of the fifty-yard line. "Hello, everyone!

I'm Randy Wright. Congratulations on making it this far!"

There were a few anxious cheers.

"That's the good news. The bad? We will be saying good-bye to most of you soon."

Zane sat straight up, the adrenaline pumping.

"If you're one of the two hundred fourteen who didn't finish, thanks for playing, but we ask that you exit the stadium now to receive your fifty-dollar Golly gift certificate. We will have another announcement soon. Everyone else, sit tight."

"Only seven hundred eighty-six left," said Zane.

Elijah shook his head. "One less. Don't forget the guy who puked."

That was still too many for Zane to relax. Elijah knocked on Zane's shoulder. "You do know you're through to the next round."

"How can you be sure?"

"You got the right answer. You checked in only four minutes after I did. It all adds up."

"But you don't know how many they're gonna take. You can't be sure."

"I can't?" Elijah stared right into his eyes, almost

challenging him. It was like Zane had met his match, if you could match apples and jet planes.

Zane watched the nonfinishers, including Grace, disappear into the tunnels.

"Have you seen Braden and Cherise?" asked Zane.

Elijah pointed. Their other teammates were together at the far end of their section. "You do realize," said Elijah, "that your orchestrating everything is partially why we're all here. Toward the end—well, you saw—it was sheer pandemonium on the field. I'm just a novice at strategy, and you've already taught me so much."

Zane tried not to smile.

Randy Wright's voice helped with that. It made him sit a little straighter. "I know you're all on pins and needles. Did I get the right answer? Did I do it fast enough?"

"Relax!" said Elijah.

Zane smiled for that.

"Please look at your receipts," said Randy Wright. "If your number is five hundred or higher, I'm sorry, but you weren't quick enough. Please exit, receive your seventy-five-dollar Golly gift certificate, and reunite with your families."

At least Zane wasn't gone yet.

"Good," said Elijah. "You're not like a steel rod anymore. Just a wooden plank."

"I assume that's a positive?"

"It is. You're still in this, but the negative is, you're going to need your brain cells to function at a higher level. You should see the data on how stress affects productivity."

"Then why am I better on the football field when I'm all amped up?"

"Different kind of stress. Physical stress. Your adrenal glands were designed to prepare you for physical fight or flight. And despite the wheel challenge, which wasn't all that physical for you, this isn't physical today."

A few stragglers still headed into the tunnels.

Zane sighed.

"Stop it," said Elijah, "or I'll make you stop it."

"How?"

"Hold up your receipt." Elijah held his next to Zane's. "See? Further proof you're in."

"What am I missing?" said Zane. He'd never known a guy who made him feel utterly moronic and totally confident at the same time.

"The numbers and letters under the bar code. Your string is the same as mine except where I have oh-oh-oh-three and six-fifteen, you have oh-one-five-one and seven-nine-eight, our check-in numbers and our wristband numbers."

"I'm starting to believe you, Elijah." He felt himself melting from a wooden plank into an over-inflated football.

Elijah was about to point out something else, but Randy Wright came back. "There are nearly five hundred of you left. And now I can tell you, that with ties, one hundred eighteen of you have made it to the next round."

"That's not good," Zane said.

Elijah gave him a look.

"Okay, okay."

"Freeze!" said Randy Wright. "I see some of you getting up, but this still isn't over. Now please get out your receipts, because they tell you if you're staying for the next round or if you're going home with a hundred-dollar Golly gift certificate."

"I could live with that," said Zane.

"Why, when you can get more?" Elijah pointed to the

writing under the bar code. *SECD0151798RND02.*

"And that means?"

"S-E-C-D. Section D. Then our check-in numbers and our contestant identifier. And surely, you can figure out the rest."

He could? Zane stared down Elijah, who just smiled. Fine. What was the rest? RND02. Was that 0 a zero? If it was and he put a space between the letters and numbers . . .

But he needed Randy Wright to say it. "And RND02?" Randy said. "You got it! Round two!"

Zane grabbed Elijah, then together, they dodged the people trying to leave, and whooped it up with the others who'd made it through.

"See? I told you!" said Elijah.

Zane pushed Elijah in the shoulder; nearly pushed him over. "Why didn't you tell me when you first knew?"

"Didn't want to ruin the moment for you."

"Do you know everything?"

"Not yet," Elijah said.

Zane shook his head. "Enough, though. I'm thinking I should pack it up and go home with the rest of them. Who can beat you?"

"You'd be surprised," Elijah said. "I'm not Superman. Besides, *I'm* thinking you're not the type who gives up easily."

Zane pushed him in the shoulder again, but this time not too hard. "You do know everything."

The sun had shifted to a gap in the banners overhead. They scooted to catch up with the shade, then watched the expressions of the people heading out. They ranged from "don't care" to "end of the world."

This part wouldn't take long. Like Elijah said, they just needed to get rid of about thirty-eight people from each section, leaving, on average, eleven point eight of them in each.

"Who's the point eight, do you suppose?" asked Elijah.

"In this section? I'd say it's you, you scrawny thing."

They both laughed.

If the JZs could see him hanging around with the likes of Elijah, they'd tease him endlessly. But underneath his awkwardness, Elijah was inexplicably cool. Really cool. And Zane didn't quite know what to think of that.

First came their shadows, then came Cherise and Braden, down the aisle. They took seats in front of Zane and Elijah.

"See?" said Cherise. "I told you they wouldn't kick us out for moving."

Braden looked up at them. "But Randy Wright told us to sit tight."

"And yet we're not kicked out," said Cherise.

They sounded like they'd formed an unlikely relationship, too. And just as unusual-looking a pair. Him, all blond and freckled and round faced and reserved, and her, all dark-skinned and angular and smiling at anyone who might catch her eye.

"You know it's your fault we're here, Zane," said Cherise. "Tell him, Braden."

Braden gave a slight smile and looked down. "She made me admit that I'd probably still be waiting for a team if you hadn't grabbed me. Satisfied?"

Cherise nodded. "My confession? I'd never have thought to do the wheel first. So it's your fault we're still here, Zane."

"I think they're trying to thank you," Elijah said.

"I get it," said Zane, "but, really, it was me being selfish. I needed you guys fast. I just guessed right."

"Instincts, I tell you," said Elijah. "The guy has amazing instincts."

"Okay, Answer Man," said Zane. "You know what I think? They should let us form our own team. We'd do good."

"Well," said Elijah.

"Well, what?"

Elijah looked startled.

Zane laughed. "You didn't mean to say 'well' out loud. You were correcting my English. Then fine, Elijah. I will use proper grammar. We'd do *well*. Better?"

Elijah was saved by Randy Wright. "And now the final round of the day."

The scoreboard lit with a nine-by-nine grid of numbered squares.

Zane leaned in to his group. "If we have to answer eighty-one questions, Elijah wins."

"And no," said Randy Wright, "it's not an eighty-one-answer challenge."

Elijah nudged Zane. "You're turning into a steel rod again."

Zane took a couple of deep breaths while Randy Wright continued.

"Each square represents a question. You must correctly answer five questions whose squares all share at

least one side. Touching at the corners doesn't count. And . . ." He paused.

"Once five of you have correctly answered a question associated with a square, that square will go dark. No one else will be allowed to choose it. Our guides will hand you each a GollyReader, which you will use to claim your questions and type in your answers."

Elijah looked up to Zane. "This is where your strategy comes in."

"I know."

"Not that I'm asking for any hints."

"You don't need them."

"I know."

"But if it's not me, I want it to be you," said Zane. "Stay away from one through thirty-one. Too many people will pick their birthdays. Also stay away from the middle. They'll be scared to get boxed in. You can answer anything, though, so start on an edge. Number sixty-three's good."

"Thanks," said Elijah. "You're doing that?"

"A modified version. I'm not as smart as you."

Cherise turned. "What are you two whispering about?"

Zane liked Cherise and Braden, but he had to keep some advantages for himself. "He's trying to convince me not to freak out."

The Golly guide handed out GollyReaders. "You look like a cozy group," she said, "but start saying your good-byes. We're about to split you up." The woman turned.

"Wait," said Cherise. "How many people after this round?"

The woman looked over her shoulder. "I don't exactly know, honey. That's above my pay grade." She winked and left.

"Did she really not know?" asked Braden.

"She knows," Zane and Elijah said at the same time.

Within seconds, Randy Wright was back. "Look at us. We have sixty-five rows of seats in the stadium, and we've bunched you up. Not for long." Randy Wright had them power up their GollyReaders. "Your opening screen should now have your assigned row."

The four of them compared numbers: Braden, 12; Cherise, 37; Elijah, 4; and Zane up top at 65.

"Get going and take any seat in that row," said Randy Wright.

Elijah and Braden didn't even say good-bye. They just shot down the bleachers.

"That was a little awkward," said Cherise. She gave Zane a hug. "Thanks again. I'll think about you when I'm spending my gift certificate."

Zane smiled. "You never know. Maybe I'll see you around."

He went up two rows and chose a shaded spot. His GollyReader vibrated. Zane touched the screen. On it were the instructions, basically what Randy Wright had said about answering five questions in adjoining squares. Also, he wouldn't know if his answers were right or wrong until the end. If he was working on a question that was no longer available, his GollyReader would tell him. The full, updated grid would only appear on the scoreboard.

Zane put his game plan together. He'd normally start with square twenty-one, his jersey number, but twenty-one was a day of the month, probably someone's birthday, and a multiple of lucky seven. He'd move it down two rows to thirty-nine. An unlikely number. Third from the left, fifth from the top. He'd start there and work his way to the left edge—thirty-eight and thirty-seven—then see what was available.

He was ready. He took in a few deep breaths. Poised his finger over the keyboard.

"You may start," said Randy Wright, "in five, four, three, two, one, GO!"

Zane punched in the three, then the nine.

QUESTION 39

———

OIL–

ILL

"Oil" minus "ill"? But why would the minus sign be in the wrong place? "Oil" dash "ill"? And what was that line at the top? If it were a math problem a line like that would be at the—

He turned his GollyReader upside down.

᧐᧐|

-᧐|O

———

Easy math. Zane typed *61* in the answer box, then glanced at the scoreboard. Question 38 was still open. Zane requested it.

QUESTION 38

THERE WAS ONE PRODUCT THADDEUS G. GOLLIWOP REGRETTED NEVER HAVING MADE. (HINT: IT WAS A VERSION OF THE FAMOUS TOY WITH COOKIE-SHAPED DISKS AND A STRING IN THE MIDDLE.) NAME IT.

Thank goodness for the hint. Thank goodness Zane had spent a year obsessed with yo-yos. With *yo-yo* typed in, he stole another glance at the scoreboard. He was still good.

QUESTION 37

FIVE FOOTBALL PLAYERS ARE LINED UP IN THIS ORDER:

WHEN THE SIXTH PLAYER SHOWS UP, WHICH NUMBER SHOULD BE ON HIS JERSEY?

Great. Distract him with thoughts of football. But this wasn't about football. This was a number sequence. Okay. To get from eight to ten, add two. To get from ten to eighteen, add eight, the previous number. To get from eighteen to twenty, add two. To get from twenty to thirty-eight, add the eighteen. But wait. Was that the eighteen itself or was it the sum of the two previous numbers? It didn't matter. It was time to add two again. He typed in *40*.

Three down, two to go. The grid was starting to blacken at potential birthday numbers and right in the middle. He went down.

QUESTION 46

IF A BAT AND A CAT WERE ON A HAT, WHERE MIGHT YOU FIND A DOG AND A FROG?

(MULTIPLE ANSWERS POSSIBLE. GIVE US ONE.)

Seriously? Could it be that easy? In a bog? On a log? He chose "log" over "bog" because "bat," "cat," and "hat" progressed alphabetically. "Bog" wouldn't have.

Just one more. An easy one, please.

The grid was even darker. In fact, he had only 40, 46, and 56 touching his other numbers. And there went 40. He went with 56.

QUESTION 56

NAME TWO TYPES OF MAZES YOU MAY HAVE GONE THROUGH IN THE PAIRS CHALLENGE.

Zane was whipping through these like smashing down tackling dummies. He entered *corn* for the one they'd gone through and *glacier* for the one he'd wanted. He looked up at the scoreboard. Square 56 went dark.

*C*ongratulations! flashed his GollyReader. *Five right!*

Either Zane was a genius, his method worked, or he got lucky. That couldn't have taken more than five minutes. Exactly what were they testing?

Elijah probably knew. There he was, legs propped on the bench in front of him, elbows on the one in back, looking as relaxed as if he were on a beach chair. He was probably the only relaxed person in the place.

Braden had just finished, but Cherise was still hunched over her GollyReader. She needed to hurry. The remaining squares—most around the edges— were going black every few seconds. Soon the entire scoreboard went dark to the sound of scattered groans.

Randy Wright trotted to midfield. "And the squares are gone! Time to look at your GollyReaders, and hit the What's Up button."

Zane did.

WHAT'S UP? YOU COLLECTED FIVE ADJOINING SQUARES. PLEASE STAY WHERE YOU ARE.

He looked toward the lower rows of bleachers. There was Elijah turned toward Zane, his arms straight above his head, both hands clutching his GollyReader. Zane mimicked his pose. But Cherise and Braden were heading out with almost everyone else.

"Sorry to say good-bye to so many now," said Randy Wright. "Enjoy your two-hundred-dollar Golly gift certificates."

Zane counted. Only twenty left in the stadium. It was still too many, but hadn't Randy Wright said something about this being the final round of the day?

His GollyReader vibrated in one quick pulse. The

screen went dark, then came back with WHAT'S UP? again. Zane touched it. The screen blinked TOP 20! EXCEPT . . .

Except what?

Zane poked the screen again.

. . . ONLY 8 WILL BE FINALISTS AND 2 WILL BE ALTERNATES. THE OTHER 10 WILL HEAD HOME WITH $1,000. HARD TO SEPARATE WHO'S WHO, SO . . .

C'mon. He jabbed at the screen.

THE FIRST 8 TO REACH THIS SCREEN . . .

Jab.

YOU'RE NUMBER 2!!!

That was it? He was in? Zane's metal rod became a pogo stick, and he was riding that thing.

And there was Elijah, jumping himself!

"And now that you know your fate," said Randy Wright, "you—"

A kid in Section C had slammed his GollyReader into the bench.

"I saw that!" said Randy Wright. "Looks like you might have made a big mistake, Section C guy, because the GollyReaders are yours to keep.

"As ten of you exit, remember to spend your

thousand dollars in cash wisely. Meanwhile, top ten? Please join me on the field."

It turned out the guy who slammed his GollyReader was actually number nine. "I don't want to be an alternate," he grumbled when he reached the field. "I do not want to be an alternate."

"Nice to meet you, too." Randy Wright stuck out his hand. "I'm Randy, and you are?"

"Berk. And I—"

"I know," said Randy. "You do not want to be an alternate. We can arrange that. You are free to go. We will call back number eleven."

Berk reeled like someone had slapped him, but didn't make a move to leave.

"Ahh!" That had to be Elijah jumping all over Zane's back.

Zane turned, and they clasped in a brief bear hug.

"I told you," said Elijah. "Now, will you listen to me?"

"I'll listen, but I can't promise I'll believe."

"Fair enough," Elijah said.

The midday sun shined between the banners like a spotlight. Cameras circled the winning group, recording this moment from every angle. One cameraperson looked like that Cameron kid from last year, but before Zane could find out for sure, a man in a gray suit strode toward them like he was totally in charge.

"This is great, this is fabulous!" said the man. "I am Bert Golliwop. Welcome to the Gollywhopper Games. Our third. Last year we had six girls and four boys in our finals. This year, it's just the opposite." He stood beside Berk and beckoned to another guy.

"I want you all to give a round of applause to our alternates. Just hundredths of a second separated them from you."

Zane hated the pity clap.

"Now, which of you finished first and second?"

Zane stepped forward, and a girl with silky black hair and a huge smile raised her hand.

"Congratulations, Hanna Lee, number one, and Zane Braycott, number two!" Bert Golliwop led the applause. "Only one one-hundredth of a second separated you two, but it was two seconds later before we heard from number three, Elijah McNair."

"Elijah!" Zane gave him a high five.

"Here's the question, Hanna, Zane. How'd you manage to tap in so fast?"

"I was just paying attention," Hanna said.

"It was basically an adrenaline thing," said Zane. "I had nothing to lose."

"Perfect," said Bert Golliwop. "We love people who take reasonable risks."

"It makes good TV," said Elijah.

Bert Golliwop laughed. "So it does, my friend. Well, we won't keep you here. Momentarily, you'll join your families in the air-conditioned tents. They haven't seen anything since you started the question grid. So might I suggest you burst in at once and give them all a grand surprise?" He motioned for a couple of Golly guides. "These are Sharryn and Wanda, two of our best Games people. They will tell you all you need to know. Until tomorrow." Bert Golliwop bowed out and trotted away.

Sharryn and Wanda stepped up.

Zane could walk into any locker room and tell you who the captains were. No doubt Sharryn was the leader of these two.

"Top ten!" she said. "Congratulations!"

"Yeah, right," Berk said under his breath. "Big deal."

"It is a big deal," said Sharryn. "If you don't think so, no one's keeping you here."

No sympathy for that big doofus? Zane was liking this place more and more.

"All morning, we've purposefully kept every family from knowing exactly where you stood," said Sharryn. "Right now they believe we're organizing you according to airport schedules—which is, in fact, true. You're just not heading to the airport today."

That brought a round of cheers.

"Instead," said Wanda, "you are headed to a hotel where the only guests are people involved in the Games. Feel free to get to know one another. Talk at dinner, meet up at the hotel pool afterward. Then tomorrow. Ah, tomorrow!"

Sharryn laughed. "Don't expect what you've seen in the past. Not at all. But that's tomorrow. For now, let's go!"

Most of them were jumping and running, but Zane was weirdly calm. He'd just defeated a gob of people, but it didn't feel like he'd really won anything except for the chance to play.

The ten of them, though, burst into the family tent, where all the whooping and shouting ignited the energy and flipped Zane's switch. He screamed and jumped and high-fived anything that came his way, even Berk's forehead. And he didn't care.

It was like they'd all become one huge family; one team, all with a team's goal: to win. He'd never celebrated with his competitors before. Zane couldn't wrap his head around that and didn't think he'd be able to. Ever. Right now, it didn't matter. He was here. And he was going to win.

After
THE STADIUM ROUND

Bert sat at his desk, pulse racing, head spinning about what might go wrong tomorrow. He'd scrutinized the footage from all eight spy cams, but no one had entered the two final challenge areas.

Danny came in and tossed Bert a bag of pretzels. "What can I do for you?"

"You can tell me why it hasn't worked. None of it. I thought it'd be foolproof."

"Nothing's foolproof. Maybe Ratso had a change of heart and has no plans to ruin you."

"And maybe it's like that old practical joke, where someone tells you they're going to prank you. It's coming. It will be epic. But the joke is that there is no prank. They just wanted to make you go crazy waiting for it."

"If that's the case," said Danny, "by this time tomorrow, you won't care. We'll be in full celebration mode, the Games will be a success, your trusted team will remain in place, and the world will smile on you."

"You're right, you're right." Bert tried to rub the headache away from his temples. "No, you're wrong. Something's going to happen." Then his face took on a big smile as his executive team came in. He couldn't let on that he suspected any one of them. But someone here was Flummox's little pawn, and he was going to find out. Somehow.

CHAPTER 17

The luxury bus took them straight to their hotel, which, with only Games people staying there, was weirdly quiet. They'd gathered the ten contestants in a dining room. Zane and his dad chose an empty table in the center of the room, and Elijah, his parents, and older sister joined them.

Elijah's family wasn't as scrawny as he was, but they weren't big people, either. Zane's dad towered over them, but they had this powerful presence that made them seem just as tall. Zane had seen that before with a quarterback on an opposing team. To look at him, you'd think he'd fold under a feather, but with a ball in his hands, he was totally in charge.

Zane didn't come close to making an interception that day.

Before Elijah's dad sat, he grasped Zane's shoulder. "Thank you, son, for getting Elijah started on the right foot." He shook his hand. "But what made you pull in a skinny little black kid when there were so many others to choose?" His laugh was larger than he was.

Zane laughed with him.

"In all honesty, though, what did?"

"I was looking for people to balance me out," said Zane. "I was hoping that someone so small had big brains."

"Smart son you have there," Elijah's dad said to Zane's.

"I've been told you have the same."

"Don't always know what to do with it," Elijah's dad said, "but we love it."

Elijah rolled his eyes.

It was easy being with Elijah's family, easier than being with his own. They'd called his mom on speakerphone as soon as they'd checked into the hotel.

"I knew it!" she said.

"You did not," said Zane.

"Oh, yes I did. And I can prove it. Look in the outside pocket of your duffel."

Zane went over and unzipped it. "Underwear?"

"Three extra pairs because you only packed one. There's also an extra shirt for you."

"They already gave us one to wear tomorrow."

"Doubtful they'll let you wear it home. You know how they keep everything secret. I was just making sure you were well covered, so to speak."

"Don't turn him into a wimp," Zane's dad had said in that loud voice he mostly reserved for money issues.

"It's fine," said Zane. "And thanks, Mom."

When they hung up, Zane's dad was gritting his teeth. "She can be a little smothering."

Zane didn't need this. "She was looking out for me."

"Sure," his dad had said. And Zane headed out the door for dinner, early. Why couldn't his parents be like Elijah's, who were laughing and touching and—

The room went pitch black. Gasps. Music. Spotlights. The old contestants! How'd they get here?

Gil Goodson, star of the first Games, came front and center. "And the drama begins," he said. "I'm Gil. And to my right are Jig, Estella, Cameron, and Clio from last year. To my left, Bianca, Lavinia, and Thorn, my competitors.

"We are missing two people. You may remember a little incident that makes Rocky unwelcome at Golly Toy and Game Company."

Clio stepped up. "And if you heard the recent buzz, you might think Dacey was also uninvited. It wasn't her fault, though, that she accidentally received a picture of our obstacle course. Cameron?"

That *had* been the kid with the camera, only he was a few inches taller, and something else. He almost had a swagger.

"I'm Cameron Schein. And I was also a victim of some sabotage. Golly has taken steps to prevent anything like that from happening again, but if something seems wrong, speak up right away. It worked out for me, didn't it?"

They all clapped.

"If you're wondering," said Clio, "Dacey moved to Colorado where, this minute, she's smiling for the pageant judges. In her words, 'Good luck, y'all.'"

"If you ask me," said Estella, "she didn't want to face us again."

"Face *me*, you mean," said Jig. "Tell them what you told me, Bianca."

"Oh, no," said Bianca. "I'm not getting in the middle of this, Jig. I'm too smart."

"Don't know about that, Bianca, but you said Dacey had a crush on me, and I just didn't crush on her back. Embarrassing."

"So you can see this is just like school," said Clio. "The Gollywhopper Games rumor mill moves ten thousand miles per second."

"And we don't want to tarnish you yet," said Lavinia.

"So we're outta here," Thorn said. He turned to leave, then looked back. "But we may see you tomorrow."

The room went dark, the music came up. When the lights came back, the contestants were gone, but a team of waiters paraded in with dinner.

Steak! Zane downed his and a second one, plus salad, a potato, and a flaming dessert. He was all carb- and protein-loaded for tomorrow. Maybe too loaded and too amped up to sit in a hotel room.

No one was in the pool when he and his dad got there. Zane dived in, breaking the smooth, still water, and took half a lap before surfacing for air. By the time he'd lapped back, that alternate, Berk, and Tay, the girl who'd come in seventh, were calling at him to play Marco Polo.

Zane wanted to ignore Berk especially, but he didn't want to make enemies. "I'll play when there are five of us. It's not fun with fewer than that."

In quick succession, in came number one, Hanna with her friendly eyes; number four, Becky, the blonde who walked like an athlete; and number five, Ryder, with normal brown hair who'd buddied up with his near look-alike, Josh, number eight.

"All right!" called Berk. "And because it's my idea, I'm Marco Polo first." He cannonballed into the water.

"Seriously? Start a game by becoming dictator?" said Becky.

"Exactly," Zane said. "Apparently, Berk needs a power rush."

"There's a girl on my soccer team like that," she said.

"There's a person on every team like that."

She and Zane high-fived.

They all went with it, though, and splashed around blindly trying to tag Berk or catch him out of the water; nearly impossible because he answered "Polo!" only three of the dozen times they called "Marco."

By now, except for the skittish girl, Leore, and Gary, the other alternate, everyone was there. With Berk ignoring the rules, it was becoming a bonding-type joke. "Marco!" Zane called.

Nothing.

"Marco!" called one of the girls.

"Marco!" called a guy.

"Polo!" Berk finally replied.

"Out of the water?" Zane said.

"No!"

"But I'm standing right next to you," came another voice.

"My foot's in the water and—"

"Got you, anyway!"

Zane opened his eyes.

"Only because I let you," Berk said to Tay.

Which was good because Tay, who was now Marco, turned the game from joke to competition. She was the type Zane wanted on his team tomorrow. Or Becky, who was apparently some fierce soccer player. Or Hanna, who laughed easier than anyone he'd ever heard. They could—

Thwuck!

"Help!" yelled Hanna.

Zane opened his eyes. Tay was lying by the side of the pool, her head near the edge.

The adults rushed over. One of them got on the phone with 9-1-1. Zane swam there as fast as he could.

Tay was totally still.

Elijah knelt over her. "Don't move her." His parents, who seemed to know what they were doing, took his place.

Hanna wedged in to Tay's side. "You're going to be okay," she whispered although Tay probably couldn't hear her. She gently held her hand even after Tay's mom got there.

Ryder and Josh were standing far away, murmuring to each other like Thing 1 and Thing 2 always did. Becky, in the pool next to Zane, was gripping the ledge so hard her knuckles had turned white. Berk was sitting at the pool's edge dangling his feet in the water, looking totally unconcerned.

Tay came to, but Zane recognized her faraway look. Berk must have, too, because he broke into the biggest grin. "I'm in," Zane heard him whisper. Had Berk figured out some way to trip her, then manage to scramble way over there before the rest of them opened their eyes?

The paramedics took Tay to the hospital as a precaution. "It could've been me," Zane said to his dad when they were back in the room. "I could be in a hospital with almost no brain left." He lay flat on his stomach and covered his head with a pillow.

His dad sat on the edge of the bed and put his hand on the small of Zane's back. The even pressure was reassuring. Almost.

After a few minutes, Zane moved his head from under the pillow, but he curled his arm around his face and head. "Things can change so fast. It's so scary, Dad."

"I know."

His dad did know. One minute he'd been playing in an NFL preseason game, the next minute he pulled a hamstring, and the following minute, the Patriots cut him. After that, according to his dad, what other skills did he have? He'd never imagined he'd need to take college classes seriously. He'd be smart and rich with all those millions he'd make in football.

"Here's the positive and the problem all at once," said his dad. "You, son, are smart. And smart people can see consequences coming faster than the rest of us. So all the possibilities out there? They're scary, and they can paralyze you if you let them. But if you let fear win, what kind of life would you have?"

"But still . . ." Zane let it hang there.

So did his dad, but he stayed with his hand on Zane's back, which was the last thing he remembered until he woke in the morning, thankfully headache free, but still a little freaked.

Then they got to breakfast. Zane had barely put a couple slices of pineapple on his plate when Berk burst in.

"You all ready for me?"

Zane took in a deep breath. Game on.

CHAPTER **18**

Sharryn joined them midbreakfast and confirmed what Zane already knew. "Tay suffered a concussion and will be fine, but she needs to go home. We've already awarded her the same prizes as our third-place finisher, and if there's a fourth Gollywhopper Games, she will be a finalist if she wants."

"That's so totally fair," said Hanna.

"Fair?" Berk said. "She gets to be in two Games? Win double prizes? Why can't I have a concussion?"

Zane stared at him. "You don't want one."

Berk stared back.

It got really quiet.

"This isn't how we wanted to start the morning," said

Sharryn. "We wanted to see smiles and nervousness and laughter and anticipation. We wanted you to be so excited we'd need barricades to hold you back because one thing hasn't changed: The Gollywhopper Games are so ready for you, they're nearly breathing on their own. You'll see stuff you couldn't possibly dream up. Do things you never thought you'd do. Win money, lots of money. A million dollars for one of you. And the title of champion."

Zane looked at Becky, who was looking at him just like a JZ might. He could feel his blood start to pump. This could be good! "This is gonna be great!"

"Yes!" came the voices of the others.

Sharryn wrapped an arm around his shoulders and gave a squeeze. "To start, a fleet of limos will whisk you to Golly Headquarters. So take that last bite, then hold on to your hats. You don't have hats? Doesn't matter. This'll be one of the best days of your lives, win or lose!"

Zane put down his fork. He was ready. Focused. He moved to the lobby. Paced. One side. The other. The JZs would know he was getting in the zone. His dad did. But Elijah didn't.

He matched strides with Zane. "I've been pondering gym class."

Huh? Zane looked at him.

Elijah took that as a cue to go on. "I have no problem when the guys pick me last. Most of my life I've been half their age and half their size. But if we pick teams today, by virtue of you coming in one-two, they'd have Hanna and you—"

"Elijah McNair!" called the limo driver.

Elijah smiled up at Zane. "See you."

"No worries, buddy."

Even before Elijah was out the door, Berk moved over. "Love it, dude! Letting him get all delusional that you'd pick him when you know we'd be awesome together."

"Right."

Berk could interpret that any way he wanted, but if he seriously thought they'd make a good team, *he* was delusional. Maybe they were both athletic, but Zane needed an Elijah.

His driver called, and Zane ducked into the limo.

"You are into this," said his dad, not hopeful, not questioning, just a statement of fact.

Zane nodded.

"Good to see. Not too shaken by Tay's concussion?"

"Been there, done that."

Aside from the past few months, he'd never held back a moment in his life, and he wouldn't today.

They pulled up to Golly Headquarters. A mob of people lined the block, holding signs and balloons and cameras.

Zane turned to his dad. "Let's do this."

Before
THE COMPETITION AT
GOLLY HEADQUARTERS

Danny rushed in to Bert's office at five a.m. "It wouldn't be foolproof if the rat had sabotaged the challenges before they were moved into place."

"What?" Bert swiveled in his chair. "And why are you here this early?"

"I figured it out in my dream or something. Did you build the final challenges where they sit now?"

"No."

"What if the final challenges were sabotaged during the construction process or when you moved them into the final areas or anytime *before* we set the surveillance trap? Maybe that's why Ratso didn't take the bait."

"We would have caught it," Bert said. "I had two different inspection teams in yesterday. Neither had a chance to confer with the other. Both groups found that Flamethrowers were still throwing flames, safely. The Sink or Swim whirlpool was whirling both clockwise and counterclockwise. All the Extreme Machines gears were meshing. They did find a broken scissors at Merry-Go-Wow, but we fixed that."

"Merry-Go-Wow? That's not on the list."

"I thought it wise to have a secret backup, but pretend you didn't hear that. No one knows. Well, almost no one. Sorry to deprive you of your beauty sleep."

Danny nodded like a disappointed little boy. But then he looked up. "You tried them, right? You actually tried Flamethrowers as if you were a contestant?"

"They inspected the structures and—" Bert shot out of his chair. "No."

The two of them wound around the building and down three floors. Bert stopped and pulled out his cell phone. "I need Plago. He's the only one I trust to work these all."

"What if he's Ratso?"

"If he is, I'll know."

Bert paced back and forth along a ten-foot path between a somersaulting baboon and Saturn's outer ring, then nearly tackled Plago the moment he arrived. "Don't ask questions," said Bert. "Just run our final challenges like you were playing them."

Plago didn't hesitate. He warmed up Flamethrowers. It shot flames as they'd tested it, but when he started the launch sequence, the flame shot so far, it almost burned the baboon.

"No!" Plago raced to shut off the flames. "What just happened, Bert?"

"Sabotage."

No way could Plago fake the horror in his eyes. He wasn't Ratso, thank goodness.

They hurried over to Sink or Swim. The third press of Panel 2 sent Plago reeling back with a shock. He huffed and puffed and finally caught his breath. "Is this whole place rigged?"

Bert could barely see straight. It's like his blood was boiling, about to erupt from his ears. He almost wanted to call it quits, stop the Games entirely. He couldn't do that. Not yet. They moved on to Extreme Machines.

Plago shook his head. "If this kills me, tell my wife I love her."

But Extreme Machines worked perfectly!

Meanwhile, with instructions from Plago, Danny had gone to check the identical challenges on the other side. None of those had been rigged.

Bert shook his head. "Ratso is very smart."

"Who?" said Plago.

"The bad guy knew to sabotage only one of each pair. Even if it didn't hurt the kid, any malfunction would have given the other contestant an unfair advantage. We'd need our third do-over in three Games. We'd be a laughingstock. I need both of you to confirm you're absolutely sure there's been no sabotage to Extreme Machine."

"None," Danny said.

"You saw it," said Plago. "I suppose we're running with that?"

"I suppose so." Bert sent them back upstairs, but lingered to walk past his secret backup. "No one sabotages my Games and gets away with it."

CHAPTER 19

Their limo had barely come to a stop in front of Golly Headquarters when Sharryn opened its door. "Zane!"

The enormous crowd surrounding the red carpet started chanting his name. If he never made it to the NFL, at least he'd gotten a taste of superstardom. Too bad he liked it so much.

Zane posed for five pictures and signed six pieces of paper, a forearm, and the back of a shirt before Sharryn moved him through the unassuming glass doors of Golly Toy and Game Company Headquarters.

What first hit him was the smell of gingerbread,

followed by a kaleidoscope of light bouncing off every surface. This was like no place on earth that Zane had ever seen.

He stood hypnotized by the skylights that were catching the sun and painting prisms around the octagonal room. He didn't even realize Ryder was in there, too, until the left wall slid partway open. Behind it was Carol, the famous Golly guide. "If I'm ever feeling blah," she said, "I come here and leave different."

On any other day, that would sound totally cornball, but here, Zane felt it.

"I could stay here forever," said Carol, "but it's time to move on. Ready?"

"Let's do this," said Zane.

"What he said." And Ryder shot through the door in front of Carol. He stopped.

They caught up with him, but there seemed to be nowhere to go in this dimly lit area. Carol kept moving as if she were either going to crash into the far wall or walk straight through it. It opened just in time for her not to lose stride.

"Okay," said Zane. "That was creepy."

Ryder nodded. "And cool."

Beyond the creepiness was a well-lit hall with weird pictures on the walls. Ryder pointed to a portrait of a very old woman with spiky green hair and an extra eyeball in the middle of her forehead. "We never saw her on TV."

"We don't show you everything," said Carol. She led them through a small waiting area and held open a door for them. "Go in. Sit tight. I'll be back with our other victims."

Elijah and Hanna were sitting tight at the large table, chatting about marine biology. Becky and Josh sat next to each other, their chairs turned so they could punch the bounce-up gorilla back and forth. They were joking about geometry.

Zane was about to spar with a five-eyed monster, but the door opened again. In came Berk and Leore. While Berk was all in-your-face, Leore barely looked you in the chin. Maybe in her element, she morphed into someone more energetic—someone with a pulse. If he and Hanna were picking teams like Elijah had suggested, Hanna would go first, and Zane would probably get stuck with Leore. That meant only one thing.

He sat next to Leore, who had moved to a chair away from the group. "Are you as nervous as I am?" Not that he was nervous; just looking for common ground.

She stared at her hands, folded on the table. "Somewhat."

"I can talk too much when I get nervous," said Zane. "Am I bothering you?"

"Not exactly."

"Good. Because if we end up on the same team, I don't want to annoy you. You'll tell me if I do?"

She nodded.

"Should I leave you alone?"

She shrugged.

He'd have more fun with the others, but Zane didn't want Leore to think he was giving up on her. Now what?

He was saved by Carol and Bill, the other guide, who burst in with more energy than Zane had ever seen off any field or court.

"We are ready for you," said Bill.

"Are you ready for us?" Carol said.

"Is this when you divide us into teams?" asked Ryder.

Carol raised her eyebrows three times and laughed. "Where shall we start, Bill?"

"Let's start with the past couple years. Carol was always in charge of one team, I was in charge of another, and we had our friendly wagers. The first year, her team won, and I had to shave my head. Last year, my team won, so she became my maid for a year."

"We spent so much time together," said Carol, "we decided to get married, and the good people at

Golly didn't want any friction to come between us."

"The problem is," said Bill, "our relationship thrives on competition. And yet they have failed to give us teams to manage."

"No teams?" asked Berk.

Bill shook his head. "Not initially. We have something else up our sleeves first."

"A little something," Carol said, "we call Friend or Foe." She let out an evil-movie laugh.

Bill's eyes opened wide. "I married that?"

"Yes, you did," said Carol. "Now, Friend or Foe will pair you with a different contestant for four challenges. Each time, you'll decide who of you plays in Friend mode and who plays the more difficult Foe version."

"The four with the best cumulative times following all rounds will be on one team and will have an advantage over the four who have been less successful," said Bill. "And that may leave you wondering, why on this Gollywhopper of an earth—"

"Gollywhopper of an earth?" Carol shook her head.

"Yes," said Bill. "Why on this Gollywhopper of an

earth would you choose a harder challenge over an easier one?"

"Good question, Bill." Carol chuckled. "It comes down to points. When you successfully finish a round, whether you've played as Friend or Foe, you'll earn one hundred points."

"But these timed challenges," said Bill, "will award you additional points for every second you beat the clock. For example, if you finish your challenge with two minutes remaining, you will receive two hundred twenty points; one hundred for completion plus one-twenty for the number of seconds left on the clock."

"However," said Carol, "if you choose to play in Foe mode, you'll have more time to complete your task, so the potential is there to earn more points. Got it?"

They did.

"In order to know who plays who—"

"Or is it whom, Carol?"

"Give that man one hundred points. In order to know who plays *whom*, we have a handy-dandy pairing chart." She held up a GollyReader with some sort of grid, but brought it down before Zane could make any sense of it.

"To make this totally random, you are identified with contestant numbers, which you'll receive right now."

"It's not as confusing as it sounds," said Bill.

"Unless you're often confused, like he is," Carol said.

"And this is what I put up with at home."

They both laughed. If only Zane's parents would laugh like that again, and not just when one messed up.

Bill then held out a block of wood with eight jester heads. "Each of these poor guys has a numbered stick for a body." Bill went up to Hanna. "Pick a head. His body will reveal your contestant number for this round."

She closed her eyes, whirled her finger around the block, and let it land on a head. Number four. Bill held the jesters out to Ryder, who pulled number one.

"And so if we look at our handy-dandy chart"—and Carol referred to her

GollyReader—"we see Ryder, who's number one, will meet in Round Three with number four, Hanna, and will be joined by Friend or Foe number four."

"Friend or Foe number four? What's that?" said Berk.

Carol came around and clamped him on the shoulder. "Oh, you perceptive soul. We were about to tell you."

"So let's just tell them, Carol." Bill came around in back of Berk and joined Carol. "We need a little help to pull off the Friend or Foe element of each challenge, so we've enlisted people to help you."

"Or hinder you," Carol said with a voice of doom.

Hanna raised her hand.

"Yes?" Bill said.

"Will we get to know how they'll hinder us? Or help us? I mean, before we decide Friend or Foe?"

Bill and Carol looked at each other. He nodded at her.

"We are evil," she said. "You'll get a little information, but not too much."

Bill continued around the table with the jesters, then hit a button on the remote. The schedule was projected on the wall. "Take a minute to see who you're facing."

In Round One, Zane—who pulled number 8— would be against Berk; in Round Two, against Ryder; in Round Three, Leore; and in Round Four, Elijah.

If it were up to him, he'd never go against Elijah, partly for the buddy aspect, but mostly because of his brains. He wouldn't have picked Berk, either. Berk was like that football player who'd targeted Zane's helmet with his own (and it hadn't been an accident like the other guy had claimed) to give him his first concussion.

Leore and Ryder? Leore seemed so tentative and Ryder, so reckless. Then again, they probably thought he was a dumb jock. Maybe he wasn't as smart as everyone here, but he did have one advantage. He knew strategy.

Berk came up to him. "First round, pal. You're going down."

First strategy—don't let him see you sweat, mostly because you're not sweating. "Bring it, pal."

CHAPTER 20

Bill and Carol led them in relative silence down four hallways into a waiting elevator. Without anyone pushing a button, the large elevator rose up and up and up until the doors opened to an area glowing with color. Was it . . . ?

"That's right," said Carol. "You don't start every day at the top of the Rainbow Maze."

"This isn't a challenge," said Bill, "just an opportunity to take the ride of your lives into the competition area. Contestant number eight. Zane. You're up!"

Zane vaulted onto a golden ledge and launched himself down the chute.

He twisted, he spiraled, taking hairpin turns at

breakneck speed. Around, around, down, down, around. "Whoo, baby!" To the right, to the left, down, down, down. "Oh, man!" Around. A huge fall. Then slower, slower, slower.

The slide deposited him somewhere new; not the wacky warehouse area with all the random, giant objects. The sight, though, nearly took Zane's breath away.

Colorful beams of light shot from the floor to a ceiling that had to be at least five stories tall. Each light beam was probably three feet in diameter, and the columns of light sort of formed walls and hall-ways as far as he could see.

A rumbling came from the slide. Out tumbled Elijah, backwards, but apparently okay.

"Yeah! Buddy!" Zane came over and high-fived him. "How great was that?"

"I'll let you know as soon as the room stops spin-ning and these colored lights go away."

Zane laughed.

"Holy quark! Those lights are real!" Elijah ran toward them, stopped short, then seemed to sneak up on one of the blue ones. He reached his hand toward it, as if the light might burn him. Then he stuck his whole hand in, giggled, and started back to Zane.

Zane looked away to Josh coming down the chute. He gave Josh a high five—might as well high-five everyone—and waited to see his reaction to the light. He pretended to not notice, but his eyes gave him away.

Berk's eyes showed nothing, though.

"You're not impressed?" asked Elijah.

"No," said Berk. "I could do the same with flashlights and colored lenses."

"Right," said Elijah. "And I could build the Pacific Ocean with a bucket of sand and a hose."

Good for the kid, but he probably didn't want to get on Berk's bad side.

"Or a replica of Mount Rushmore out of GollyGlop."

Zane gave him a little nudge.

"I know," Elijah said. "I couldn't help it."

Zane gave Elijah a stealth low five.

The other four—Hanna, Leore, Becky, and Ryder—ran the high-five gauntlet, then paused to stare, openmouthed.

"Our grand illusion of the year," said Carol,

walking in. "These beams are walls of sorts that separate the spaces for the Friend or Foe challenges." She waved her arms. Four of the lights turned white and now had writing projected on them. The first white beam had an arrow curling to the right. It read:

Area #1
Players 1 & 2
Ryder and Becky

The next white beam pointed the way to Area #2. Then came the one for #3, then Berk's and Zane's names for Area #4.

"It's time," said Bill, "to follow your arrows to the land of challenges. Off with you!"

Zane and Berk, already elbowing for position, followed their arrows between light columns, which finally curved into an open area about half the size of a school gym. On a table several steps ahead sat a square-based, two-foot-tall pyramid of eyeballs—probably marbles, but still freaky. Zane would eat eyeballs if that's what it took.

He waited for Berk's reaction. "Cool. Eyeballs."

"Drat!" said Bianca, coming from nowhere, Jig in stride. "We wanted to gross you out."

"Not these tough guys," said Jig. "The others'll give us what we want, though."

"What're you doing here?" said Berk.

"We're your Friends," Bianca said.

Jig sneered. "Or your Foes."

"So if you guys don't know, I'm Bianca LaBlanc from two years ago, and this is Jig Jiggerson from last year, and this is so much less pressure than when I had to talk in a hot-air balloon. Or when I auditioned for that TV pilot last week."

Jig nudged her.

"Anyway, at this station, your challenge is called Googly Eyes because Golly has this new marble game coming out that's really cool, even for me when

I played it with this eight-year-old last week. And she was so good, but, sidetracked! So Googly Eyes is your Round One, and we're here to help you."

"Or hurt you," Jig said.

She rolled her eyes at him. Apparently, they weren't in love like some of the websites hinted. At least she wasn't.

Zane wished they'd get to it. He wanted to strike before his adrenaline started coming down. He jumped up a few times to keep it going.

"Ooh. Zane's ready," said Bianca. "Maybe we should do this."

"Here's the deal." Jig walked up to the pile of eyeballs. "You each need to re-create this. If you do it in Friend mode, you get fourteen minutes, and we won't bother you. At the halfway mark, we'll even give you a hint. If you do it in Foe mode, you get twenty-four minutes, and we will make the task more difficult."

"And if the Friend person gets done in time, he can help us hurt you, if that makes sense."

"It actually does," said Zane.

She smiled at him. "I like this guy. I wanna be his Foe."

"They need to decide," said Jig.

"Yeah," Berk said. "So tell us more."

Jig shook his head. "After you choose."

There had to be some really funky catch for the Foe person to need ten more minutes to construct a pyramid that, by Zane's quick count, was ten by ten—one hundred eyeballs—at its base, then nine by nine, or eighty-one of them, and so on up to the one at the top. Simple. Maybe he should knock this out in Friend mode, then inflict pain on Berk.

"I'll take Friend," Berk said before Zane could open his mouth.

Zane stared Berk in the eyes for five full seconds until Berk looked away. "I wanted Foe, anyway."

The moment he said that, more shafts of light sprang from the floor, shielding them from whatever was rumbling beyond.

"So, noises, yeah," said Bianca. "They're getting stuff ready for you because you can't exactly make an eyeball tower without eyeballs."

"This sample stays here," said Jig, "if you need to see it again."

Bianca and Jig gave them exactly one minute to

study the eyeballs, but Zane had it. All the eyes on the ten-by-ten layer at the bottom were blue. The ones on the nine by nine were brown. The next layer's were green. And they continued the blue-brown-green pattern up to the single red one, like a cherry on top.

"Time's up!" said Jig. He and Bianca led them through a gap in the light that somehow felt like a door, then down a short "hall" into a "room" with two tables. Each had what looked like a square plastic serving tray with a whole bunch of indentations.

"Your eyeball bases," said Bianca. "Ha! If anyone ever told me I'd say the words 'eyeball' and 'bases' together and it'd make sense . . . Anyway, you need to start."

Jig steered Berk to the base marked FRIEND. About five yards away was a bin of eyeballs. "These are for you to use, Berk."

Bianca and Zane moved to the Foe base at the far end of the room. His eyeballs were the same, but his bin was double the size of Berk's.

"You're so cute, Zane, I hate to tell you what we didn't before," Bianca said. "He gets to carry as many eyeballs as he can hold in his hands. You are allowed to bring only five eyeballs at a time. And it gets worse. Every thirty seconds Jig and I will steal an eyeball from you. If Berk finishes before you, he'll become a thief, too. At random times we'll steal more. Well, it might look random, but actually, you'll do something to trigger our thievery. Got it?"

"I'm thinking I should just go fast," said Zane.

Bianca only smiled.

"Which means you're not allowed to answer any questions."

Bianca smiled bigger. "Ready?"

"Ready."

"Ready over here!" called Bianca.

"Ready here!" Jig said.

Bianca pointed to a countdown clock shimmering in a light beam. It was holding still at twenty-four minutes. Without a word, it went to 23:59 and counting.

Zane bolted to the bin. He needed blue eyes first. One hundred of them. That would take twenty backs and forths for the first layer. No. More. They'd be taking four away each minute; six if Berk finished first.

He grabbed five eyeballs and returned to the base at the 23:48 mark. He dropped them and paused to make sure they were settling into the base's shallow dimples. Back to the bin.

Five more blue eyeballs. Back to the base. Drop them. Back to the bin. Clock: 23:32. Five more, but why had he accidentally picked up two brown ones? Fine. He'd just start his second layer. But no more clock checking.

When he got back to the base, Jig and Bianca were dancing around with the eyeballs they'd taken. Fine. He'd just go faster. He made three more trips by the time they'd stolen the next two. He could potentially net thirty or more every minute. Thank goodness he'd started getting back in football shape before this.

And thank goodness he could handle taunts. "Losing ground over there?" Berk called. And, "It'd be tragic if you tripped and fell." And "My baby sister can run twice as fast as you." If those were supposed to psyche him out, big-time fail.

Next time back, Zane paused to check his progress. He had enough on the first level to grab any color eyeballs now. A drop of sweat fell on the base. He wiped his forehead with the back of his arm, raced to the bin, and returned with two brown, two blue, and one green. When he got back, Jig and Bianca were holding two eyeballs a piece.

"No fair!"

They laughed.

Zane didn't bother to ask why they'd doubled their take because they wouldn't tell him. And if he tried to figure it out, he wouldn't move as fast. This was all about speed. He just wiped his forehead again and ran. Back again, and Bianca and Jig were each holding another eyeball.

Zane shook his head, deposited what he had, and ran back, sweating even more buckets. Before he picked up his next five, he used his shirt to wipe his whole face.

They hadn't robbed him this time.

Back, forth, back, forth, again and again and again, with Bianca and Jig each stealing on the half minute and sometimes more between. What was the trigger?

"Whoa!" Berk called. "I am cruising over here. On my five-by-five tier."

Fabulous. Zane was still on his eight-by-eight. He couldn't help himself. He looked to the clock. Just over six minutes gone. At this rate, Berk would finish with, like, a zillion seconds left, a zillion seconds of him stealing Zane's eyeballs.

Zane amped it up a notch, but by the time he got back, Jig wasn't there. He was whispering something in Berk's ear. Hint time?

"Oh, man!" yelled Berk. "You've gotta be kidding me. I gotta start over?" Apparently, Berk hadn't noticed the color layers.

"Ha!" Zane said loud enough for Berk to hear.

But what was that metal-on-concrete dragging sound?

Zane refused to look up.

"You can't move your bin," said Jig.

"Who said?"

"Who had to say?" Jig said. "It's implied, like you shouldn't punch me in the face."

Then came the sound of eyeballs plunking into the bin. After that, footsteps away, probably Berk running to check the eyeball model.

Zane's time suddenly felt better, and his energy

picked up. Could he beat Berk head-to-head? Not with Berk's bin right next to his pyramid. The dragging sound came again.

Then footsteps. "Got it!" Berk called. "Man! You put my bin back. And gave it a sign. 'No moving me. That means you, Berk!' Very funny."

Zane allowed himself a small laugh. Things were suddenly fair again. The eight-by-eight row, done. The seven-by-seven, partially done and going so much faster; just forty-nine eyeballs. The next would be thirty-six, the next twenty-five, then sixteen, nine, four, and that one red one.

Had he seen any red ones? Was there only one in all those eyeballs? He needed to keep an eye out. Ha!

He raced back and forth, back and forth, gathering, placing, wiping sweat, having more eyeballs stolen.

Ding-ding-ding!

That came from Berk's area when Zane was just starting his four-by-four layer.

"Yes!" screamed Berk. He trotted over right at eyeball-stealing time.

After Zane's next trip back, Berk was staring him down. "You look extra sweaty."

Zane wiped his face again, and when he came back, the three of them were each holding eyeballs. Aha! He ran back to the bin. "If I wipe the sweat off over here," Zane called, "you don't penalize me."

"Oh, man!" said Berk.

"Thanks for the hint, pal!"

Zane picked up five more blue eyeballs and deposited them on the fourth layer. One more blue, then on to the nine brown ones. Factoring in the ones they'd take away, he'd hopefully need only four more trips. He placed those five eyeballs. Another set of five. Only eight eyeballs left with the ones they'd steal. If he went fast enough, and if he happened to see the red eyeball immediately, only two more trips. Back with three browns and two greens. Time for the red one. He sunk his fingers deep into the remaining eyeballs. He swirled them right, left, right, left, and there! He moved the red one to a safe spot in a corner. He'd first need to replace the ones they'd stolen on the half minute.

He ran back and filled in everything. Now the red one! It was right where he'd left it. He ran it back with four extras just in case. He plopped the red eye-ball on top and *ding, ding, ding!*

Done. Clock: 4:47.

He moved away from the base. Needed to walk. Needed to breathe. He'd run fast. Could anyone do it faster? No way to tell now. Berk's clock had already reset for the next person.

Zane walked toward the light beams in the far corner, his huffing and puffing fading, his mind clearing.

"Are you okay?" said Bianca.

"Yeah." Zane started to wipe his face, but stopped. "Penalties for sweat wiping now?"

Bianca threw a chilled towel over his head. It felt good. It smelled good. These people thought of everything.

"What'd you think?" Bianca said.

"Didn't have time to think," said Zane.

She sidled up to him close enough to whisper in his ear. She smelled good, too. "You had the brains to figure out the color thing."

"Hey!" said Berk. "No whispering allowed."

Bill stepped in. "And let's talk about what actually isn't allowed, Berk. You may want to rethink little stunts like pulling your eyeball bin over."

"No one said it was against the rules."

"Technically, yes. It wasn't against any stated rules, but you were treading a thin line."

"What does that mean?"

"It means if you do something like that again, it might bite you in the rear. You got lucky. And you got one hundred points for completion plus two hundred seventy-eight for the number of seconds you had left."

Zane finished the math in his head. Yes! A nine-point lead was a nine-point lead. He stared until he got Berk's attention. "Next victim?"

CHAPTER 21

That cold towel had been nice, but Zane needed real water. Bill led him to a bathroom.

Zane stuck his whole head under the faucet and realized he couldn't shake his hair dry as he normally would this time of year. Without football, he'd let it grow.

He rubbed the towel over his head and assessed his performance. What could he have done better? Figured out the sweat trigger earlier? Looked for the red eyeball all along? Moved his bin before it became illegal? There were no do-overs, but it never hurt to learn.

Bill sent him to a chair in one corner of their

original starting space. Berk was already in the seat next to his, and two of the other pairs sat in separate corners. "We're just waiting for Josh and Elijah. Sit, and no talking for now."

Zane wanted to talk. He wanted information. At least he didn't have a long wait. Josh and Elijah came through their light path, with Carol behind them.

"Ahh!" Carol's ear-piercing yell made them jump. "It's too quiet in here!"

"Agreed," said Bill, "which is why we're doing something about it."

"Thank you for stating the obvious."

"Now that you've had a taste of Friend or Foe," said Bill, "it's time for your next challenge. Almost. First, no talking to anyone about any challenges, no exception."

"This," said Carol, "is our little way of keeping you in the dark." On cue, the lights went out. Even Zane gasped. "It's fun to have friends in the control room." The lights came back. "The second piece of business." Carol put her arm around Berk. "You need to leave any props or equipment or challenge items in place unless, of course, moving them is part of your challenge." She thumped him on the back. "If in doubt, ask. That, we will answer, okay?"

No one said a word.

"What?" said Carol. "Did we scare you into silence?"

Pretty much all of them nodded.

"Then scream or shout or somehow use those vocal cords."

The area turned into a hooting, hollering match that somehow morphed into a barnyard track featuring a rooster, dog, horse, and other indistinguishable animal sounds. Zane provided the quacking.

Carol and Bill stepped forward, and they quieted immediately. But it had felt good.

"And now, you animals, time for Friend or Foe, Round Two." Bill waved his arms like he was conjuring magic, and the light beams changed their messages. Zane was now paired with Ryder.

"Go to your areas," said Carol. "Your Friends and Foes will fill you in. Now scat!"

This "hallway" went straight back to a "room" where Lavinia, who'd been totally by-the-rules in her season, and Cameron, the silent kid, were engaged in a chat-a-thon. Zane expected they'd jump to attention and grow all serious like he'd seen at school. Two or three quiet kids would be yakking in a classroom like any of his football friends, but when the JZs walked in, they'd grow quiet, as if they'd suddenly remembered their places in the school hierarchy. Either that, or they held a secret to the world they weren't ready to share.

Cameron and Lavinia, though, burst into laughter, as if he and Ryder were the joke.

"What's with them?" he said to Ryder as they paused at the edge of the room.

"Sorry." This was Cameron, right? The painfully shy guy came right up and stuck out his hand. "I'm Cameron. And this is Lavinia."

Had he gone through a personality transplant?

The four of them shook hands all around.

"You caught us in a bad moment," Lavinia said. "For that I apologize. We're supposed to take this seriously, and we thoroughly do, but um . . ."

"Yeah," Cameron said. "I've had a hunk of pancake in my hair all morning, and Lavinia finally let me know. Just. Now."

"To ease any concerns," Lavinia said, "your clock won't start until I say go."

Cameron nodded. "She's our Go Girl. I'm the Summoner." He raised a hand. From his right a cart with two containers rolled out on its own. "And the other one, please." Another cart rolled in from the other side. This one held a stuffed alien creature about the size of a chimp.

"This is Eep," said Lavinia, "the main character of Planet Golly, a board game that may seem lame now, but was popular fifty years ago."

"We're thinking people weren't so smart back then," said Cameron, "because Eep is a Martian who needs to find his way from the lost-in-space station to his home on Planet Golly. And if his home planet wasn't Mars, why did they call him a Martian?"

"We just realized that, thus the other reason we were laughing," said Lavinia, "but I remember how you must feel right now, so on with the show."

Cameron stood between the carts. "Here's the story. Our Martian Eep is all saggy because he's very low on Gloop, the Ultimate Martian Fuel. So using only the provided containers as measuring devices, you need to refuel him with an exact amount of Gloop."

Lavinia stood behind the cart with the two containers. They were both clear. The one marked with a big black *4* was about the size of a paint can; the other, marked with a big black *7* was about three inches taller and bigger around. "These numbers refer to the units of Gloop each container holds when filled to the bottom of the red band." She ran her finger around the red line circling each container.

"If you play in Friend mode," said Cameron, "we give you one starting hint, then we leave you alone. You will have ten minutes to complete your task. If you play in Foe mode, you have fifteen minutes, but you get no hint, and there may be distractions."

"So Ryder, Zane? Friend or Foe?" asked Lavinia. "You have thirty seconds to decide starting . . . now."

How much Gloop did they need to measure? Definitely a weird amount. They wouldn't say, "Give me eleven units." Any doofus could figure that out. This one could be tough.

Ryder stepped up. "I've got this. I want Foe."

"Perfect," said Zane.

"Then it's go time," Lavinia said. "Ryder, come with me."

"This way, Zane." Cameron led him toward a gap in the light beams. He was so different from last year's guy, the one who seemed to shrink every time he talked. "How's it going?"

"Hard to judge," Zane said. "I beat my first guy by nine seconds, so there's that."

"And no matter what happens, you'll always have bragging rights, being one of only eight in this year's finals."

Zane gave a small "Holy cow!" under his breath. His odds of making it to this point were scads less than his odds of making it to the NFL.

They stepped into a classroom-sized area divided in half by a light wall that came only to his shoulders. On this side was a cart with the two containers, the 4 and the 7. The 4 was already filled with green glowy stuff. Zane pointed. "Gloop?"

"Gloop," said Cameron. "That's your advantage. Ryder won't see this first step in measuring exactly five units to feed to Eep. If you need more Gloop, or if you need to get rid of some, bring one container at a time over here."

They moved to a steel counter with a sink, but instead of a faucet, it had a hose.

"Dump what you don't want into the sink. Use the hose to get more. When you've measured exactly five units, bring just one container around the light wall"—Cameron went around the partition—"then feed Eep. If you've fed him too little, it'll run right through him and he'll deflate again. If you've fed him too much, stand back. He'll barf it all up."

A withered Eep was propped in a chair, a giant funnel stuck in his mouth.

"Any questions?"

"Five units, right?"

"Exactly five units. Okay, come back around. One more thing. The first forty units of Gloop are free. If you need more, we'll deduct one point from your score for each extra unit. On the flip side, for every unit you don't use, we'll add a bonus point."

"So figure it out first?" said Zane.

"Your call."

"Which means," said Zane, "that you can't answer."

Cameron stayed silent for a moment. "Everything I've said will be projected on the wall." He pointed to the back wall, and the instructions appeared. "These are in black. Any further instructions will appear in blue. Got it?"

"I'm ready."

Cameron stepped away. "Then go!"

Five units? They'd already filled the 4. If the word "*exact*" weren't shouting at him, he'd pour those four units into the 7, fill the 4 one-quarter of the way, add it to the starter units, and feed Eep. But the walls of the containers were thicker on the bottom and thinned out considerably at the top, so eyeballing it was out.

This had to be some sort of math equation with

filling and pouring and dumping to get five units. What if he started by pouring the Gloop from the 4 into the 7? Zane needed to try it. Worst case, he'd pour it all back and wouldn't waste any units.

Okay. Now he had four units in the 7 and nothing in the 4. If he filled up the 4 and poured enough in to fill the 7, there would be one unit left inside the 4, right?

Right. He was so close he could taste it, but he couldn't hold all the reasoning in his head.

Zane ran the 4 to the hose and filled it. He ran it back to the 7 and poured it in until it hit the 7's red band. So now he had seven units in the 7 and one in the 4. And—

Yes! He ran the 7 back to the sink and dumped it out, ran the empty 7 to the table, poured in the one unit from the 4, filled the 4 back up, and added that to the one unit in the 7. Five units.

Zane bolted around the light partition and poured the contents into the funnel as quickly as he could without spilling a drop.

"Eat, you little Martian, eat!"

But apparently the Gloop digested at only one

speed. Zane still had 6:53 as the last drop poured from the bucket to the funnel.

"C'mon, funnel, drain!"

A little more, a little more, a little more and—

Zane looked up to new blue instructions flashing on the wall.

Good job, but Eep needs more; 4 more units, to be exact.

All right! Just fill up the 4 and feed him. Zane raced back, but the 4 container was gone. An empty 5 container was in its place. This had to be the same type of system, but which should he fill first, the 5 or the 7?

His gut told him to go with the 7. As the green Gloop oozed into the container, he tried to reason it out.

If he poured five units from the 7 container into the 5, that would leave two units in the 7. And if it followed the same system, he'd empty the 5 into the sink. Then if he dumped those two units into the 5, and if he filled the 7 again—

"Ah!" He'd been so lost in thought, the 7 was spilling over. He turned off the hose, then dumped out the overflow until the 7's Gloop reached the red band.

Back to the table. He filled the 5, then ran the 5 to the sink and dumped it out, wasted, with at least one unit he'd lost from being careless.

No time to beat himself up.

Again to the table. He transferred the two remaining units from the 7 into the 5. Now, if he filled the 7 again . . . Hmm. Yes! If he filled the 7 and used three units to top off the 5, he'd have four units.

Back to the sink! "Fill, you container, fill!"

It finally did. Back to the table. He poured. Around the light partition. Into the funnel.

"C'mon, Eep! You can do it, buddy!"

The clock was at 4:14 and counting. Eep was filling. Eep was straightening. Eep was glowing. Eep was lifting. Eep was flying around the room!

Cameron came in and thumped Zane on the back. "Good job!"

"How good? Better than your person in the first round?"

Cameron smiled. "I can't tell you that. I can say that you got your hundred points for completion, plus two thirty-seven for time remaining, plus seventeen units unused. Too bad about the overflow."

"I know," Zane said. "Can't beat myself up about that now."

"Absolutely." Cameron led him to a room with a sink, mirror, and a stack of towels. "You might want to wipe yourself down, and you'll need this." He tossed Zane a fresh Gollywhopper Games T-shirt. "Just leave the dirty one here. I'll be right outside."

Somehow the Gloop had landed in Zane's hair, on his face, and all over his arms. It came off pretty easily, though. He cleaned up, changed shirts, and emerged to a bunch of noises from just beyond one of the light walls. "Ryder?"

Cameron nodded.

"Are you allowed to tell me how you've been his Foe?"

"You can probably guess," said Cameron.

"So you can't tell me."

"I can," said Cameron, "but we have five minutes to kill, and he'll use it all. So guess."

"If I was his Foe, I'd give him a container with holes and make him search for a solid one. Then I'd give Eep a much smaller funnel."

"We did the second one. Also, his four container

wasn't filled at the beginning, and his Gloop sometimes comes out too fast and sometimes turns off
altogether. And that's your five minutes' worth, or so
they tell me. Apparently, they have people testing all
this stuff out."

"Did you get to test?"

"No. But Gil does. He lives in Orchard Heights,
so he's at Golly all the time."

A buzz came from somewhere on Cameron. He
stood. "I need to be a Foe one more time. Stay here."
Cameron trotted off.

Zane started to play Monday-morning quarterback, but how much would it really help to dissect
his mistakes? Each challenge was entirely different.
For the next, the Golly people could make the contestants twirl on their heads or scale a fish or explain
Einstein's Theory of Relativity. Everything boiled
down to two key words: play smart.

If he did that, he'd never need to second-guess
anything.

CHAPTER 22

Cameron came back with a cold bottle of water. Zane drained it. A short time after that, Lavinia brought Ryder around, totally red faced and Gloop covered. "Zero points. Zero!" He looked at Zane. "First, I had too much, then I had too little, then just a little too little, then I got the first one with two minutes left. Tell him, Lavinia. Tell him how close."

"You told it perfectly, Ryder, but like I informed you, you were not allowed to estimate. We emphasized *exact*. We didn't ask for *close*."

"Then how do you do it?" Ryder turned to Zane.

He reined in his smile. "Math."

"Math?"

Lavinia explained.

Ryder shook his head. "So stupid. I was so stupid."

"No," said Zane. "Your mind got stuck. It won't happen next time. Believe it."

And he was saying this why? It's what he knew. Zane had tried tennis, and he'd wrestled some, but solo sports didn't do anything for him. It was football—diving for a tackle, launching for an interception, rallying behind a common goal—that felt right. When the team gelled, it was like the world was singing. And though this was one-on-one, team Games were coming.

Right now, things stayed silent until the lights showed their next assignments. He was paired with Leore, so no telling what he was up against.

Ryder's recklessness and Berk's bravado had been easy to read. At the pool last night, he'd seen Becky's athleticism and witnessed Hanna's confidence beneath her kindness. Josh loved to be front and center, and Elijah was Elijah. Leore, though, was a question mark hiding behind hair that surrounded her face like barely open curtains.

They followed their arrows, side by side.

"How's it going so far?" said Zane.

"Horrible."

"That bad?"

"Worse."

"There's still two more," he said. "You never know what can happen."

"Unfortunately," Leore said, "a lot can happen."

Either she had totally bombed or she was like that kid, Cyril, who used to be on their team. "We're going to lose," he'd moan. And "Do they have enough medics on hand?" If someone had warned him it might rain cows, Cyril would have predicted dire crushings. Zane would have said, "Milk for everyone!"

Zane couldn't let Leore's attitude bring him down. On his worst concussion days, he'd felt the negativity smother him with never-stopping waves. He couldn't let that happen now. He needed to believe—he did believe—that whatever they threw at him, whether as Friend or Foe, he could win.

But whatever Golly had placed on a pedestal in the middle of their room was completely underwhelming. It was about a foot long and made of pieces from the Doohickey Builder Set. Not that he held anything against Doohickey. Zane had spent hours building lots of contraptions with rods and gears and cranks during commercials in college and NFL games.

Leore stopped about halfway to the pedestal. "This is not my strength," she said.

Would she even admit to a strength?

"And where are our people? What if they forgot about us?"

"If they did, I'll find them." Then Zane strode up to study the Doohickey model.

He didn't have much time. Estella and Thorn came from behind one of the light pillars.

Leore jumped.

"No worries, Leore," said Estella.

Thorn nodded. "We don't bite."

"Not much." Estella laughed and guided Leore to the model. "If you don't know, I'm Estella from last year, and he's Thorn the Rich from the year before."

"If you don't stop introducing me that way," Thorn said, "people will start thinking that's my real name."

Had Thorn spoken that much on the DVDs? Not that he'd seemed shy; more that he'd seemed bored by the whole thing. On the other end, Estella had been passionate about everything. His kind of person.

"So here's the what's what," Estella said. "See this little Doohickey prototype? You're gonna build us one of these. Everything you need is in your spaces. We've even provided you each with an identical starter piece. It's standing in the middle of your areas."

"If you choose Friend mode," said Thorn, "we'll pretty much leave you alone. In addition, you're allowed to ask one question during the challenge. Make it a good one."

"Not 'Can you build this for me,'" Estella added, "because that would be a big, fat NO."

"Exactly," Thorn said. "But if you work in Foe mode, you can't ask questions and . . ."

He paused, and some evil music came up.

"Yeah," Estella said. "We're not always nice."

If it were Zane, he'd throw the Foe extra parts to wade through. Or broken ones he'd need to replace. He could do this, though. Piece of cake.

"For this challenge," Thorn continued, "you'll have eight minutes in Friend mode."

"Eight minutes to build that?" Zane pointed to

the model he could build in thirty seconds.

"Right," said Thorn. "And fifteen in Foe mode."

Zane gave a low whistle. Crazy time difference. Were they going to take his model apart every time he turned his back? Would they blindfold him? Was Sasquatch guarding the Doohickey pieces in the Foe room? "We both need to build the same thing?" he asked.

"Exactly the same thing." Estella pointed to the model. "This is the prototype for both. You may come back and refer to it as often as you need. So what is it? Friend or Foe? Go."

Leore was biting a clump of hair. "I don't know how I'm going to do this either way, so what does it matter?"

"Fine," Zane said. "Take Friend, okay?"

"Whatever."

"We're set?" Estella said.

Zane nodded. "I am." He circled the pedestal, trying to memorize the details. To the left, there was a crank attached to a long rod. In between the crank and an end cap on the far side were, in order: a green spool, a hook, a blue spool, a coiled-up yellow banner, another hook, and a red spool. The hooks were attached to pieces of cabling. They'd probably need to hang their version somewhere.

Zane and Thorn headed around a circle of smaller light beams that formed a column all its own, a marker for the room with the model. "So you're my Foe today?"

"For starters," Thorn said.

"Where's the evil music now?"

"Playing in your head, I hope," Thorn said, not at all bored with this.

When they rounded the corner, it became totally obvious why it would take so much time to construct that model. His starter piece, an enormous single rod nestled in a shallow silver cup of sorts, stood upright, nearly floor to ceiling.

Before Zane got his bearings, the lights flickered.

"Your time starts now," said Thorn.

Go! First step, gather the pieces. Main rod, check. Above him, hanging from steel supports that spanned the ceiling, dangled two thick cables about six feet apart. One was just a piece of cable. The other already had a hook attached. So he'd need to attach the other hook to the cable, assemble the contraption, and get it up there. But where were the crank, the three spools, the hook, the banner, and the end piece? And he'd need a ladder. Everything had to be somewhere. It's not like they wanted him to stand there like an idiot for fifteen minutes.

Zane scanned the room. In the corner! A slight gap in the lights? False alarm. He headed back to the middle of the room, but stepped right over a fist-sized metal loop, flush with the floor. Zane pulled it. Smoke billowed. He lurched back. A triangular piece of floor started rising with even more smoke. It rose and it rose, and with a click, it stopped. Zane waved away the smoke. A closet! Zane opened its door. Cranks and hooks!

But which should he use? They came in different sizes and shapes.

He could match the hook with the one already attached to the cable, but he'd need to check the prototype for the exact crank. It'd be fastest, though, to find what choices they'd given him for the rest of the pieces and possibly make only one trip to the prototype.

Two other corners also had lift-up closets. One had all the spools—green, blue, and red—but in different sizes and with different designs. The other had a mess of banners, each tagged with a different saying.

Now Zane ran around the column of small lights. This time, the prototype was suspended from a mini scaffold on the table and had its banner unfurled: BELIEVE IT, ACHIEVE IT!

The silver crank tapered to a point. Hopefully, only one looked like that.

Spool time. The green one was largest with round cutouts. The blue one was medium with square cutouts. The smallest one, red, had diamond-shaped cutouts. Green, blue, red, in order of size and placement. Green, round like a go traffic light. Blue, square like, um, whatever. Red, a bloody diamond ring.

Back to his space. The rod was there, but the closets were gone. Cue creepy music in his brain. Thorn ambled in with an evil grin.

"So you're gonna mess me up every time I leave the room, huh?"

The grin turned into a smile.

"Maybe I won't leave." Zane relifted then opened the nearest closet, the one with the spools. Each color came in every variation of size and cut-out shapes. He sent the largest green one, with circles, rolling toward the middle of the room. He sent the smallest red-diamond one rolling, too. Then he grabbed the medium blue-square one and dumped it near the rod on his way to corner number two.

Up came the closet with about twenty hooks of different sizes and with different end points: some squared, some rounded, some pointed.

Zane ran to the middle of the room and eyeballed the size of the rounded hook already hanging. He chose three that looked about the right size, and one was. He shoved the other two toward a wall.

As for the pointed-end cranks, it'd take trial and error to see which fit. He grabbed all four sizes.

Over to the next closet. Of the dozen banners, only one had BELIEVE IT, ACHIEVE IT!

Back to the middle.

Zane expected to use all his strength to lift the huge rod and lay it on the floor, but it must have been made of hollow plastic. His only real concern right now was how to hang the thing. He still hadn't seen a ladder. Zane glanced once more around the room and focused for just a second on the clock. Somehow, nearly six minutes were gone.

First order of business, insert the crank into one end. The first crank was too loose. He compared it with the other three. The largest one fit perfectly.

Next to the crank, the large green spool. He started at the non-crank end, lined up the spool's center with the rod, and pushed it along the rod until it rested next to the crank. Next, the medium blue spool. Then the banner and the red spool. He left a space for both hooks.

Clock: 7:43. 7:42.

End cap. Where was it? None of the closets had them. And where was the ladder?

Zane couldn't leave the room. No telling what Thorn might do. Take his contraption? Hide all the pieces?

Play smart, play smart. Where would they stow a ladder? He circled the room in search of more loops to pull, but there were none, not even in the fourth corner. But that fourth corner had the odd light column made from smaller lights. Was it big enough to hide a ladder?

Zane reached in like Elijah had done earlier. Nothing bit, nothing burned. A little farther, a little farther. Metal. Zane plunged both arms in, then his head. Before Thorn could mess him up, Zane grabbed the ladder out, ran it to the middle of the room, made sure the legs were locked, climbed with the hook, connected it to the cable, climbed down, and repositioned the ladder in the middle.

He couldn't lift the main piece up yet. He needed the end cap.

Zane lapped the room again. Nothing. He stood in the fourth corner and surveyed the room. Then he bolted to the middle, to the shallow silver cup that had held the main rod upright. He should never have taken it off.

Zane reattached the end cap and picked up the contraption. With all the attachments, it still may have been light, but it was totally unbalanced. He took two shaky steps up the rungs of the ladder, which brought him eye level with one of the hooks. He positioned the first hook between the green and blue spools, laid the rod on the hook, then lifted the far end of the rod high enough to position it on the other hook, between the banner and the red spool.

Clock: 3:18. 3:17.

Why hadn't it stopped? The banner.

He moved the ladder, climbed back up, and turned the crank. The banner unrolled more and more and . . .

2:44.

CHAPTER 23

Leore was already in the model room when Zane got there. It made him wonder how horrible her previous two rounds had actually been.

Estella pointed to Leore. "One hundred five points."

Thorn pointed to Zane. "Two sixty-four."

Was Leore glaring at him through her hair? Didn't matter. Three challenges, three wins. Zane discreetly pumped his fist. "Hey, Thorn, did everyone find the ladder?"

"You did," Thorn said.

"Quickly, huh?"

"You got two hundred sixty-four points, right?"

"Oh, man," said Zane. "No scoreboard, no answers, no nothing?"

"We've been well coached," Thorn said.

"You trying to get information from him?" Estella said. "It'd be easier to get oil from a cucumber."

"Something else I haven't heard," Thorn said. "Where'd you get that one?"

"Just made it up."

They hung around for a few minutes, returned to the starting room at the same time as Ryder and Becky, and headed to their assigned corners. Josh was already in his, sitting backwards, chin resting on the chair's back, fingers running up, across, and down the cut-out rectangle near the chair's seat. Next to him, Berk was apparently feeling pretty good about himself, the way he was leaning way back, legs sticking straight out and hands folded across his belly. In the chair to Zane's left, Leore sat stone still, expressionless. If she were leading by ten thousand points, she'd probably still look depressed.

Ryder had settled in, hands clasped, elbows on knees, bouncing his heels. That mirrored Zane's own posture, minus the bouncing. It wasted too much energy.

Becky had the seat next to Ryder, and on the

diagonal from her was Hanna. Talk about opposites. Hanna, black hair; Becky, white-blond. Petite; athletic. Smiling with confidence; glaring with intensity. Hanna seemed all meadows and bunnies, but Zane sensed she had a killer rabbit tendency underneath. And Becky's stare reminded him of Jamaal—nicest guy ever until he got on the field. Then it was crush, kill, destroy.

Then there was his own opposite, Elijah, staring into space, which probably meant his mind was racing a million miles per hour.

The last challenge posted.

Zane knew he'd be paired with Elijah, but he wished they'd changed it.

"Before you get up," said Carol, "some good news. This is the last of these challenges, so once you're fully inside your separate hallways, the cone of silence has ended. Discuss away."

They weren't a step inside their hall before Zane started discussing. "So gloat, buddy. You left your three people eating dust, right?"

Elijah shook his head. "I destroyed the Gloop. My Eyeball time would have been better if these short legs could run faster. But I never found the ladder. I am in serious trouble."

"You?"

Elijah nodded. "For the first time, I'm concerned."

"You shouldn't be," Zane said. "Ryder got zero on Gloop. Leore barely squeaked by on Doohickey, and I'm practically positive she failed something else. Don't give up."

"Josh flunked his Eyeballs, and I did beat Hanna, but now I'm going against you."

Zane shook his head. "It's not really one-on-one; it's you getting your best time."

They rounded the corner toward their room. "And look, we're ending with Gil and Clio. The winners. That's you or me. Okay?"

"Okay." Elijah sounded sure, but the fingers on his right hand were tapping the side of his leg, one after another, pinkie to thumb and back to pinkie again.

"You need to shrug it off, buddy. Odds are this challenge is made for you. You're gonna go in there and crush it because I need you on my team, the top team. Okay?"

"Okay." And this time Elijah looked Zane in the eye.

"Sounds like you're ready," said Gil.

"Oh yeah," said Zane.

"Good," said Clio, "because we're ready for you." She snapped her fingers.

Rising from the center of the floor came a huge version of Golly's AlphaWheel. Of all the games he and his mom and Zoe had played before football took over his life, they played this the most. It had been his mom's favorite growing up. Their old game was so beat up, though, the alphabet spinner stopped mostly on *K*, *R*, *X*, or *W*, so he and Zoe had devised another system with a deck of playing cards. Zoe and his mom usually beat him, but only usually. Today was for money. Today was for glory. Today he'd get his points and get out of there.

"I've seen that come up four times today and four more during rehearsal yesterday," said Clio, "and it never gets old."

Gil gave the wheel a strong spin, and its pointer *tick-tick-tick*ed as it ran through all twenty-six spaces. "So here's the deal. You need to collect six letters and spell a six-letter word. Then you will eliminate one of those six letters and rearrange the remaining letters to spell a five-letter word. Then eliminate another letter and use those four to spell a four-letter word. Repeat the elimination process again to spell a three-letter word, then a two-letter word, like this." He snapped his fingers.

An example appeared on the wall.

PRICES
PIERS
RISE
SIR
IS

"In this example," said Clio, "more than one way works." She snapped her fingers and a second list appeared:

PRICES
PRIES
PIES
SIP
IS

"Once you've made one word list, you'll get six new letters and do it a second time." Clio looked over to Gil.

"In Friend mode," he said, "you will spin the wheel four times and play with those four letters, plus any two you choose. You will have six minutes."

"In Foe mode," said Clio, "you'll have nine minutes. You will spin the wheel to collect all six letters. And before you ask the logical question—what if my letters don't spell anything?—don't worry. The AlphaWheel has its own dictionary. With every spin, it will show only those letters that would finish fairly common words."

"Fairly common?" asked Elijah.

"You don't know all the words in the dictionary?" Zane said.

Elijah shook his head. "I'm getting there."

"So now it's time to decide," Clio said. "Friend or Foe?"

"Do you mind if I take Friend, Zane? I'm still concerned."

"No problem." This challenge was something he'd unintentionally studied for.

"If we awarded points for the easiest decision," Gil said, "you guys would win."

Clio took hold of Zane's elbow and positioned him next to the AlphaWheel. "We're staying here. See you, Gil! See you, Elijah!"

They disappeared around the light wall.

On the opposite wall, rising through the floor, came a huge stand with six monitors, each flashing a different letter. On the stand were four labeled buttons: Backspace, Scramble, Eliminate, and Enter.

"As you spin, your letters will appear on the touch-screens. When you know which word you want to spell, touch the letters in order. Watch."

Four monitors lit up with letters: *A, E, N, Z.*

"If you want to spell your name," said Clio, "you would hit the *Z* first." She did, and the *Z* jumped to the first screen. The *A, E,* and *N* slid to screens two, three, and four. "The red light around the *Z* means it's ready to be locked in. If you change your mind, though, hit Backspace." She hit it, and the light disappeared.

"If you're stuck, hit Scramble, and the letters will randomly rearrange." She did and they came up *N, E, Z, A.* Again: *E, N, A, Z.* Then Clio tapped, in order, *Z, A, N,* and *E,* and they rearranged themselves

in order, each letter bordered with a red light. "When you're ready to lock in your answer, hit Enter. If it's a word, you're good. If it's not a word, fifteen seconds flies off the clock. So far so good?"

"Yep," he said. "But what's Eliminate?"

"When you go from your six-letter word to your five-letter word, and your five to your four and so on, you'll need to get rid of a letter. When you're sure which letter needs to go, tap that letter, then hit Eliminate. It will disappear. Forever and ever. You cannot get it back." She looked at him with her big, brown eyes.

"Got it."

"All the instructions will be projected onto the

wall if you need them. Lucky for you, this Foe mode is straightforward. I won't stare at you or freak you out or otherwise throw any monkey wrenches into the works. Your time will start with your first spin of the wheel. And the wheel must go around at least once each time. Good luck."

"Thanks, Clio."

Of all the contestants in all the seasons, she might have been his favorite. She was smart and cute, and she was nicer than he ever could have been. But he couldn't start crushing on her now. He had words to spell. Ten of them in just nine minutes.

He put his hand at the edge of the wheel to give it a strong spin, but paused. The harder he spun, the longer it would take for the wheel to stop.

"Here goes." He gave the wheel a medium spin, and it went around at least five times. *R.* Great start!

He spun it much easier this time. *T.* Yes!

O. Good. It already spelled "rot."

U. "Rout." With letters like these, he could rout the competition. Next!

Q. Seriously?

He went to spin again, but the wheel was dark.

"What's—"

The sixth monitor now had an *E*. That had to be the only letter he could add to make a six-letter word. Reading the letter from each monitor, the list read R T O U Q E.

Having the *Q* was actually a positive. It would be Q-U regardless. He tapped those two, hoping a six-letter word would jump out at him. The monitors read Q U R T O E. Nope.

He'd need a vowel next. He tapped the *E*, but didn't lock it in. Q U E R T O. He didn't know that word. Or "quetor" or "querot." Maybe he needed to swap the *E* for the *O*.

Zane hit Backspace, then tapped the *O*. Q U O E R T. And if this word ended in –E R, it'd be "quoter." Was that a word? Like, someone who quotes someone else. That had to be it unless the word didn't start with Q U.

Every instinct told him to lock in "quoter." He did. The red borders gave way to green borders, which flashed very fast, then disappeared.

Time for a five-letter word. "Quote" was most

obvious, but he didn't see a four-letter word in it. He eliminated the *Q*. The letters came back up U O T E R.

If he could find the five-letter word, he'd already figured out the four, three, and two while he was collecting letters.

The −E R ending had worked once. Zane wanted to lock those two letters on screens four and five and scramble the other three, but they gave him no button for that. He'd have to do it in his head, scramble O T U. T O U. O U T. Out! Outer!

Zane locked that in. Then "rout." And "rot," not "rut." He needed the *O* to spell "or" or "to."

He entered "to," and all five monitors flashed, then came back with the same message: *Congratulations, Zane! Spin the wheel to get six new letters.*

He had the spinning motion down. The first spin went around only twice. It landed on *H*. He could work with that.

Next, *R*. Even better.

E. He had a two-letter and a three-letter as long as "her" worked with the next three.

Y. Not what he had hoped. But "her" could also be "hey" now.

He cheered the wheel like it was a teammate. "Good letter! Good letter! Gimme a good letter!" *P.* Was that a good letter? No time to think. The wheel would think for him. This time it only had *C, S,* and *Z.*

S would have to be easiest. "C'mon, *S.*"

Z? Seriously? The letters on the monitors looked hopeless, but they had to make a word or the AlphaWheel wouldn't have given him *H, R, E, Y, P,* and *Z.*

Clock. He was down to 3:49 and counting. He just needed to get his hundred points.

He hit Rearrange. E Z Y P R H. Nothing backwards or forward. Rearrange. Z P H E R Y. Nothing. Rearrange. Y E P R E Z. Rearrange. Z H Y P E R. There it was! The five-letter word just past the *Z*—"hyper." Without the *R,* "hype"!

Zane had everything but the six-letter.

2:28.

Did he even know this word? Was there such a word as "hyperz"? Doubtful. What about "phryze." You want some "phryze" with that burger? No time to joke.

2:14.

Rearrange. Z Y P H E R. No. P H Y Z E R. No. And neither spelled anything backwards.

1:49.

Why had he agreed to Foe so easily? He wasn't going to give up. Rearrange. P E R H Y Z. Rearrange. R Y H P E Z?

1:01 left.

He had to try something. What, though, what? Fine. The backwards version of the last one.

He tapped in *Z*, *E*, *P*, *H*, *Y*, and *R*. Might as well lock it. Green? Green! That was a word? Didn't matter now. He knew the rest from here.

Z. Eliminate.

"Hyper."

R. Eliminate.

"Hype."

P. Eliminate.

"Hey."

Y. Eliminate.

His screens went blank.

CHAPTER 24

Zane didn't ask what happened. Clio's face said it all. He needed to hear it, though. "Zero?"

She nodded. "When you got 'zephyr,' I thought you might do it. No one pushed those buttons faster. My heart's still thumping."

This was worse than the overtime loss against Carlton, when his momentary brain burp allowed their mediocre wide receiver to catch the ball in front of Zane. So why did Zane know "mediocre" but not "zephyr"? "Did everyone know it was 'zephyr'?"

Clio shook her head. "I figured it out, but Gil didn't. Neither did the producers working with us. And they're adults."

"What does it mean?"

"We think it's a type of wind."

"Yeah. And it blew me right out of the sweet spot."

Elijah ran up to him as soon as they rounded the corner. "Zane! Zane! Thanks! I—" He stopped. His eyes widened.

"I must look really bad," Zane said.

"You don't look good."

"So if we're together in the bottom, we'll just use our different strengths to crush the other team. Recalibrate." Recalibrate? Why'd Zane know a word like that, but not—? Forget it. That play was over. He focused forward.

They were first in the meeting room, but theirs had been the shortest challenge. Carol and Bill motioned them over.

"Elijah!" she said. "A minute thirty-three for your spins and only fifty-nine seconds to solve. You're the man!"

"Seriously?" Zane said. "You are the man."

"This won't make you feel any better, Zane," said Bill, "but half of us didn't get 'zephyr.' Not only was it the toughest word all day, it was the toughest in all our trial runs. You're a competitor, though, and this thing isn't over for you."

"I know."

"You'll know soon. In fact . . ." Bill spoke into his headset. "Light it up."

With that, writing projected on one of the beams.

Elijah XXX
Zane XXX
Hanna XXX
Becky XXX

Josh XXX
Berk XXX
Ryder XXX
Leore XXX

"Nothing like a scoreless scoreboard," Zane said. "I'm assuming Elijah and I are on top because we're the only ones who finished all four rounds?"

"Yep, but I don't want to talk about that now," said Bill. "Let's talk about your biggest comeback."

Now? "Why not," said Zane. "We were down

twenty-seven to three. First play of the fourth quarter, I intercept the ball and run it in. Twenty-seven, ten, and it's like we're all amped up. We stop them after three plays. We get the ball, and our running back immediately takes it to the house. It's twenty-seven, seventeen."

"How much time left now?" Bill asked.

"Six forty-two."

"I love how you guys know that. Keep going."

"Then nothing much happens until they punt with two minutes, ten seconds left—a really great punt, forty-two yards—but he outkicks the coverage, and our guy runs it back. Touchdown. Twenty-seven, twenty-four."

"You stop them in three, score, and win?"

"It wasn't that easy. They're driving, picking us apart, eating the clock. It's third and fourteen at our twenty-yard line, with fifty-eight seconds left. We call our last time-out. If they make a first down, game over. So Coach reminds us to cover the end around—they've been beating us with that all day—but I'm thinking they'll fake the end around and the quarterback'll take it up the gut. So I say something.

Coach revises our defense, and it turns out I'm right. Our two tackles converge on the quarterback, cause a fumble, and one of them picks it up and takes it back to their thirteen-yard line. We score with seven seconds left on the clock. Final, thirty-one, twenty-seven."

"And how'd you feel?"

"We were jumping and whooping it up so long and hard, I don't remember starting or stopping that day. It felt good."

"So tell me this," Bill said. "When the jumping and whooping stopped, and you had a chance to think about it, how did you feel?"

"Smart. I felt smart."

"Because you are. You remember that." He pointed to the scoreboard.

Zane's name had slipped below the red line.

After
THE FRIEND OR FOE CHALLENGE

What did that Harvey Flummox have up his sleeve? Why had he scheduled "an urgent phone meeting" today? Didn't he realize the Games were in full swing? Of course he did. Maybe he'd grown a conscience and wanted to come clean about the sabotage. No other reason would pull Bert Golliwop away from the Games right now. If only he could legally record the conversation without that lunkhead knowing. At least Bert could have surveillance equipment capture his side.

The phone rang. Bert took a deep breath and waited for Flummox's voice, which, undoubtedly, would be laced with haughtiness or, in evil villain terms, would carry a certain mwah-ha-ha quality.

"Happy to talk to you, Bert," Flummox said, like he truly was happy to talk to him.

"Though this is unusual for us," Bert said, already puzzled. Time to clear up one thing. "Thanks for the back scratcher, by the way. What possessed you to send it?"

"I heard about your hives and the pen-and-duct-tape stand-in."

"Amazing how word spreads." Bert's heart pounded harder in anticipation of his next question. "Who told?"

"One of our counterparts at United GameCo. Or was it McSwell? Or Rinky Brothers? We were trying to conjure up a plan to offset your Games. Anyway, one of them mentioned it. Danged if I remember who."

Someone at Golly, someone inside, *was* talking to a rival. Or was Flummox lying? Regardless, Bert had to play it cool and drop the subject for now. "What can I do for you?"

"First, let me apologize for the awful timing of this call. I know you're busy, but there's something I've been pondering for a while, and I suddenly reached a decision."

A decision to try and sabotage the Games?

"You see, my puzzle creators and I have come up with a humdinger, a real doozy. This baby has the potential to triple our sales from last year. And it could spawn ideas that will keep this puzzle chain going for years."

That wasn't a confession. It was a boast.

"However, we both know I don't have the sales and distribution force of a Golly Toy and Game Company. And the truth is, this might be bigger than I can handle."

"And?"

"And the other truth is, I'm getting old, and my kids, frankly, don't want the business. The daughter has a small ski resort in Vermont; the other daughter is a nuclear physicist; and the son is a poet. They still provide puzzle inspiration, but they have no interest in owning a company. It's time for me to stop working so hard, start playing with my grandchildren, and consider my future beyond the corporate walls."

"And?"

"I know how your puzzle division has been underperforming."

Did he have to rub that in?

"So I'm offering this: Might I tempt you to rename your division Golly Puzzles by Flummox?"

"You mean sell me your company?"

"I would insist on heading that division, at least for a while."

"So you can . . ." Bert let his voice trail off. If this offer was on the up-and-up, it'd be foolish to accuse Harvey Flummox of being Ratso.

"You were saying, Bert?" said Flummox.

"So you can transition into retirement?" Bert said, as if he'd meant that all along.

"Exactly," said Harvey. "I don't need an answer today; it can wait until after your Games. I'll be rooting for them to be huge, so you can make me a generous offer."

Bert felt as if the office were swirling around him in the best possible way. He could finally own the Flummox genius machine, and do it legally. He rubbed his hands and smiled. Except—

His cheeks went cold. Could Flummox be setting him up for something? Could this be part of the ruination of the Games?

It didn't feel that way. If Flummox wasn't the rat, though, which company was perpetrating the evil— McSwell, Rinky Brothers, or United GameCo? Or could it be that Ratso was working solo?

All Bert could do was to wait. Maybe the rat would still make a fatal move.

CHAPTER 25

What Bill just did, have Zane replay that amazing game, might have been the best thing anyone had done for him in a long time.

Zane didn't wait for instructions. He glanced at the scoreboard, then corralled Josh, Ryder, and Leore into a huddle. "Here's the deal. The other team already thinks they can run right over us, but we're strong. We each have skills that, combined, can generate the power to make *us* the final four. Got it?"

The others looked like they'd never heard a pep talk before. Zane stuck his hand in the middle, anyway, then Ryder put his on top, and Josh and Leore followed. He'd have to explain the next part. "On three, we all say 'Team!' and lift our hands. Ready? One, two, three, team!"

It wasn't bad for a first try, though with a little extra force, they could have flipped Leore backwards.

Everyone else in the room was staring at them.

"See?" Zane said to his people. "We have them stunned already."

Bill nodded at Zane. "Our friend Zane has already helped us separate you into two teams. The scoreboard, of course, tells the story." Bill pointed to it.

Zane didn't want to look. He never wanted to look when he'd lost—but you couldn't move fully forward if you were blind to what was behind you.

Hanna 1236
Elijah 1002
Becky 917
Berk 908

Zane 905
Josh 742
Ryder 696
Leore 465

Berk. If he hadn't moved his bin, Zane would be above the line. But like his parents said, "Life isn't fair." Neither were penalties for pass interference when Zane had been the one interfered with, yet he always managed to move forward.

The way Carol was looking at his team—with eyes nearly as sad as Zoe's when their dog had died—one thing was for sure. It wouldn't be easy. "The good news is this. If we'd stuck to our original plans, the four of you would be heading home. And yet, you're still here."

"And the evil news?" said Josh.

"Friend or Foe continues. To survive the team challenge, you will need to play in Foe mode, head-to-head with the other team."

"Yes!" Berk kept pumping his fist.

"It's not impossible, though," Bill said. "If you watched the last Games, you'll remember that the Orange Team—sorry about that, Carol . . ."

"Yeah, like you're really sorry, Bill."

"But the Orange Team squandered their lead, and the rest is history."

"As for the colors you'll wear this year . . ." Carol reached inside a gear bag that was slung over an unoccupied chair and pulled out two T-shirts, one silver, one gold. "My team, playing in Friend mode, will choose . . ." She held the jerseys out to them.

Berk snatched the gold one. "Is it even a question? Gold is more valuable."

The other three let him have his way.

Zane smiled. Berk had put him in the bottom, but Berk was also Zane's hope. Could Hanna control such a wild man? Possibly. Could Becky? More probable. But not Elijah. Berk would eat the kid for breakfast. And Zane couldn't save Elijah unless he sacrificed his own self. Maybe that would be the Gold Team's downfall. Chemistry. Without it, anything could happen.

Zane slipped the jersey over his head. It was solid

silver. Tough as steel. Hard-working. Like they'd need to be.

"Gold, you'll stay here," said Carol.

"Team Silver, follow me." Bill skirted one bank of lights.

"Banished," Leore said.

Bill shook his head. "Nope. Promoted to a better space." He led them around two light-beam corners to a large living room. Although it had funhouse mirrors and a variety of stuffed animals somehow floating in the air, this room was comparatively normal. Except the deep red couch where Zane sat might have been the most comfortable one in the world. "Are you trying to put me to sleep?"

Zane moved to a throne next to a table with fruit and muffins and cheese and crackers. Hadn't they just eaten breakfast? Maybe not. They'd gone through all those Friend or Foe challenges.

"Is this lunch?"

"Not even close," Bill said. "A midmorning snack if you need one."

Zane eyed the muffins but grabbed a couple cubes of cheese instead. "I can't tell you what to do," he said to the other three, "but I'm gonna say this. Eat the muffins if you want, but sugar can make you crash. Stick to the cheese and a little fruit if you need to eat something."

"Like that's really going to help," said Leore.

What a piece of work. "It can't hurt."

"Means more muffins for me." Bill took a big bite of one. He held up a finger, chewed, then swallowed. "So after this break we will send you into the famous warehouse area, where you might see anything: mountains, broccoli, snot noses, palm trees, bowling alleys—you name it. This year, though, you will share the space with the Gold Team."

"What if we need the same things at the same time?" asked Ryder.

"I was getting to that, my man. Both teams will run similar challenges, but the puzzles will lead to different answers and different stunts. Do note: This is a shortened team challenge. You will only go through three puzzles and their ensuing stunts."

Zane's stomach dropped. Just three? "Three opportunities for Team Gold to fall on their faces!"

Leore looked almost happy. "And only three opportunities for us to fall on ours."

"Don't even think that," said Zane. "Not unless you want to lose. Do you?"

"Of course not," she said.

"And with that," said Bill, "I'm going to leave you four to stand on your heads or twiddle your thumbs or get better acquainted. But first, more rules." He handed out a stapled set of papers to each of them. "Read and sign, please."

The info was basically what Zane had seen on TV. Each team would get a puzzle whose solution would be one of three Golly games or toys. Inside the corresponding box was a stunt card. If they opened the wrong box, they'd perform the wrong stunt and have to try and solve the puzzle again.

Then there was a paragraph about making a real effort to solve each puzzle and the fifteen-minute penalty they'd receive if they didn't. The next page was all about cheating. If you did, gone!

Zane signed. Leore and Josh were still reading. Ryder was pantomiming his desire to fold the papers into airplanes and toss them at the other two.

It didn't feel funny, but Zane pretended to laugh. This wasn't the time to tick anyone off. This was the time to develop a well-oiled machine.

"You know," he said after both Leore and Josh were looking up from the rules, "we're still in this. It might not be easy, but if we work like a team, you never know what'll happen."

"I hate to disagree," said Leore. "Our only chance is if the other team stumbles."

"We can only control ourselves," Zane said. "If we focus, we'll always have a chance."

"He's right," said Ryder. "Let's get in there and get it done."

"Seriously?" Josh said. "You guys are too intense.

Why do you think they call them Games? If they wanted us to be serious, they'd call it Homework." He laughed too hard at his own joke.

This wasn't going the way Zane had hoped. Only Ryder agreed with him. Then again, Ryder was the guy who hadn't bothered to reason out the Gloop challenge. Time to try something else. "So Bill said we should get to know one another."

"Or twiddle our thumbs." And Josh started twiddling his.

"So we know you love to crack jokes, but you . . ." Zane looked at Leore. "What's your favorite thing? Or your favorite class in school?"

She almost smiled. This was good. "I like to write poetry."

"You're good with words?" said Zane. "So lucky! I totally messed up the AlphaWheel. I mean, does anyone know what a zephyr is?"

"You mean the breeze?" Leore said.

"Man!" said Zane. "You probably slayed the AlphaWheel."

She actually smiled this time. "Though I did luck out with easy letters both times."

"It's good to be lucky," said Ryder. "Maybe you can rub some luck on us." He held the back of his hand out to her, but she didn't move. "Rub it."

Leore gave a shy laugh and rubbed the back of his hand.

Zane stuck his out. So did Ryder. It was like the ice was broken. They needed to ride this momentum.

"So can we count on you to lead us on word puzzles?" asked Zane. "They always have word puzzles, and I stink at those."

"Me, too," said Josh. "Communication arts? Bzzz! Wrong again."

"You can't be that bad," Zane said. "None of us can. I say I am, but that's compared to someone like Leore."

She blushed a little.

"If we take advantage of each of our strengths, we'll have a great chance. So Leore is our go-to person for word puzzles. You're okay with that, right?"

"I'll try."

"Perfect!"

"Josh, you're funny. The funny people I know see things differently."

"Yeah," he said. "On TV I spotted Estella's tape bumps—you know, some of the starting places to solve puzzles—before those teams did."

"Great! So you'll be on the lookout for things that are a little odd. Ideas that might get us pointed in the right direction."

"And Ryder?"

"I'm gonna be the time cop."

"Quick! Give the deputy a badge!" Josh laughed. "But how's that gonna help us?"

"If we get off track, I'll blow the whistle."

"Forget the badge," Josh said. "Give him a whistle."

"Great," said Zane. "Don't let us get away with anything. Keep us focused." He'd rather have known how Ryder could actually help them solve puzzles or do stunts, but his skills would reveal themselves. Jamaal had never intercepted a pass until that playoff game was on the line.

"So what are you good at, Zane?" Ryder said.

"Math. Also the physical stuff. Anything mechanical or that needs muscle."

"Just look at the guy," said Josh. "I could've told you that."

Where was Ryder's whistle? The last thing they needed were even minor put-downs.

"Let's hope you're good at that," Leore said, "because that's where I particularly stink."

"You're probably better than you think. Wasn't there a time in math or science when you aced a test you didn't feel comfortable about?"

"That's like every test," Leore said.

"Exactly my point," Zane said. "We are four of the only eight people in this universe to be right here, right now. And it wasn't luck. Even if you think that you stink at one thing, you've already proven you're good enough at *everything* to advance this far. So believe you can do it."

Leore was about to roll her eyes.

"You may not be able to do it alone, but together, we can lift our team over every hurdle."

Bill whipped into their room. "He's one hundred percent right. If you remember the past Games, no contestant took the lead on every challenge. They contributed as they could, sometimes surprising themselves. You can do this. Oh, and please, please win for me."

"What's the bet this year?" Josh asked.

"Honeymoon location," said Bill. "If Carol wins, we go to Paris and eat ze French food and view ze French museums. If I win, it's the beaches in Maui. Sun, surf, sand, and plenty of relaxation. So help me, guys. I need a break. I need a beach chair. I need pineapple."

He collected the papers. "And that's all I have to say except . . . it's go time!"

Team Silver traveled down a light-beam hall-way until it dead-ended in a semicircle of more beams. A series of chimes reverberated around them, and the wall of lights evaporated to reveal an area with real trees and real birds. And the other team.

Zane felt like the main character in the movie *Back to the Future*, who seemed to have been born into the wrong family. He belonged on that team, not this one.

"It's you!" Carol pointed at Team Silver.

"It's us," said Bill. "Do not underestimate those with the Foes. Gold may be inherently more valuable, but the world has much more silver. There's power in numbers."

"It appears your numbers are exactly the same as ours," Carol said.

"In bodies, yes, but in skills, we'll see."

"We will."

Carol and Bill glared at each other. And though her eyes crinkled and his lips wavered as if they'd burst out laughing, they maintained the stare until they both looked up at the same time.

Carol turned to her team; Bill, to his. "They're ready for you," he said. "Go in and make me proud. No. Forget about me. Make yourselves proud. And may Foe mode reign!"

A silver-and-gold door slid open from a seam in its middle. It was enormous enough for the eight of them to walk through side by side.

Zane expected a mass of odd objects, but instead came face-to-face with two billboard-sized arrows— one silver and one gold.

Without words, the teams divided. Zane bolted to the left, footsteps right behind him. About ten feet away was a huge silver T-shirt suspended above a silver-lit table with a silver envelope. He grabbed it, ripped it open, and handed the card to Leore. This needed to be about the team, and she needed the most convincing.

"Supposedly, our choices are under the table. And there's this list of random words."

Reckless

Vertical

Younger

Mister

Flawed

Late

Common

Dangerous

The Games DVDs had made the puzzles look easy. One person had a flicker of an idea, then another person built on it, and through the magic of TV, they solved it. But here? The magic needed to flow through them.

Zane brought up their choices in one swoop: Chompers, WordsWorth, and Silly Stacks.

"Somehow these words are supposed to tell us which game to open."

"That's how it worked in the past," said Ryder. "But if we don't figure it out in five minutes, we need to open whichever makes most sense."

"How do we know which makes most sense without solving it?" said Leore.

"Easy," Josh said. "We'll do eeny, meeny, miney, mo; catch the right stunt by its toe."

What part of not wasting time did they not understand? "Let's just solve it," said Zane.

Leore was looking at that word list without blinking.

Zane stood next to her. "I bet you've already ruled out that the first letters or last letters don't spell anything."

"Also," she said. "I don't see any common definitions, languages of origin—"

"Have you been watching the National Spelling Bee, too?" said Josh.

"I've participated in the National Spelling Bee, but I never got to Washington, DC. Almost, though. 'Effulgent' kept me."

"What does that mean?" Ryder said.

"Time police," said Josh. "Blow the whistle on yourself."

Good. "So, Josh. What's weird about the list?"

"Outside of the fact that the words don't have anything in common?" He shook his head. "But we're playing this in Foe mode, right? That could mean the other team has the same type of word list, but their words are simpler."

"Simpler than 'late'?" Leore asked.

"He means," said Ryder, "simpler than the longer ones."

"You don't know what the longer ones mean?" asked Leore.

"I know them," said Ryder. "Like, 'reckless' is out of control, not being careful. And 'vertical' is up and down and not sideways. And 'younger' is more young."

"More young?" said Josh. "That's good. Young means young."

"Because I need to explain 'young' to you? It's the opposite of older, by the way."

Zane whistled a halt.

"Maybe he should be the whistle cop," said Josh.

"We need to focus," Zane said. "So we were at 'younger.' Why do you think they gave us that instead of 'young'? Does the –E-R change anything?"

"Not that I see," said Leore.

"Maybe it's a Foe thing," Zane said. "A longer word looks harder. Keep going with the rest of the words, Ryder."

"Okay, so there's 'mister' as opposed to 'miss' or 'misses.'"

"Or it can be *a* mister," Leore said, "a device you use to, say, spray plants with water."

"Or run under when it's a hundred degrees at Six Flags." Now Zane was wasting time. "After 'mister' there's 'flawed' as in not perfect."

"And 'late,'" said Josh, "as in not early. And do you hear ourselves? Not, not, not. We keep repeating 'not.'"

This time Leore really smiled. "They can all be opposites." She grabbed a pen from the table and started writing words in a neat column to the right of the original list.

Reckless	Safe/Careful
Vertical	Horizontal
Younger	Older
Mister	Miss/Mrs./Ms.
Flawed	Perfect
Late	Early
Common	Unusual
Dangerous	Safe

"You guys are geniuses!" Zane said. He grabbed the Chompers box.

"What do you mean?" said Leore.

"Look at the initial letters on your list of opposites."

"S-H-O-M-P-E-U-S?"

"Use 'careful' instead of 'safe,'" said Zane. "And what's an *R* synonym for 'unusual'?"

"'Rare,'" she said.

"Exactly. Use 'careful' and 'rare,' and it spells 'Chompers,' which I'm opening, okay?" He didn't wait for a response before he pried off the lid.

Inside was a card.

Stunt #1
＊ ＊ ＊ ＊ ＊ ＊ ＊ ＊ ＊ ＊

We chomp our Chompers day and night;

Eat everything within our sight.

A goat, a boat, a puck, a truck;

We eat until the food gets stuck.

And then we scream and shout and pout;

No more to eat till it's all out.

We have no hands! We're at a loss!

We need you, please! Come help us floss!

"We're coming, giant teeth!" Ryder started running, but Zane caught him by the elbow.

"Where are you going?"

"In search of teeth."

"We need a strategy." Zane pointed to his left. "Head to that corner and yell your name if you find them." He let go, and Ryder sped away. "I'm heading way back, left. Josh, back, right Leore, front, right. Work your way to the middle. If you find the teeth, yell loud."

"Loudly," Leore said.

"Right," said Zane. What was with these people and grammar? Didn't matter. He sped off.

The famous mountain from last year remained in the middle of the vast space that rose to a glass ceiling many stories up. He raced by a hippo, a fire hydrant, a barn, three fireplaces, a giant hot fudge sundae, a tower of pizzas, a chair-sized pincushion, a rack with hundreds of hats, hovering spacecrafts, and a wall of mattresses, maybe, where Team Gold was doing some stunt with pool cues.

Zane picked up the pace. Giant teeth, giant teeth. He'd assumed they were giant. This was Foe mode, but they wouldn't be so cruel as to hide normal-sized teeth in a place like this.

He passed a group of purple things: robot, minivan, tent in midair, unicorn in a bubble bath. Then came the orange things: a barrel of basketballs, person-sized pad of sticky notes, steamroller—

"It's Ryder!" The voice came from behind Zane. "I'm under the fire truck in the ceiling."

There! Zane raced over and pulled up, right behind Leore, at the Chompers—eight teeth on top, eight on the bottom, all about the size of refrigerator doors. Between some of them were traces of color, probably whatever was stuck.

Zane took the big silver card from Ryder. *Let the flossing begin!* That's all it said.

Go time! Zane grabbed both coils of rope sitting on the floor in front of the Chompers and tossed one to Josh, who had just gotten there. "You and Leore floss the bottom. We'll take the top, Ryder, but we need to find ladders first. When we bring them back, Josh and Leore'll give us their dental hygiene tips."

"Good one," Josh said.

Ladders. What was with Golly hiding ladders? Nothing here, nothing—

"Here!" Ryder called.

Zane went around a pine tree, where Ryder was already pulling on one of a pair of stair-step bookends.

"Take yours around front," Ryder said. "Opposite side of her." He pointed to Leore, who was pulling the rope through the base of the left molar, then letting it disappear back through the teeth like a tug-of-war.

"Any advice, Leore?" Zane said, pushing the stairs to the front.

"Just start near the gums. That's the only way to feed the rope to the other side."

With the rope looped over his shoulder, Zane climbed the stairs and fed one end between the first two teeth.

"Got it!" called Ryder.

"Tug like your life depended on it."

Ryder's tug nearly slammed Zane into the teeth. He tugged back, and within seconds they had a smooth sawing motion. "Perfect," Zane said. "Work it down."

"Finally got something," Leore said. "A boxcar."

"Like from a train?" Ryder called.

"Yes, and it says, 'Instruction one of two. All aboard, but order them right.'"

"Keep going!" Ryder tugged even harder.

Three more backs and forths, and something smashed into Zane's stomach. He let go of the rope, and it zipped back through the teeth. "You okay?" Zane called.

"I'm fine."

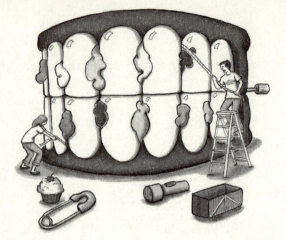

"Something hit me. Some sort of stuffed-animal fly. Eyes bugging out and everything. Move your stairs to the next tooth."

Ryder was ahead of him. By the time Zane positioned his stairs, Ryder had already fed the rope through the next gap.

Except for a little grunting, they all stayed quiet except to announce what else they'd flossed from the Chompers: miniature wheelchair, cupcake, cotton candy, flashlight, flyswatter, enormous safety pin, and another boxcar on Ryder's side that said *Instruction 2 of 2: Then keep the train within your sight.* All the objects were made of some expanding foam that compressed between the teeth, but puffed up once they came out.

Zane repositioned his ladder and fed the rope

through a tooth gap. It took only six tugs to get a lighthouse.

"Just two more places to floss down here," called Josh.

"Us, too!" Zane put even more effort in his tugs.

"Now one. We have a jar of apple butter," said Leore.

"How do you know it's apple butter?" Ryder said.

"I can read labels."

A big piece of green came through the next tooth on Zane's side. "I think the guy ate some rolled-up spinach." Three more tugs. "Or not. It's a yellow flower on a green stem."

"Last one!" said Ryder.

"Ours is almost out," called Josh. "What is it, Leore?"

"A pinwheel."

"And we have something round," said Ryder.

It fell out on Zane's side. "One of those caramel apples on a stick. Now, grab everything and meet behind the teeth."

They looked like shoplifters from a randomness store.

"Where's the train?" said Leore. "They said there would be a train."

"Exactly," Ryder said. "'All aboard, but order them right. Then keep the train within your sight.' I don't see anything."

"Not true," Josh said. "You see the cupcake you're holding."

"Seriously—"

"Shh!" Zane held up a hand. "Hear that?"

Arms still loaded, they moved to the front of the teeth.

From way back, coming around the mountain, was a train engine made from an oversized Go-Golly-Go Car. In front of it, floorboards were flipping over to reveal more train tracks as the cars needed them.

The engine stopped in front of them. The open-topped boxcars behind it were numbered one through fourteen.

Leore held up a boxcar from the Chompers. "I just noticed. This is labeled number six."

"And this boxcar is eleven." Josh dropped it into the number 11 boxcar.

"So where do the rest of these go?" Ryder dumped his four objects into different boxcars.

"Whoa!" said Zane. "What are you doing?"

"Seeing if it's random."

Leore put a hand on her hip. "When has anything ever been random with the Games?"

"Fine." Ryder took out the pieces. "Satisfied?"

No one answered. Instead, they lined up the pieces across the floor. Next to Ryder's cupcake, flashlight, and wheelchair were cotton candy, flyswatter, lighthouse, flower, pinwheel, apple butter, safety pin, and bug-eyed fly.

"Any others have numbers?" Ryder asked.

"Not on mine," Zane said.

Leore shook her head. "Mine, either."

"Hey, you Golly jokers!" Josh called into the atmosphere. "Isn't this supposed to be a stunt? What's with the puzzle?"

"You didn't see?" Ryder pointed to the side of the engine. It said *Puzzle #2*.

From above came a Tarzan yell. Bill swung in on a rope and landed in front of the engine. "For being Foes, you killed the first puzzle and stunt. But hurry! You're still playing catch-up." Bill and his rope lifted toward the ceiling and disappeared behind the mountain.

"We'll never make it," Leore said.

"We're not giving up." Zane squatted and moved the fly next to the flyswatter.

Josh pointed at Zane's pairing. "That's just wrong."

"No," said Leore. "It's very right."

Leore? Something positive?

"It's like wordplay. Here's a flashlight, there's a lighthouse."

Zane moved them next to each other. "Get together everything that matches."

They matched the caramel apple and apple butter, then strung together the safety pin, pinwheel, and wheelchair. That left the cotton candy, flower and cupcake unmatched.

"Maybe they're using different names for these," said Leore.

"Like pretty flower instead of yellow flower?" Josh said.

Did the guy know he wasn't funny?

"And instead of cotton candy, sticky stuff that's impossible to get out of your hair when you're eight and think it might make an awesome blue wig?"

That was funnier. But funny needed to wait. Zane stared at the objects and where they'd ultimately go—the train with its engine, five empty cars, the number 6 boxcar in place, four empty cars, the number 11 boxcar—

"Hey! We need to string together five objects, then a new set of four, then three." He pointed to the sequence of filled and unfilled boxcars.

"We already have a three," said Ryder. "Put 'em in!"

"No, Ryder," said Leore. "Just because there're three doesn't mean the string's done."

"Then let's get it done," Ryder said.

"I'm trying," she said. "For one thing, unless this has another name, the flyswatter is at the end of one string because nothing else here starts with swatter. So before it, housefly . . ."

"*House*fly?" Zane added the flashlight/lighthouse pair to the front of the housefly and flyswatter. "And unless the flower's real name is like 'yellow flash' to go in front of the flashlight, this string is done."

"So let's pretend for a minute that we have our string of four and our string of three." Leore moved the safety pin, pinwheel, and wheelchair to the side, then grouped the caramel apple, apple butter, cupcake, cotton candy, and flower.

"Maybe that's a caramel cupcake," said Josh.

"Right," said Ryder, "because we need two things that start with caramel."

Zane stayed quiet for Leore, who was shifting the objects like a sleight-of-hand artist.

"There!" she said.

"Are you sure?" Zane asked.

"Positive. We call these candy apples where I live. So we have cotton candy, candy apple, apple butter, and this flower has to be a buttercup, then cupcake."

"Load the train, Ryder!" said Zane.

Within seconds, the train blew a warning whistle, then chugged off, floorboards flipping in front of it, floorboards flipping back over behind it.

"Why can't it move faster?" said Josh, following it in slow motion.

"Or tell us where it's going," said Ryder. "We could meet it there."

But they could only walk alongside it.

"They're still on the train!" came Berk's voice from around the bend. "Woo-woo! Suckers!"

"This is not good," Leore said.

Zane slowed a step until she caught up. "But you

were brilliant. And they could mess up or get penalized or trip over a groundhog and roll up the side of the volcano and fall in."

"Like that would happen," she said.

"It's not over till it's over."

"How cliché."

"But it's true. Isn't that how clichés start?"

The train took them to the far side of the warehouse, probably much farther than it had taken the other team. It finally stopped past a Ferris wheel and a merry-go-round, at a table with a choice of three Golly boxes: Long Train Running, Running Waterfalls, and Watch Your Step.

"I thought we solved this already," said Ryder.

"We cracked the code," Leore said, "but we still need to open a box."

There'd been five objects strung together, then four, then three. "It has to be—" Zane and Leore reached for it at the same time. "Go ahead," he said.

"Why that one?" said Josh.

Leore looked at him. "Running water. Waterfalls. It fits the pattern."

"What's wrong with long train and train running?"

"Train running isn't exactly a common phrase," Leore said.

"Here!" Ryder had been opening the box through the explanation.

Stunt #2

* * * * * * * * * *

The well is dry, but water's near.
Our buckets aren't the best, we fear.
Please use them, though, for your next task.
Go fill the well! That's all we ask.

They raced off. The waterfall flowed from one of the ledges that crisscrossed the warehouse, stories high, then landed who knew where. They were about to find out.

Zane stopped short of the huge pool at the waterfall's base, and for half a second, inhaled the mist that hit his face. "Where's the well?"

"Over here!" Ryder's gift: finding anything. He handed out buckets to them all.

Zane dragged his through the pool, but water nearly poured through the ill-fitting wooden slats.

"These buckets aren't the best? That's an understatement." By the time he ran his to the stone well, barely one-quarter of his water was left.

When he zoomed back past them, the other three were only partway there, wearing . . . what? Zane glanced back. Yellow slickers. There was one more hanging in a free-standing closet next to the waterfall.

Forget wearing it. Zane dropped his to the ground, then swiped the bucket through the water and wrapped the raincoat around it. The three others returned.

"The raincoat genius strikes!" said Josh. "Now we don't need galoshes."

Zane must have dumped three times more water into the well this time. He still couldn't see where it landed, but he did notice a blue laser beam rimming the inside of the well, about four feet from the top. A sensor? A warning not to reach below it? Probably so. Wouldn't come into play until they had enough water, anyway.

Zane dashed away, working silently. The others, now using his method, kept calling him the Raincoat

Genius until Josh switched to His Muteness. Zane was just saving his breath.

After his fifth trip, the water level had risen enough to reveal a bucket floating on the surface. And after his tenth, he could make out a laminated card inside the bucket that was about three feet below the laser line. *Puzzle #3.* He ran back and refilled. "About six more trips," he said, overtaking Leore and Josh on their way to the waterfall.

Zane closed in on the well again, but why were Ryder's raincoat and bucket on the ground? And why were his feet in the air and his belly on the well's—

Zane dropped his bucket and shot over. "Ryder!" Zane lunged and caught an inch of his T-shirt. But it slipped out of his hands. "Stop!"

Bzzz!

Ryder rocked to his feet and glared at Zane. "Why'd you do that?"

"Didn't you see the blue laser? You can't reach in."

"Who said?" Ryder raised his face to the rafters. "Don't tell me there's a penalty."

Why hadn't Zane warned them about the light? "There's always a penalty."

"What? Like two minutes?" Ryder said.

Josh came racing up. "What'd you do? Contaminate the well?"

"Worse." Zane pointed down. The laser beam was now at the top of the well. "But it's okay."

Leore pulled up and sighed. "I heard. Even more water?"

"More water," said Zane. He looked at her. Dared her to be the voice of doom and gloom.

"Then I guess that's all we can do," she said.

"Exactly. Go!" Zane didn't think he could move any faster, but he almost lapped the other three on his fourth trip. He may not have been in two-a-days, but this was probably the hardest series of wind sprints he'd ever run.

Back, forth, back, forth. Back, and the rest of them were standing there. "We just need yours," said Leore.

Zane poured it in, and the water cleared the line. "Take it, Ryder."

CHAPTER 28

Ryder was still trying to free the puzzle envelope from some sort of impossible shrink-wrap when Bill hopped over on a pogo stick. "Messing up, Ryder? Yowza!"

"Don't rub it in."

"Good news, though," Bill said. "I'm not going to Paris yet. The other team, well, I'll just say . . . embarrassing! You still have a chance." He jumped off.

While the others wrestled with the Foe-mode shrink-wrap, Zane went in search of a knife or scissors. It took him two seconds to stop looking for the needle in a haystack. But if he unscrewed one of the raincoat hooks from the closet, it—

The screw did have a pointed end! Zane ran the hook over just as Josh had managed to claw and bite the thing open.

"What's it say already?" Ryder asked Josh.

The guy needed to slow down.

"Makes no sense, like something I'd write." Josh held it out.

A corny of my father's was given the potion of either raising toters (the river mammals that glide through murky waters), dyeing them with satin, or even signing about them.

"What's a corny, anyway?" said Josh.

"I think it's a typo," said Leore.

"A type o' what?" said Josh.

"No. A typo, an error," she said. "The word should probably be 'crony.'"

"Like a witch?" Ryder asked.

"I can't believe your jokes!" She shook her head. Zane, though, had been thinking the same thing and not in a joking way.

"A crone is a witch. A crony is an old friend."

"I'm still confused," Ryder said. "Even if you fix the typo, it says the friend was given a potion that would raise some sort of animals from the dead or something and cover them with satin or maybe sing about them instead."

"It's not sing," Leore said. "It says 'signing,' maybe like in sign language, but wait." She pulled Ryder's hand closer, then took the card from his grasp.

"So he's going to learn animal sign language?" Josh said.

Zane stayed quiet. If he'd learned nothing else from football, he knew to respect the guy with the talent. Let him work his magic. Or today, *her* magic. Leore pulled a pen from her pocket and underlined some of the words in the sentence.

A <u>corny</u> of my father's was given the <u>potion</u> of either raising <u>toters</u> (the river mammals that glide through murky waters), dyeing them with <u>satin</u>, or even <u>signing</u> about them.

"I'm not certain these are technically typos. They seem deliberate."

Ryder was kind of jumping his shoulders. "Get to the point."

Zane put a hand on his arm and nodded at Leore.

"Without the mistakes, this could say, 'A crony of my father's was given the option of either raising otters (the river mammals that glide through murky waters), dyeing them with stain, or even singing about them,' which does make sense in an odd sort of way."

"So now what?" said Ryder.

"Now we see our choices." Josh moved to a glowing silver table.

"That seriously wasn't there before," Zane said.

"It wasn't," said Josh. "It sort of rose from the dead. Or the floor."

On the table was only one package, the retro three-pack from the Golly ServiceLegend Series. And it was bound in the same shrink-wrap.

Zane pulled the hook from his pocket. "I've got it this time." He ran the point of the screw as parallel as possible to one edge of the big square box until it made a small tear. He dropped the hook and pried the plastic open with his fingers and his teeth. Inside: Cavalry Cavalcade, Renegade Rangers, and Tango Troop.

"Cool!" said Ryder. "My grandfather still has these. When he was a kid, his favorite was the Cool Canadians of the Cavalry Cavalcade. But he and his brothers used to argue over who was tougher—them or the Rough Riders of the Renegade Rangers or the Military Men of Tango Troop."

"Thank you for the history lesson, Sir Whistle Blower," said Josh.

Ryder glared at him.

Leore didn't appear to let the joke or the tension derail her. She kept writing the corrected words with their typos:

corny   portion   toters   satin   signing
crony   option   otters   stain   singing

"Now what?" Zane asked.

"I'm thinking either the wrong letters or the corrected ones will spell the answer." She scribbled the wrong typo letters: *OR, PO, TO, AT, GN*.

"Are those all the letters in Tango Troop?" said Zane.

Leore scribbled some more. "There!"

RO OP OT TA NG
Tango Troop

Zane hugged her. "You are amazing." He wanted to add, "Just stop being so negative," but it wasn't the right time, it wasn't the right place, and he wasn't the right person. Anyway, Ryder had the box open.

Stunt #3
✱ ✱ ✱ ✱ ✱ ✱ ✱ ✱ ✱ ✱

Tango Troop has set the target. Demolish the airfield to cripple the enemy.
Your ammo? You already loaded it into the train.
Your destination? Look up.
X marks the spot.

It had to be on one of those crisscrossing pathways. "But how do we get up there?"

Ryder pivoted. "This way!"

"Wait!" Zane said. "We need the ammo first!" He grabbed his raincoat and bolted back to the train. Their fourteen objects were still there. They weren't heavy, but they'd be bulky. And the others still looked gassed from running the buckets.

Zane dropped the raincoat to the ground. "Pile a bunch of them on here. I'll take as many as it'll hold; you guys carry the rest. Which way, Ryder?"

"This way!" He had them backtracking past the waterfall, probably saving a few of the minutes he'd lost them at the well. "I saw a spiral staircase when we were looking for the first thing. Whatever it was. It seems so long ago."

"Seriously?" Josh said. "You can't remember?"

"Remember what?" said Ryder.

Zane wished they'd save their breaths and run faster, but it would be counterproductive to waste his and tell them. If he were coaching, though, they'd hear it after the game.

Two tight and winding staircases came into view, one marked with a gold *X*, and theirs with the silver. Zane leaped past Ryder to go up first and check it out. Even if that saved only one second, that second could make a difference.

Their stairs continued about a story higher than the gold one's. At the top, at least three stories up, the bird's-eye view was probably fascinating. Zane ignored it, but hoped Team Gold was so complacent, they'd stopped to sightsee.

He ran down a caged-in pathway with the raincoat slung over his shoulder like Santa Claus hopping over rooftops. The path led across the entire width of the warehouse floor, took a hairpin turn, and came back the other way. His teammates, single file, were only halfway down the first path. Maybe Zane should have lagged, inspiring them to move faster. This way, though, he could have a strategy in place when they got there.

The path took another hairpin turn. Below, and at a distance, he could make out Team Gold looking over the side. What was their advantage here besides being one level closer? Fewer targets to hit?

Another turn, and Zane reached a domed platform—a cage, really—five yards by three yards, made of clear plastic, and with a view to the ground that buckled his knees for a moment. Its walls had basketball-sized holes every six inches. Zane stuck his head through one of them.

Below was an airfield that had circles numbered

one through eight. He brought his head back in and saw a huge toy chest. Inside were massive amounts of water balloons and a card lying on top. The three others pulled up as he was reading it.

> Your mission: Strike all eight targets
> within the circles.
> Your ammo: The fourteen objects
> you carried here.
> Your auxiliary ammo: Water balloons.
> Your instructions: Each of you must hit two targets. First, use the objects from the train. You may all drop at the same time if you wish. If they strike fully within the eight circles, mission complete. If not, you must strike any missed targets with three water balloons each. Water balloons may only be dropped one at a time.
> GO!!!

"Let's drop 'em!" said Ryder.

"Absolutely!" Zane said.

"Bombs away!" said Josh.

Zane dropped the pinwheel, which drifted far

off course, then the cupcake, which almost landed inside, but the lighthouse was a direct strike. The circle turned red. "Got it!"

One down.

"Ah!" said Josh. "So close."

"Me, too," said Ryder.

Zane turned and grabbed the only thing left, the flower. He didn't even stop to see where it landed. Time for water balloons.

"Woo-hoo!" shouted Ryder. "She got it with the apple butter."

"Stop looking," Zane said. "Load up with balloons, but only one person drops at a time."

"Does that mean we need to wait until they hit?"

"Didn't say," Zane said. "But we can't risk penalties. I'm dropping now because I'm ready. Then Ryder, Josh, and Leore last, because she only needs one more target, too." His first balloon hit on the number seven's outline, but the water nearly covered the entire target.

"Do you suppose that counts?" Leore asked.

"We'll see when it lights up."

Ryder's struck dead center on number one.

"Josh, wait," said Zane. "Go again, Ryder. You have the aim nailed."

The second one was off center a little, and his third hit near the edge, but apparently that was good enough. It lit up red. Three targets, done!

Josh missed with his first.

"But I know where to go now," he said. "I'm dropping again."

That one was close, but his third was dead-on. That was the way to do it. They fed him three more balloons until target number two was bathed in red.

Leore was ready to go with hers. She missed the first and the second, but her third, fourth, and fifth were dead center.

"You're done!" Zane said, and dropped above the number seven target that was still wet from his first balloon. Direct hit! Same with balloon number three.

"Ryder, you're up!" He dropped one. Missed. Two, hit. Three—

Trumpets sounded. Lights flashed. A platform rose.

On it, Elijah, Becky, Hanna, and Berk were jumping and fist-pumping and hugging and shouting.

CHAPTER 29

Leore slunk to the ground and hid her face on her knees. Ryder and Josh mumbled and turned away. All Zane could do was watch the celebration.

Team Gold's platform nearly reached the glass ceiling before a group of people in black Spider-Man–like suits rushed on. Within a minute, the platform fell away, and Elijah, Becky, Hanna, and Berk were hang gliding around the warehouse, shrieking and laughing.

Zane had had enough. He doubled over, hands on his knees, head down. Even when they'd been forced into Foe mode, even when the water line had risen, Zane had never imagined they'd lose, not until the horns sounded.

At least he'd battled to the end. He wouldn't look like a fool on TV when they showed the losers—no, they weren't losers—the losing team. And he wouldn't turn into a weeping, sulking, object-kicking mess.

Zane straightened. He gathered the other three, who did look like the losing teams he'd seen. "I need to say something." He took a deep breath. "Probably no one bet we'd come close."

Josh pointed at Ryder. "Especially after—"

Zane grabbed his finger and forced it down. "We're not doing that. I could blame myself for not saying anything about the laser line in the well. We all can blame ourselves for something, but it will never change the fact that we have a lot to be proud of. We almost made it. And, yes, almost isn't good enough, but here, now, we can walk back into our normal lives knowing we gave this a real shot."

Zane felt a pair of hands clench his shoulder. "I swear this guy's gonna steal my job." Bill turned him around and gave him a big hug.

Then he hugged each of the others. "Can I tell you a secret? Not that I wanted you to lose, but I'm happy to go to Paris. Carol really, really wanted to go there, and if you think she's all bubbly now, you should see her when she's really giddy."

And there she was, running toward them, smiling, but not giddy.

Zane gave a "what're you gonna do?" shrug, and she nodded. "I need to tell you, Silver Team. When Golly approached us with Friend or Foe, maybe three of us thought Team Foe would stand a chance. And even though a close loss can sting more than a bad one"—and she looked directly at Zane—"that close call is going to make you heroes in your hometowns and even beyond.

"So when you leave here, hold your heads high, take advantage of those bragging rights, and enjoy your winnings—three thousand dollars—"

"Three thousand?" said Ryder. "Woo-hoo!"

Three thousand wasn't life changing, but three thousand dollars? "Oh, yeah!"

Carol hugged each of them, then she and Bill herded them from the platform to the pathway, but stopped abruptly and had them turn back. Team Silver's clear dome was opening at the top and folding underneath the platform. One by one, the hang gliders hovered, then landed there.

Zane rushed over to Elijah. "Way to go, buddy!"

Elijah's face went tight, then exploded with giggles. "Sorry," he managed.

"No," said Zane. "It's good."

"It's the relief after the scare," Elijah said. "Our egos were enormous until we had the two mess-ups and saw you'd pulled nearly even with the water balloons."

Becky shook her head. "We could've put you guys away early, but it wasn't easy for some of us to focus." She glared directly at Berk.

"What?" he said. "I wanted to kill 'em from the beginning."

"It doesn't matter," Hanna said. "You all were amazing."

"We still lost," Leore said, huddled on the ground again. But then she lifted her face. "But we did try. We tried very hard."

"Absolutely." Zane leaned down and almost gave her a "way to go" backslap, but remembered she wasn't in football pads. He patted her shoulder instead.

Then he pulled Elijah toward him. "You're gonna be incredible. And I will be right here, cheering you on."

"I'd be cheering you if the roles were reversed, assuming that's allowed."

Zane turned to Carol. "We can watch, can't we?"

She shook her head. "Not exactly."

"You're kicking us out?"

"First, there's lunch."

"Then you're kicking us out?"

Bill shook *his* head. "We need you to stick around a little longer."

"For what?"

Bill smiled. "Let's go eat."

They wound down two of the ramps—Team Gold dancing around Carol, and Team Silver hovering around Bill—then into a huge and previously hidden elevator.

"About lunch," Carol said. "We're breaking with tradition. First, you're all eating together. Second, there'll be a viewing area with early Games highlights for you. Check it out."

No, thanks. Not now.

"Finally, about the obscene display of food we've become famous for? We've scaled it back significantly."

"To what? Bread and water?" said Josh.

"There'll be a little more than that," said Bill. "It's just that all our past contestants, excluding one who is not here today, have told us it's too much between rounds."

"How many did we need to wake from food comas, Bill?"

"Four? Five?" He laughed. "We promise we'll feed you very well after this last round."

Zane wasn't that hungry, anyway. Part of him wanted to stomp out the frustration, part of him wanted to flop on the couch and take a nap, but all of him, he suddenly realized, was happy that they weren't shipping him straight to the airport.

They came out of the elevator, and Zane lagged behind. He needed a few seconds to mourn his loss before he got to lunch.

Elijah had other plans. He stopped and waited for Zane. "So, what is it?"

"What's what?"

"Your eyes. Your mood. I know you wanted to win—we all want to win—but you had some higher stakes in this, didn't you?"

How could someone so awkward know so much about people?

"I like the glory." And that's where Zane wanted to leave it. "But you, buddy," he said to change the focus, "have a chance to claim it. Are you ready for the next round?"

"I don't have any expectations, really," said Elijah.

"Why not? You'll kill it."

"Maybe the mental stuff, but there's more to this than brainpower. Look at me. I'm four foot five inches. I weigh seventy pounds."

Zane couldn't help but laugh. "I weigh more than two of you?"

"Yeah, and you're more than a foot taller, and you have a bigger bone structure, which is beside the point. I'm concerned I may not be fast enough or strong enough or spatially smart enough to see this through till the end."

"I don't know what the spatially thing means, and don't explain it because here's what's important:

Golly will not give you anything that's physically impossible."

"But—"

"I know. You're thinking even if it's possible, it might take you forever."

"Exactly."

"And that, Elijah, is where you're wrong." Zane laughed. "How many times has anyone told you you're wrong?"

"Like, none."

"I'm telling you now. You're wrong," said Zane.

Elijah started to protest.

"Hear me out. If you came into a room with a monster equation covering the whiteboard, how would you feel?"

"Ready to take it on."

"That's how you need to go into this next round."

"If only it could be math."

"No matter what it is, treat it like a math problem. Attack it logically. If you don't have all the physical tools you need, look around. These people give you everything. I mean, what did you do with Chompers? How did you reach the top set?"

"Top set of what?"

"Of the Chompers. Flossing the giant teeth to get the objects for the word chain."

"We didn't floss giant teeth. We poked objects out of a foam wall with pool cues."

"Right. But we did have to floss between giant teeth, and none of us could possibly reach the top ones. Behind the teeth were huge bookends we used for stairs."

"Really?"

Zane nodded. "They'll give you the tools. Just think outside the box. You may only weigh seventy pounds, but your brain is probably ten percent of that."

"Actually, no, but I'm assuming we're not being technical here."

Zane gave him a little push and laughed, and they went into the dining room, where all the parents rushed them.

"You were a star!" Zane's dad said.

Zane nodded, but couldn't smile. "It never entered my mind that we wouldn't win."

"It never does. That's why you're such a competitor."

His dad put his arm around him and led him deeper into the room. "I have never seen you as focused and on task and as such a leader as I did today."

"I really wanted it," Zane said.

"I know."

"You probably don't." Zane shook his head. "I wanted more than three thousand dollars."

His dad laughed. "Don't we all."

"But we really need the money."

"Why?" asked his dad. "We have a house and food and two cars that work most of the time. We scrape together enough to put you both in sports. We're fine with what we have."

"If we had more, Mom wouldn't be yelling at you, and you wouldn't be yelling at Mom about bills and new shoes and everything."

"Seriously, Zane?" They walked toward a table at the back of the room, but Zane veered away to another one, away from the highlight reel. His dad motioned for him to take a seat. "If it were about money, your mom would never have married me. She knew I was washed-up in the NFL and I'd be just another boring, middle-class guy."

"But you're always fighting about money."

"And you thought your winning could stop our little arguments?"

Zane felt the blood rush to his face. "Little?"

"We're loud about everything," said his dad. "And we're fine, we love each other. You know that."

"Doesn't sound like it."

"I am so sorry, Zane. And I can reassure you there is no divorce in our future, not even close. If we had more money, we'd still disagree about other things. It's what we do. We both need to be right." His dad leaned back. "Sometimes we laugh about it, how you and Zoe wouldn't be as competitive if you didn't come from us."

"You laugh? I don't remember the last time you laughed."

"I laugh all the time."

"But you and Mom don't laugh together."

His dad blew out a deep breath. "I promise everything's fine."

It was good that Zane had finally said something, but his stomach was still churning.

His dad tried to catch Zane's eye. "Is this really about your mom and me?"

"I thought it was."

"Then what?"

Zane shrugged, but he knew. "It hurts to say."

"Which is why you need to."

"I know." Zane rubbed his finger back and forth on the table's edge. "Two seasons ago. Remember when our team got knocked out of the playoffs?"

His dad nodded.

"I recovered fast. There was next season, always a next season. Then I got the first concussion, and the one after, and I was pretty depressed."

"That's an understatement."

"Then the Games got me out of it." Zane took a deep breath. "But suddenly there is no next season. No Games, no football, nothing. Now what?"

"It'll get better. I promise."

"How? Because you're not gonna tell me I can go home and put on pads."

Right then, his dad looked down into Zane's eyes. "It often felt there wasn't much of a future for me right after football, but I'll make sure there's something for you."

Maybe Zane should have thanked him and moved

on, but he couldn't. Not yet. He tried to smile. "But how can I keep from turning into a Daryl?"

"What's a Daryl?"

"You remember Daryl, my linebacker friend who stopped playing after he broke his leg."

"Whatever happened to him? I can picture him coming over on crutches . . . What? About a year or two ago, and then . . ."

"Exactly." Zane shook his head. "He had to miss all those practices. And when he did come back to the locker room, I still remember. We were laughing at some inside joke that he wasn't in on, and it was like he started fading away in front of us. Maybe we tried to include him—I hope we did—but right now, I couldn't tell you whether he's still at my school or he completely dropped off the face of the earth." Zane puffed out a breath. "I don't want to fade away. I don't want to drop off the face of the earth. I like my friends. I don't want to lose them. I mean, how do you start over? How did you start over?"

"I had your mom. She made it easier." His dad shook off some memory. "Hey, you can always find Daryl again. He'd understand." His dad grew a bit of a smile, but Zane knew he was only half joking. "And you can go to all the games." Even his dad didn't sound convinced.

Zane just gave him a look.

"Okay, yeah. The good stuff happens during workouts and practice and team meetings."

"And?"

"And you refuse to fetch water and bandages and smirk on the sidelines like those managers. What do you call them?"

"Thing One and Thing Two."

His dad gave a small laugh. "Maybe it won't come to that. I have to believe it wasn't only you shutting out Daryl. He had a say."

Daryl probably did have a say. He'd said to himself that he didn't belong anymore. Would that happen to Zane? And then what? There was always that Kelly from the School Round, but her giggling would drive him nuts. What if there were other Elijahs, people he'd never considered before? That could be cool, but would he get tired of them? Would they even want to be around him?

Zane felt his head give a slight shake. It wasn't

that he'd have to trade the JZs and their crowd for another one. He was Zane. He wouldn't retreat like a Daryl. If he needed to bring new friends into their group, make inside jokes with them, he could. But that wasn't the total issue. He took a deep breath. No. It was like football, itself, was one of his best friends. And Zane couldn't bear the thought of abandoning it.

"Just for now, just for today," said his dad, "focus on the spectacle, get into the competition. Smile, cheer. I know you'll do that, anyway. I also know you'll fool a lot of people, make them think you're still all positive. Your mom and I and everyone who truly knows you, though, will see how much it hurts. And together, we will start working on the rest of it. Okay?"

Zane nodded. It had to be okay.

CHAPTER 30

Lunch was a lot more than bread and water. It was like an entire deli collided with a burger restaurant, then careened into a bakery.

Elijah was at the end of one table, balancing a sandwich thicker than both his arms put together.

Somehow that kid gave Zane a spark of energy. He laughed. "You gonna eat all that?"

"Probably not, but it's a work of art. Andy Warhol would've loved it."

Andy who? Zane didn't bother to ask. His stomach had opened a bit. He started to grab two plates, but one would be enough. He wasn't in training.

His sandwich—turkey, corned beef, and salami with lettuce, tomato, pickle, and mustard—might not have been as thick as Elijah's, but balanced by salad, tortilla chips, and cookies, it was his own work of art.

Zane found his dad at Elijah's table.

"You remember Dr. and Dr. McNair from breakfast this morning, Zane, don't you?"

"You're both doctors?" He turned to Elijah. "No wonder you're so smart."

"Except for a gene or two, we can't take any credit," said Elijah's mom. "He could pretty much explain Einstein's Theory of Relativity from birth."

"Mom!"

"He learns fast," she said. "He learned from you today, Zane."

Elijah rolled his eyes. "Can we talk about something else?"

"No," Zane said. "I could use that right now. What'd you learn?"

"I don't know. What did I learn, Mom?"

"Well, before today," said Dr. McNair, leaning in, "he wouldn't have told off a big guy like Berk."

"You what?" said Zane.

Elijah shook his head. "I got caught in the heat of competition. It was nothing."

"It wasn't nothing," said Elijah's dad. "You should have seen him. Berk started preaching his version of logic, reached for the wrong box again, and it was like someone put a superpower cape on Elijah. He shot forward just in time, grabbed the box from Berk's hands, and told him to shut his trap. This was the way things were going to be."

Elijah was looking meek and shaking his head, which only caused Zane to laugh out loud. "I didn't mean to teach you to be an enforcer."

"It's what I needed to win."

If nothing else, lunch brought Zane from ditch-deep to level ground. After two cookies, the sugar spike was about to kick in. Zane picked up his third when Bill came to their table. "Five-minute warning, you two. We'll meet by the door."

"I still don't know why you need us," Zane said.

"But you'll *want* to know." Bill left with a wink.

Zane put the cookie down.

Inside
THE EXECUTIVE VIEWING AREA

Something must have been hilarious over there. The five members of Bert's executive team were sitting back, laughing, nearly licking the plates that had held the huge lunch they'd catered in. Even Plago. Maybe he was celebrating the fact that he was still alive. But how could they even smile at a time like this? All Bert could swallow were three cinnamon-raisin pretzels from the bag Danny had given him earlier.

Bert paced back and forth in front of the four monitors in their viewing area. Should he even stay here? Or should he go to the control room instead, where he could watch each camera angle from forty different feeds? Maybe he'd see something that would avert any disaster before it happened.

Then again, he'd had people randomly assigned to each monitor, ready to stop the Games if they saw something. His own eyes couldn't be in forty places at once. They needed to be here, to watch Tawkler and Morrison and Jenkins and Lorraine. At least he'd ruled out Plago, unless that man was one of the greatest actors in the world.

Bert looked at his watch. These Games couldn't be over soon enough.

CHAPTER 31

Carol and Bill had brought them into what might have been someone's large family room if that room had eight recliners with attached TV monitors.

"Consider this home base for the rest of the Games," said Bill. "Two bathrooms in the back. A refrigerator with plenty to eat and drink if you're still in consumption mode. And"—he tapped Hanna's monitor—"entertainment."

"But don't get too comfortable, not even you, Silver Team," Carol said. "You need to help us for this next—"

Huh? The room was spinning. Another concussion?

Bill and Carol laughed. "You should see your

faces," she said. "Yes, you can pretty much count on this room to move every time you're in here."

"It's our preferred means of transportation to your next stop," said Bill. "And, by the way, we're not done with Friend or Foe."

"That's right," Carol said. "Each person on Team Gold will pair up, as Friends, with a member of the Silver Team. Team Silver, here's what's in it for you: If your pair comes in first place, you'll win ten thousand dollars. Five thousand for second place, four thousand for third, and three thousand for fourth."

It was like someone had switched Zane's power strip back on.

"Now who plays with whom," said Bill, "is entirely up to . . . Team Silver."

Berk zeroed in on Zane with a "you and me" look.

"And we start with the person from the Silver Team who earned the most points in Friend or Foe. So, Zane, who do you want to work with?"

This was a no-brainer. The combination of Elijah's genius and Zane's athleticism could produce some sort of supercontestant. Were the rest of them blind to that? They were all basically holding their breaths and staring. Except Leore, who was looking down as usual.

"Before I pick, I've gotta give props to the star of our team. We wouldn't have come as close if it weren't for Leore."

She snapped her head up.

"So whoever gets her is truly lucky. That said"—Zane put a big smile on his face and looked toward Berk—"my pick, no question, is my man . . . Elijah."

Berk gasped.

"Me?" Elijah said. "I always get picked last."

"Not today."

Elijah leaned way back with the biggest grin on his face. He kept glancing at Zane while Josh picked Berk—guess he thought that brawn would beat brains—and Ryder chose Becky. Zane understood the logic, wanting her competitive edge, but she wouldn't balance him. Not unless she could remind him to stop and think. Or he could remind her.

Zane would have picked Hanna if Elijah weren't available. She had this spark in her eyes, she moved quickly and decisively, and besides, she knew how to win. She was the only two-time first-place finisher—at the stadium and also here, in the first Friend or Foe round.

"You're stuck with me, Hanna," said Leore.

"Not stuck at all," she said. "We've got this, okay?"

Leore nodded.

The room stopped moving. Bill peeked out a door that had slid open. "Hanna, Leore, you're up! Go out and have a seat in the waiting area. When you hear chimes . . ."

On cue a loud set of chimes sounded.

". . . you'll receive an envelope and get under way. See you soon."

They dropped off Ryder and Becky, then Josh and Berk.

"By the way," Bill said as Zane and Elijah went out, "no chairs for you because—"

The chimes sounded. A rope dropped from far above their tiny room. Zane grabbed the large, attached envelope and handed it to Elijah. "It's your show, buddy."

"You'll help like it's your show, right?"

"That's the only way I know."

Elijah pulled out a card and held it above his eye level.

Zane pushed down on the card. "Make it comfort-able for you. You're gonna figure it out faster than I will."

Bridge Builders
(Coming soon from Golly's
new Virtual+Reality series)
.uoy no sdneped taht ?uoy tsum ro ,seof ruoy
ecaf tsum uoy ,osla
.gnitoof ruoy rof sdraob egral-muidem-llams
esu :tsum uoy
.raelc eb lliw egassem eht noos .ereh ot ereht
morf nruter neht .ereht ot ereh morf egdirb a
dliub :weivrevo

"Easy," said Elijah.

"Maybe for you."

"It starts with a period, so it's just written in reverse order."

"Do you have refocus, see-all, superpower lenses in your eyes or something?"

"You're wired for some things. I'm wired for others."

Zane nodded. "So what's it say?"

"Top line, from the right: 'Also, you must face your Foes, or must you? That depends on you.'" Elijah paused for a second. "I need to start at the bottom right. It says, 'Overview: Build a bridge from here to there. Then return from there to here. Soon the message will be clear. You must: use small-medium-large boards for your footing. Also, you must face your Foes, or must you? That depends on you.'"

"That's it?"

Elijah nodded. "How do you suppose we avoid the Foes?"

"No telling till we go in."

Zane ducked through an undersized doorway in the wall to a concrete floor flanked by trees and bushes. It was like someone's large patio, but without the furniture. The trees and bushes continued at the patio's width to a forested dead end, almost half a football field away.

Zane rushed the seven yards to the end of the concrete, and the solid patio beneath his feet dropped off beyond that. A set of metal railroad-type rails may have started inset into the patio, but they were seemingly suspended in midair over the valley below, then stretched as far as all the greenery. About every six feet, vertical rods topped with circular, flat caps rose above the hand railing that paralleled the tracks all the way to a forest at the end. The rods on the right side, though, extended three feet taller than the ones on the left.

"From here to there," Elijah said. "How far do you think that is, Zane?"

"Forty yards. That's gotta be our bridge, but we need something to walk on or"—Zane strode to where the rails started—"or we fall about eight feet into— Is that a real river?"

No answer. Elijah was rooting around in the bushes. He pulled out a couple of wooden boards about one foot long and four feet wide, with deep sets of grooves running along both of their short sides. "Our footing, I presume."

"Keep pulling them out. I'll check." Zane ran them over and fit their grooves perfectly over the rails, laying their path from here to there. He trotted back to Elijah. "The boards *are* our footing. Pull 'em all out first and—"

Clio and Gil some-
how flew down from
the treetops on the left and
landed at the start of the bridge.
Clio grabbed the second plank
off the rails and handed it to
Gil, who flew back up through
the trees. She winked. "Your
Foes have arrived." Then she,
too, lifted up and away.

Elijah pulled out another board from the bushes.
"What was that?"

"Weirdness." Zane looked over Elijah's shoulder.
"Read me the message again."

"'Overview: Build a bridge from here to there.
Then return from there to here. Soon the message
will be clear. You must: use small-medium-large
boards for your footing. Also, you—"

"That's it!"

"What's it?"

Zane pointed to the middle of the card:
egral-muidem-llams. "We need to do it in that order;
otherwise, we get board-stealing Foes."

"And we don't know how to get them back."

"We will."

Elijah laid another board onto the haphazard pile he had going.

"Tell you what," Zane said, diving into the bushes. "Start stacking them near the bridge. I can pull out more at a time." He shrugged off the scratching branches and sailed the boards out, each time with an "Incoming!" warning. He didn't want to kill the guy. When he'd tossed all he could find, he emerged from the branches, then carried five boards over to Elijah's three piles. "What's what out here?"

"We have a small, a medium, and a large pile. I put the heaviest ones closest to the bridge so we wouldn't have to carry them as far."

"Good thinking."

"I extrapolated that idea from your telling me to stack them close."

"Save the compliments for later and keep stacking. I'll get the rest."

By the time they'd

sorted all the boards, counting the one already on the rails, there were eighteen large ones, eighteen medium, but only seventeen small.

"How do we get the last one back, Zane?"

"We'll figure it out. Right now, let's build a bridge and hope they don't steal more." Zane loaded a set of three boards—small, medium, and large—onto Elijah's arms.

Elijah didn't say anything, but he was struggling under the bulk. Zane grabbed six, plus took one off Elijah's hands. In a flash, they'd placed those nine pieces of bridge without a Foe in sight.

They were working like a machine, Zane taking six boards to whatever Elijah could handle. They stopped, laid the pieces in place, then took a couple seconds to breath. Repeat, repeat, repeat until Elijah dropped his next set of boards and stood there, his arms rising, then lowering, then rising at his sides. "They feel like they're floating."

Zane had to laugh, but they needed to get back on it. He started jogging to the patio at a slow enough pace for Elijah. "Just eight more boards to bring over. I'll manage them. You search the bushes for the stolen one." Zane raced ahead.

Clio was dancing on the patio with the stolen board.

Zane bolted toward her, but at the last second, she sailed it across the patio to Gil.

Elijah pulled up. "Please! Not keep-away!"

"Apparently," said Zane. "I don't have time, and I know you can handle it, buddy."

"But I'm short—"

"No, you're smart. You'll get it. They'll always give you what you need." Zane raced onto the bridge and glanced back before he set down the remaining eight.

Elijah was jumping at the board Gil waggled above his head. Worse case, Zane would come back after he'd placed these boards, and they'd outwit their Foes together. But Zane had laid down only five when Elijah returned victorious.

"How'd you do it?"

"I thought I'd need to slay a dragon, but then I asked the price of getting it back."

"Which was?"

"Answer why they stole it from us, the small-medium-large sequence."

"Good job, buddy. I'd still be there trying to— what'd you say?—slay the dragon?"

"Metaphor."

"Right." Zane covered the last bit of rails with the large board. "Now what?" He looked at Elijah.

Elijah looked right back at him with a blank stare that turned into a lightbulb moment. "The card said, 'Then return from there to here. Soon the message will be clear.'"

Without a word, they started sprinting. When they reached the patio, there was nothing but a pad of paper and a couple pens on the floor. Zane flipped through the pad, but the pages were blank. He stuffed it and a pen into his pocket, just in case. "We missed something."

Elijah nodded. "We need to go back."

They sprinted back to the far end of the bridge.

"Now what?" said Elijah.

"Look around, I guess." Zane lifted the three boards closest to them in case he'd missed some message underneath.

Meanwhile, Elijah stooped to inspect the underside of the handrail. He shook his head.

"Nothing here either," said Zane. He ran his hand up one of the tall vertical rods that connected the bottom rail with the handrail, then rose about level with his head. It was smooth all along, until his fingers reached toward the flat top.

Zane stood on his tiptoes. "There's writing up here! There's a *W* and something else that isn't a letter. I need to be like half an inch taller."

"How do they expect *me* to see up there?"

"They don't," said Zane. "There has to be another way. A ladder or . . ." He didn't have an "or." He looked up. Looked around.

Elijah was at the other handrail, the side with the shorter vertical rods. "No writing here, but wait." He ringed one of those rods with his thumb and forefinger and slipped it off the top.

"What are you doing?"

"I'm going to compare the circumferences of the rods on this side to the rods on the other side. There has to be a reason why the ones here are shorter and the ones over there are taller. Maybe these telescope up some way or those telescope down." Then he moved across the bridge to a taller rod, but didn't come close to reaching the top.

"I can do that." Zane gauged the circumference of the short pole, then reached up to slide the ring his fingers made down the tall pole. "Definitely smaller up top, and—"

Elijah had started running his fingers up the rod. "There!" He pulled on a small clip, and the tall rod telescoped down into itself. The cap at the top read:

".W

One by one, they telescoped the poles down. Each one brought them closer to the patio, and each had three letters or letters and punctuation marks on its cap. Elijah wrote as Zane called them out.

".W ORR OBN ACE WTA HTL LAT UBE VAH EWS NIA RBE HTE SUY LNO TON DLU OHS EW"

"They're reversed again," said Zane. "We just need to figure out where to break up the letters into words that mean something."

"I already did that," Elijah said.

"Of course you did."

"But where do we give our answer?" asked Elijah.

Zane pointed to the patio. "What's that?"

They raced over. Half hidden in the bushes was

a small table with a GollyReader. Its screen said, EVEN FOES CAN BECOME FRIENDS. There was also an answer box.

"Tell me what to type," Zane said.

"Forward or reverse?"

"The way normal people would understand."

"Okay. First, quotation mark. Then I'll just read the sentence. Let me know what you want me to repeat."

"Go!"

"We should not only use the brains we have but all that we can borrow."

Zane typed then held it out to Elijah. "This is for you. Hit Enter if you think it's right."

Elijah added the period and the quotation mark at the end, then hit Enter.

They got five words in return. QUOTE FROM PRESIDENT WOODROW WILSON

Chimes sounded. The small door opened.

CHAPTER 32

Zane ducked back through the small door, into the area where the moving room had dropped them off. It now had four chairs and a table, but no other opening.

"Isn't this a firetrap?" said Elijah.

Zane peeked his head back out to the patio. "Guess not. And we could always jump into the river. Did we decide if that was real water or not?"

"It's real," said Gil. He and Clio were suddenly standing behind them.

"Where did you come from?" asked Elijah.

Gil snapped his fingers. "It's magic."

"No, really."

"I parachuted in from way above there." Clio pointed to the ceiling. "And Gil rose from the floor."

"They're not gonna tell us, Elijah. And it's not what you really want to know, is it?"

"Yeah. It is."

"Don't you want to know if you're still in this?" Zane said.

"I'm still in."

"That's confidence," said Gil. "How do you know?"

"Several factors. First, Zane didn't try to chase you when you stole our board, so I didn't either. One pair or another probably did. Maybe even climbed a tree."

"Which would have been more fun for us," said Clio.

Gil smiled. "At least we got to steal one board from you."

"That *was* fun." Clio nodded at Elijah to go on.

"Second, only Berk and Ryder could have gotten the boards down the bridge faster than Zane did practically alone. Third, I deciphered the reverse writing instantly. Then there was Zane, who kept me on track the whole time."

"Besides," said Zane, "if we were last, you wouldn't be stalling for time now, right?"

They didn't answer. They didn't even change expression. The only thing that gave it away was Clio's eyes. They danced.

"You're good, little dude," said Zane. "You're still in this."

Clio looked at Gil. Gil looked at Clio. They shook their heads. "We honestly don't know how everything stands."

"Maybe not everything," Zane said, "but enough. So what's next?"

Gil sat. "We wait."

They all sat, mostly quiet. Zane downed a bottle of water, happy for Elijah but gearing up to be a mere cheerleader for his one-man team.

A *beep-beep* came from the closed end of the room, then the wall slid open.

"You decent in there?" Bill leaned out of his golf cart and laughed. "Hop on."

Clio sat next to Bill and told Zane and Elijah to take the backseat. Gil stood on the rear bumper and grabbed onto the cart's roof.

"Here we go," said Bill.

Zane expected to have a raw, behind-the-scenes look—concrete floors, steel beams, electrical boxes—but the cart zoomed through a finished series of hallways and stopped in one of the light-column rooms.

Bill faced them. "We're just pausing to time this right. Soon all four carts will converge on a platform. You'll get out and line up, Gil and Clio will disappear again, and we'll give you the results."

Clio turned. "Elijah already knows those."

"What do you know?" Bill said.

"To start, I'm safe for now."

"What else?" Bill said. "What order did the teams finish?"

"I can't say definitively, but I'm either first or just barely second over Becky. She's fast and clever. Third, Hanna. She and Leore might have been faster with their answer, but this challenge was equally about muscle and speed. Then I believe Berk was last. He and Ryder probably got slammed by their Foes." Elijah looked up at Bill. "How'd I do?"

"Let's go find out." He spun the car one-eighty, and they backtracked through the halls, through their waiting area, then over their patio, and across the bridge they'd built. Now, though, they could see three other carts on three other bridges all converging on a large center platform with eight black circles.

"Where did the trees and bushes go?" asked Elijah.

"Our little secret." Bill stopped their cart, as the others had, at the platform's edge. "Find your circle and stand on it."

The one with Zane's name was third from the end. If that meant something, it wasn't obvious. He wasn't next to Elijah, but Hanna was next to Leore. Becky and Josh were separated, but Ryder stood next to Berk in the center.

Berk just wouldn't close his mouth. "Did I get the right answer? Did I win? Why won't you talk to me? Why do I have to stand inside a stupid circle?"

"It looks good on TV," Bill finally said.

"If I watch TV, will I finally learn if I won?"

"You might find out sooner if you zip it."

Thank goodness Bill said something or Zane might've tackled the voice out of Berk.

Carol paced in front of them from one end to the

other, then turned slowly. If Zane were still in this, he'd want her to speak already. She finally stopped in the middle. "Team Silver," said Carol, "I'm not sure that I mentioned this, but your winnings for staying here and helping the Gold Team? That's in addition to the three thousand dollars you already won."

"At least six thousand dollars?" said Ryder.

"You got it!" Carol said.

Bill stood next to Carol. "As for Team Gold," he said, "your base amount was six thousand dollars, the amount you'll receive if you came in last just now."

"No bonus?" said Berk.

Bill ignored that. "I'm sorry to say good-bye to . . ."

Almost before Zane could look, the circle next to him opened, and Becky dropped through the floor. The circle closed before they could finish gasping.

"Don't be alarmed," said Carol. "She's laughing. She landed in a padded space that funneled her for one last ride in the Rainbow Maze and will be joined by . . . Bon voyage, Ryder!"

His circle opened, and Ryder was gone.

At least Zane would go out with a bang. He wished

they'd eject him already. He didn't need to hear Berk keep repeating, "Victory is within sight! Victory will be mine!"

"Not unless you calm down," said Bill.

Berk did. For a second. "I'm in the final three!"

Carol got in his face, and then he calmed down. "Now, Leore," she said, "don't look so worried. Whether or not you drop through the floor is your choice. But, Team Silver, you realize this is the point when, as Berk announced, we are down to three people. So raise your hand if you want to take the ride through the Rainbow Maze."

Zane's hand shot up. So did Josh's. Leore's hand was resting on her hair as if she was trying to decide whether to scratch her head or raise her arm.

Carol gave her the warmest smile. "It's fun. I promise."

Leore nodded. And with that, she dropped.

Then Josh.

Zane took a deep breath and steeled himself against the fall.

It didn't come. And it didn't come. And it still didn't come.

"His trap door stuck?" At least Berk finally asked a good question.

"No," Carol said. The way she and Bill were smiling at him, they were up to something.

"In fact," said Bill, "we're gonna keep him around for a bit because here's what else you don't know. For being the Friend on the first-place team—"

"You did it, Elijah!" Zane couldn't help himself. "Sorry, Bill. Go ahead."

Bill laughed. "On top of the ten-thousand-dollar bonus, Zane, you are—

Horns sounded. Lights flashed. His circle became a tornado of confetti.

"You are," Bill continued, "back in the competition."

Zane wished someone were there to measure his vertical leap. Elijah's too. The kid was jumping in circles, his arms thrust in the air. "Zane's still in!"

"So that's the good news," said Bill.

"The bad news is I've still gotta beat three people to become the champion," said Berk.

"Not true," Carol said. "There are only two more elimination rounds left, which also means we say good-bye to the third-place finisher on Team Gold."

And Berk's floor dropped.

Zane couldn't help himself. Neither, apparently, could Elijah or Hanna.

"He's gone!" she said.

"He's gone!" Elijah echoed.

They jumped and high-fived until Bill stepped in, doing a victory dance his own self. "And then there were three." He and Carol gathered them around. "I pretty much had you all pegged for the final group. Right from the start I told Carol—"

"Liar! Granted, you had one of the three, but I had two."

"Which one, Bill?" said Hanna. "Which two, Carol?"

"That's our little secret." Carol pointed to a golf cart driving up a bridge, driverless. "Your chariot awaits!"

Carol took the driver's seat with Elijah next to

her. Bill stood on the bumper, which put Zane in the back next to Hanna.

"Leore was good, wasn't she?" Zane asked her.

"And she can't admit how amazing she is. She might deserve this more than I do."

"You can't say that. You made it on Team Gold all by yourself," Zane said. "You need to own your abilities."

"Oh, I do." Hanna's eyes shone bright, but didn't reveal her story. What was her story? Her strengths, her weaknesses?

She had to be smart, and strong enough for the physical stuff, or she'd be gone. If only she would talk, he might know what he was up against. "Well, let's say I made you brag."

"Fine. I get mostly A's, I speak fluent Korean—but I was born in Korea—and I taught my mom's old dog a new trick."

That gave him nothing. "You call that bragging?"

"I call that being smart. The less you know about me, the better. For me."

Zane shook his head. "With you and Elijah, no wonder your team won."

"And we messed up twice," she said.

Elijah turned around. "But it wasn't you and it wasn't me."

Zane almost asked what happened, but he'd find out on TV. He needed to get his head back in the Games. He gave a couple of small, tight fist pumps. He was ready. And this time, he was in it till the end.

The cart returned them to the room with the black recliners.

"Weren't all eight of us supposed to come back here?" said Hanna.

"We may have alluded to that," Bill said, "but we can be tricky."

"From here on out, though," said Carol, "no tricks, no twists, no Friends, no Foes—just traditional, single-elimination Games."

Bill nodded. "Here's how it'll work: When the doors to this room open next, you'll walk out, wait for the chimes, then tackle your challenge. The two who finish first, or fastest after any penalties, will continue to the next round. All three of you will return to the Room O' Movement this time. Ready?"

"Ready."

"Ready."

"And raring to go," said Elijah.

"Let's do this," Bill said.

The room moved to the left until it shifted backwards.

Was this real? Him? Top three? It couldn't replace football, but winning might make that first month of school better than bearable.

"And we're here," Carol said.

The room stopped, and the door opened to a small area with colorful question marks and exclamation points plastering its walls. The black door with Zane's name was third in line.

He stood in front of it, wriggled his arms, took a series of jumps. Chimes!

He burst in.

Sitting center was a solid metal cylinder about three feet high and two feet in diameter; on it, another cylinder, the Doohickey carton, Special Domed Edition.

Hanging on the wall to Zane's left was a framed box about the height and width of a single whiteboard, but this one was a foot deep and had rows of softball-sized, paper circles numbered one through fifty. The sign above the frame read PUNCHBOARD.

Against the adjacent wall sat a chair and a table with paper and pens. And a ladder! They actually gave him a ladder this time. On the wall to his right were the directions, but not on cards like they'd always been. Instead, they were on three-foot strips slid into rows of metal slots, like the ice-cream flavors at Jerome's dad's restaurant. The directions, almost to the ceiling, were definitely out of order:

Put numbers in reverse numerical order.

Degrees at which water freezes in Celsius.

First, build a pyramid using Doohickey parts.

Place rod on balance cap.

Type answer to message on keypad.

Write down the four numbers you were asked to identify.

Calculate: baker's dozen minus regular dozen, plus quarts in a gallon.

Enter four-digit pin number into keypad (two tries before penalty).

Adjust rod and cups until scale balances.

Because you stuck a letter on my front, I became an ulna.

Find revealed message.

Punch your fist through seven numbers of your choice on the punchboard.

Fit the balance cap over the topper.

Place all seven punchboard items into cups.

Unfold the remaining rod and attach cups at both ends.

Place pyramid on base.

If hint = thin, then evens = _____.

At first glance, the challenge seemed to have three steps: build and balance a scale, find and enter a four-digit pin number, find and enter a message. He'd need to organize the instructions to be sure.

Zane set up the ladder next to the wall and slid out the first two instruction strips. They were long, flexible, way too unwieldy, and thankfully had nothing written on their backsides. This would already take longer than he thought. Or—

He slid the two strips back into their slots, tore paper into short strips, then numbered them one through seventeen. He jammed paper number one into the slot that said, *First, build a pyramid using Doohickey parts.* Now he just needed to figure the order for the other sixteen.

There were six steps for building the scale, two for the punchboard, four questions with numerical answers, two steps for the pin number, then two more to enter his answers. He labeled all the slots with his best-guess order.

14 Put numbers in reverse numerical order.

9 Degrees at which water freezes in Celsius.

1 First, build a pyramid using Doohickey parts.

5 Place rod on balance cap.

17 Type answer to message on keypad.

13 Write down the four numbers you were asked to identify.

10 Calculate: baker's dozen minus regular dozen, plus quarts in a gallon.

15 Enter four-digit pin number into keypad (two tries before penalty).

8 Adjust rod and cups until scale balances.

11 Because you stuck a letter on my front, I became an ulna.

16 Find revealed message.

6 Punch your fist through seven numbers of your choice on the punchboard.

3 Fit the balance cap over the topper.

7 Place all seven punchboard items into cups.

4 Unfold the remaining rod and attach cups at both ends.

2 Place pyramid on base.

12 If hint = thin, then evens = _____ .

Time to build a pyramid. Then what? Number two: *Place pyramid on base*. Did that mean he shouldn't build it on the metal cylinder itself? Maybe he was being too literal, but Zane opened the Special Domed Edition Doohickey carton at the table. Yes! They'd given him only the pieces he needed. He fastened the three smaller green rods with the Doohickey connectors to form a triangle. Then he stuck a longer blue rod in the center of each connector, leaned them together, and bound them with a topper. He placed the pyramid on the center of the base.

Step three. That orange, groove-topped cone had to be the balance cap. It fit perfectly over the topper. He unfolded the remaining red rod, and it straightened with a snap. Now he had to attach cups to the rod ends. Where were they hiding?

The chair had four spindly legs, a flat seat, a flat back, and nothing taped to its underside. Nothing under the table, either. On top sat the empty Doohickey container, domed lid, paper, and pens. The punchboard? No. Whatever items he got from there went into cups.

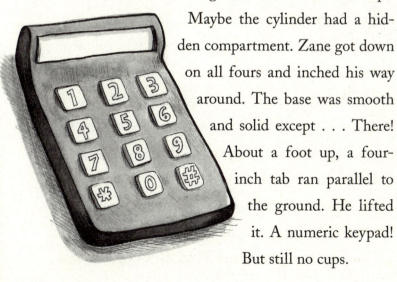

Maybe the cylinder had a hidden compartment. Zane got down on all fours and inched his way around. The base was smooth and solid except . . . There! About a foot up, a four-inch tab ran parallel to the ground. He lifted it. A numeric keypad! But still no cups.

Zane looked inside the Doohickey container again. Empty. He lifted the Special Domed Edition lid, the *cup-shaped* Domed Edition lid. He turned it over. Nestled inside were two metal cups, and the red rod fit perfectly into the notch on each. Back on track.

Step five. He laid the rod inside the groove on the orange balance cap but didn't bother to balance it yet. That would come with the seven items. Punchboard time!

Wham! He hit number two with his fist. *Pow!* Number one. *Smash! Bam! Blam! Whack!* Twenty-one, eighteen, forty-two, twelve, six, and seven. And with one final *kapow!* Lucky thirteen. Seven paper circles, totally decimated. He reached into the new holes and pulled out one item from each: a ladybug, sandwich, camera, whistle, frog, can of paint, and crescent moon, all with magnets on their backs, all about the same size, and all about the same weight.

That was a problem. How could he balance seven objects of the same weight?

The moon and whistle looked a little smaller, so he held them in his left hand with the frog and ladybug, whose shapes weren't as solid as the other three. In his right hand were the paint, sandwich, and camera. He didn't want the scale to crash to one side and destroy the pyramid, so at the same time, he opened each hand over a cup, laid the objects inside, and adjusted a couple so their magnets stuck to the metal.

With the seven pieces in, the four-magnet side was definitely heavier. He slid the red rod toward the lighter side, but he slid it too much. Now the three-magnet side was lower. He moved the rod back a little, then a little more and a little more.

Zane crouched at eye level to the scale. Were the cups even enough? He wasn't taking any chances. He stood the Doohickey container next to the three-object side. The bottom of the cup came partway down the letters in "Super." He marked that spot with the pen. The cup on the other side was at the top of "Super." Two more adjustments, and perfect!

Steps one through eight, done!

Step nine. Second from the top, the first question. Freezing point in Celsius. Thank you, Mr. Longley, science drillmaster. He wrote a big zero on a piece of paper.

Now the equation: *Calculate: baker's dozen minus regular dozen plus quarts in a gallon.*

The trouble wasn't with the regular dozen and it wasn't with the quarts—thanks again, Mr. Longley—it was with the baker's dozen. Somewhere, in the back of his mind, he remembered it was either one more than a dozen or one less.

If he were a baker, and he gave his customers eleven doughnuts when they ordered a dozen, he'd earn a higher profit at first, but he'd also make his customers mad. But if he slipped in a thirteenth doughnut, he'd have happy customers who'd be back for more.

He'd go with 13. It felt right, and he did have a couple guesses before any penalty kicked in. So a baker's dozen, minus a regular dozen, plus four quarts in a gallon. He added 5 to the paper.

Next. *Because you stuck a letter on my front, I became an ulna.*

An ulna? Wasn't that the bone Zane had broken in first grade? But how did that translate into a number?

Zane sighed. Another word puzzle. He could do this, but he couldn't start with "ulna." If he took off the *u*, "lna" wasn't a word. He wrote "bone" on a scrap of paper. That was all he needed. He got rid of the *b* and his paper now read *0 5 1*.

Last question. *If hint = thin, then evens = _____*.

Fabulous. This would take Elijah about a tenth of a second. Maybe Zane was bad with wordplay, but he knew one thing. The answer was a number, zero through nine, the only ones on a keypad. And if he combined that logic with the letters in "evens" . . .

Okay! They'd moved the *t* from "hint" to the front to make "thin." He did the same with "evens." "Seven"!

Steps fourteen and fifteen. He put the numbers in reverse numerical order—*7 5 1 0*—and punched the code into the keypad on the base.

"Please stand and step back" came a woman's voice from nowhere.

Who was he to argue?

The lights went out, but instantly a spotlight shone on the cylinder, which emitted a blast of steam. The pyramid revolved about a quarter turn, and then it started sinking, like the base was swallowing it, the mouth gradually closing on the pyramid as it tapered. The scale arms and cups would never fit.

But as the arms reached the now dime-sized opening, the red rod folded upward, then adjusted itself to allow the cups to come fully together to form a ball. In seconds, that ball was the only thing left on the pedestal.

It had to be part of step sixteen. But where was the message?

The spotlight faded to a purplish glow. The blacklight revealed letters from one edge of the base's top, up one side of the ball, around and down the other side, and across the other half of the base.

Clancy _____ the eating contest last night. After he downed a dozen half-_____ burgers, he clutched the trophy to his stomach and wailed, "I _____ _____ much _____ dinner!"

Huh? The numeric keypad was still there, which meant everything in the blanks needed to translate into a number. But how?

If this Clancy dude had a trophy, he apparently won this contest. And if he clutched his stomach and wailed, he was feeling sick. And he was feeling sick because he ate too much for dinner. Zane listened to the sound of the words rolling around in his head. Ate? Too? Eight? Two? For dinner? Four dinner?

That was it! Clancy won. Zane jotted down 1. *After he downed a dozen.* Twelve! No. Twelve was part of the sentence. *After he downed a dozen half-blank burgers.* Half what? Half one? Half two? Have-to burgers? Like he had to down them to win? It had to be more obvious. Half three? Half four? Five? Six? Seven? Eight? Nine? Zero?

None of them made sense. So what would? After he downed a dozen half-sized burgers? That might make some people sick, but not someone who entered eating contests. A dozen half-pound burgers would, though. But no matter how he spelled it, pound wasn't a number. What else? What else? He had nothing else. And he had no other blanks to fill.

Zane brought his paper to the ground next to the keypad and wrote the numbers he knew. 1 _____ 8 2 4. Why couldn't this be a four-digit code like the last one?

He wrote *12 half-_____ burgers,* then he stared at

the numbers on the keypad. He looked to the paper, the keypad, the paper, trying every number again. Eight. Nine. Wait! It's like they'd been invisible— the star and pound keys. It *was* half-pound burgers. Step seventeen! Zane typed in the code. 1 # 8 2 4.

The lights went out.

CHAPTER 34

Click! A bright sliver shone around the door. Zane opened it.

Bill leaned way in. "What took you so long?"

"I lost?"

Bill said nothing. He led Zane to the moving room. No one was there.

"I assume they didn't vaporize?"

Bill smiled. "Have a seat. Company's coming in just a few minutes. It's neck and neck out there."

"I beat the wonder kid?"

"Yes."

Seriously? "How'd that happen?"

Bill shook his head. "Using those paper numbers

on the instruction boards? How did you come up with that? I swear you are the epitome of efficiency."

"I'm not sure what I am," said Zane, "but I learned to play smart in football."

"And people say it's a sport for thugs."

"Smart thugs, maybe."

Bill tossed him a bottle of water. "You seem to go through a lot of these."

"Smart, hydrated thugs."

Bill left him alone with his water. And with silence, silence that gave way to rapid-fire thoughts he couldn't stop.

Suppose he somehow beat Elijah twice in a row. Sure, being champion of the Gollywhopper Games might make the first month of school bearable, but aside from that, what? What would he do the rest of the summer in place of two-a-days? What new inside jokes would the JZs make without him? Would they even let him hang around? Of course they would. They were good guys, the best. But would Zane, himself, feel left out? Might he fit in better with their other less-than-core friends on the sidelines? Or would they greet him with a "how the mighty have fallen" attitude? "Look at poor Zane, sitting in the stands with the rest of us." He wouldn't even be with his cheerleader friends, who were on the field during games and had practice every day after school. What did he have to practice? Would anything give him the same rush as football?

He finished off his water and paced around the room, trying to get pumped for the final challenge. It wasn't working.

Elijah barged in. "You beat me, Zane!"

"Not by much, buddy." He smiled in spite of himself.

"Sadly," said Carol, following him in, "you good buddies will be Foes in a minute. I'm off to get Hanna."

Elijah took a seat. "You're the toughest rival ever. Should I just hand you the million dollars?"

If it were anyone else, Zane would grin and nod. But this was the little guy. "Honestly?" he said. "It depends on what they have us do."

"Maybe so," Elijah said.

Carol came back with Hanna, who walked in like she owned the world. Her lips, though, couldn't quite form a smile. It was the face Zane probably had when he didn't perform like he should.

Hanna took a deep breath and nodded, almost to herself, as if she needed to move past the disappointment. Then she managed most of a smile. "You two are so great," she said. "And maybe we'll see each other next year. They seem to bring the old contestants back. Will there be a next year, Carol?"

She shrugged. "They'll decide soon. Regardless, we may use you as toy and game testers."

"Use us. Definitely use us!" The sparkle came back into Hanna's eyes. "And by the way, Zane, I can waterski, I read voraciously, I can debate with the best of them, I plan to be a trial lawyer, I am excellent at reading people. Also, though I'm great at organizing things, I may be a little too careful, which I was with this last challenge, but if I had it to do over again, I'd learn from my mistakes. And I'm not afraid to own who I am. See?" She gave Zane and Elijah each a hug good-bye, then walked out the door with Carol and Bill.

Zane shrank back into his chair. Could he own who he was without football? Did he know who he was?

"Ahem!" Elijah was standing next to him, holding out another bottle of water.

"Thanks, buddy." Zane sort of stared into space.

"So what is it?" said Elijah.

"What's what?"

"You're suddenly like a withering plant that stopped producing chlorophyll."

Zane sat up straight, smiled. "It's nothing."

"It's not nothing."

Fine. He'd give him something. "It's just, well. I'll miss you, buddy."

"Me?"

Zane nodded.

"Then visit me in Chicago."

"You live in Chicago? We stay with our cousins there every year."

"Visit me, too. Come to school and see the little freak dwarfed by the big kids. Or wait and get a look at me in college. That'll be funny."

"You in college." Zane shook his head. "Medical school after?"

"No. My parents are the doctors. I have my own path. People like Bill Gates and Steve Jobs—oh, and

Charles Babbage—merely set the groundwork for me. There's so much else to do, and I already have scholarship and grant offers, so if I win the million dollars, it's seed money for my company."

"You're eleven. You have a company?"

"I will soon. I've been amassing and testing a myriad of ideas. First, though, school. My parents insist." Elijah sat up a little straighter. "Hey! You're good in math. When you go to college, get an engineering degree and come work for me."

"I'm still in middle school."

"Not forever. When you get old enough, I'll give you a summer job."

Zane shook his head.

"Why not?"

"I'm a football player. I've always dreamed I'd play for my Tigers, then get drafted by the NFL." Zane let it drop.

"But what?" said Elijah.

"I didn't say 'but.'"

"You implied it."

Maybe he had, but Zane didn't mean to. He needed to gear up for one last challenge, one last play. He needed to feel like he was still in competition. The Games deserved his best.

"C'mon, Zane. Tell me." Elijah leaned over in his chair; practically fell out.

Zane laughed, but not even Elijah would get him to spill his guts now. The only thing he wanted to spill was enough fire to win the next challenge and the Games.

"So you're clamming up on me, huh?"

"Just gearing up for this last challenge. It's what I do."

"If I had to guess, though, you're not afraid of a little bet."

Zane looked into his eyes. "I wouldn't have taken you for the betting type."

"Not money; things you can't buy. If I win the last challenge, you'll tell me what's bugging you. Deal?"

"What do I get if I win? It has to be big because with so much physicality so far, chances are they're hitting us with something in your power alley. So what do I get?"

"Name it."

"A lifetime of on-demand tutoring."

"You don't need that. Besides, wouldn't that be a

little lopsided? A quick confession to hours of talking you through school?"

"Timewise, yes." If Zane both lost and had to spill his guts, it'd take more than a quick minute to heal. "But take it or leave it."

"Deal!"

They shook on it.

"Good," said Elijah. "Now I know, for sure, you won't give up if it's in my power alley."

"I only have an On switch, buddy. I'm heading out there to win. Me with my brawn because we both know you'd win Battle of the Brains."

"It all comes down to what they have planned for us."

"And what we've planned," said Carol, standing just inside the door, "was decided long before we knew who would be in these Games."

"When did you get here?" Elijah said.

"You know us," said Carol. "We're like atmosphere. We're always here."

"But never fear." Bill came up behind her. "We will not follow you home."

"Nope," she said. "We're going to Paris."

"Yeah, yeah, yeah." Bill's voice might have been

dripping with boredom, but his eyes shone. "So this is it. Silver versus gold. Friend versus friend."

"I don't think we've had two people become such fast friends," Carol said. "Clio and Estella hit it off last year. Gil and Bianca had a strange kind of immediate bond. And everyone stays in touch online, but this friendship is different. I don't think anyone would have guessed."

"Especially me," said Zane. "It probably wouldn't have happened anywhere else."

"And now that we've finished with the ultimate bonding experience, you two need to fight it out to the death. Danny, bring in the swords."

Some guy barged into the room, waving swords like a samurai in early training.

"I don't seem to have this down yet," Danny said. "But you two will figure it out. We hope. Paramedics are on standby."

Elijah gasped. "Have you lost your minds?"

Danny, Carol, and Bill burst out laughing.

"You should see your faces," Carol said. "Too bad they won't show that on TV. No cameras in here except for us monitoring you, and that stays private."

"Though I wish, in some cases, we could," said Bill. "But no samurai swords, no cage fighting. There will, however, be amusements. Ready?"

"Ready."

"Ready."

"Let the last challenge of the third Gollywhopper Games begin!"

Before
THE LAST CHALLENGE

The thought hit Bert like a giant flyswatter. Why was Extreme Machines the only sabotage-free challenge? It was like Ratso had pointed a big arrow its way, blinking, "Pick me, Pick me!" Bert needed to think. He left the executive viewing area and came down to his office.

Danny popped his head in. "Need anything?"

"I need to make a decision."

"I thought you already did."

"I thought so, too," said Bert.

"Maybe you need one more tour around the area."

"I do. I do." Before the second "I do" Bert was out of his office, nearly running for the final challenge area. He rang the Bell Tower and set the gears in motion for Extreme Machines. He was about to pat the goat's behind on Merry-Go-Wow when Walt Rusk, chief of Security, rushed up to him.

"No one's supposed to be—" Walt stopped himself. "Oh, it's you, Mr. Golliwop. Is this young man okay?"

"He's fine. He's with me, but no one else should be in here."

"Does your 'no one else' include Ms. Jenkins?" asked Walt.

"Jenkins?"

Walt pointed to his right. "About a minute ago, she rushed over to Extreme Machines, the one on the other side."

The three of them trotted over there.

Jenkins was already moving toward the door.

"You're supposed to be upstairs," Bert said.

Jenkins nodded. "I know, and you're going to think I'm crazy, but I was worried. One of my workers just told me she'd seen some strange guy around here yesterday. I decided someone needed to check things out, and you'd left the viewing area."

"Yesterday? Then no worries," Bert said. "We checked everything earlier today. Let's go back and finish these Games."

Bert led Jenkins and Danny back to the viewing area. He'd barely made it through the door before he cleared his throat. "We are scrapping the Extreme Machines challenge! More important, Plago, immediately instruct our factory to start quadruple production on Merry-Go-Wow!"

"What?" said Plago.

"Merry-Go-Wow!" said Bert.

"It's just cleared Legal," said Morrison.

"I know," said Bert.

"So that's the way it's going to end?" said Jenkins.

"Absolutely," said Bert.

"But we've barely started the marketing plans for that," said Tawkler.

"Or the financials," said Lorraine.

"Then fast-forward it all."

"But, Bert," said Plago. "We haven't finished developing it yet."

A clattering came from the other side of the room. Old Man Golliwop grazed a food table with his wheelchair. "Yes, we have," he said. "I have. I may be old, but I still have a brain or two left. And it feels good to get back into the game. Merry-Go-Wow. It's all WOW!"

"And one more thing," said Bert. "We're going into the puzzle business with that lunkhead Harvey Flummox." He didn't wait for a reaction.

"But forget that now. We need to finish these Games right!"

CHAPTER 35

The room started moving forward, then suddenly stopped to let Danny out.

Bill and Carol had each put a hand to one side of their headsets.

"We are having a few technical difficulties," Bill finally said. "So we're in a holding pattern for several minutes."

"Hope you don't mind," Zane said. "I need to stay in game mode." He'd turned his chair away from Bill and Carol and Elijah, put on a pair of headphones, and cranked up the music to drown out any negative thoughts. After five minutes, he started flexing his legs. After a few more, he jumped in place and wriggled his arms. And now, the football warm-up habit kicked in.

He dropped to the floor for sit-ups and leg stretches and torso twists, and he felt a tap on his back.

Carol motioned for him to take off his headphones. "Good news! Back in your chair, please. We're ready to roll."

"Finally!" Elijah said, echoing Zane's own thoughts.

The room moved backwards, to the right, then stopped, letting them into a small rectangle of a space with two doors. The wall between the doors—about twice as high as the doors themselves—didn't reach the ceiling, which rose many stories above.

"Inside," Carol said, "are two identical areas divided only by a wall that runs down the middle of the space. You will have the ability to see what the other is doing, so in the spirit of Friend or Foe, we offer you this."

"If you are stuck," said Bill, "give a shout and ask permission to get a one-minute glance at your opponent. If the opponent allows that, you will incur a five-minute penalty. If the opponent says no but you look anyway, that's ten minutes. With the talents we have here"—Bill looked at Elijah, then at Zane—"ten minutes could be deadly."

Carol stepped forward. "Ready or not, your challenge starts NOW!"

No time to wish Elijah luck. Zane barged through his door and grabbed the card off the rope that hung all the way from the many-storied ceiling.

**An unsealed letter with debatable news
was scattered at sea on a sightseeing cruise
by a brat with a goatee and bowl-styled hair
who first cowardly hid it—"No reason to share."
But a kayaking girl brought ten pieces she found
and gave them to beasts on this merry-go-round.
Go! Find them yourself, yell the message out loud.
If you do this the fastest, you'll be doggone proud.**

"Word stuff," Zane said into the air. If he weren't so competitive, he'd sit back and watch Elijah take this one. But he'd seen bigger upsets.

Zane stuffed the card into his pocket, then raced around a wall of light columns, around a second bend, and into a smaller version of the warehouse area. There were still the hippos and solar system and mountain, but another wall of lights led him past a big dance floor with a zebra band playing that Mercy Neptune song, a brick tower, a restaurant, and a huge pond with swirling water and bodies bobbing in it. All along were security guards. Were they guarding the million dollars? Were they even real? Or were they lifelike mannequins?

It didn't matter because there! Ahead! Past huge gears and arching flames was the biggest merry-go-round ever. Zane shot forward. No way had Elijah made it here as fast.

To call this merry-go-round big was an insult to the word "big." Not only was it enormous, but it had three levels, and as it spun, and spun fast, Zane didn't see one horse. Okay. There. One horse among at least a hundred animals—normal ones, and others he couldn't name.

And he had to find the right ten pieces of a message?

Zane couldn't beat the little guy with smarts, but he had speed and strategy on his side.

There might've been a way to stop the merry-go-round and hop on, but Zane ran alongside it, took a leap, and grabbed onto one of the brass poles attached to a panda. Above it, too high for Zane to reach and *way* too high for Elijah, was a green ribbon threaded through some sort of translucent green tube. Inside the tube was a small scroll of paper—pieces of the letter from the poem, had to be. The ribbon, like every other one he could see from this vantage point, was tied in a big bow at the very top of this level's ceiling.

Zane jumped onto the panda. He gripped its pole. As it moved up and down, he wrapped both legs around it, shimmied up, and came eye to eye with the tube. The ribbon was threaded through and wrapped around a clamp that held the tube shut. He went a little higher. It wouldn't take much to untie the ribbon to get it down. No way did Elijah have the arm strength to do that, not ten times.

Even if Golly gave them another way, and they probably had, Elijah would need extra time to figure that out. Right now they were evenly matched. And Zane could race ahead if only he could unravel the clues in the poem.

Zane sat on the panda and reread the puzzle. For some reason, he kept staring at *brat with a goatee*. To him, a brat was a kid, and if a goatee was what he thought—one of those pointy beards—that kid

would look very, very strange. But Golly hadn't randomly chosen those words. What did they mean?

No clue. He needed to do something. Zane jogged around the first floor of animals, hoping that would jog something in his brain. Before he got back to the panda, he climbed the narrow brass staircase to check out the second floor. It was smaller in diameter; in fact, the merry-go-round was sort of like a three-layer cake, each floor smaller than the next.

It was on the third floor, sitting on a rhino, that Zane caught a fleeting glimpse of Elijah's merry-go-round, which revolved the opposite direction. Any one-minute glance would be worthless, so that play was out. He looked away fast.

Focus, focus. Brat with a goatee? That had to mean something. And Zane couldn't just sit here. He knew he shouldn't, but he climbed the rhino's pole, untied its purple ribbon, came down, freed the tube, and looked inside at the scrolled piece of paper.

Wrong guess. One-minute penalty. Now he knew. He was sitting on a rhino with a one-minute penalty,

and he was staring at a sheep and a moose and thinking about a kid with a goatee. A goatee. A goat-ee. A
goat! He'd seen a goat on the first tier.

He looked at the puzzle again.

An unsealed letter with debatable news
was scattered at sea on a sightseeing cruise
by a brat with a goatee and bowl-styled hair
who first cowardly hid it—"No reason to share."
But a kayaking girl brought ten pieces she found
and gave them to beasts on this merry-go-round.
Go! Find them yourself, yell the message out loud.
If you do this the fastest, you'll be doggone proud.

The second word! Another animal. There had to
be a seal somewhere. What else? "Brat" hid "rat."
That was three. Had he cracked it?

Zane bolted down both spiral staircases and ran
halfway around the first floor. There was the goat. He
climbed the pole, worked to untie the ribbon, and—

"Ow!"

Something nailed him on the back. He dropped
to the ground.

In
THE EXECUTIVE VIEWING AREA

Bert blanched. "What just happened?"

"Huh?" said Tawkler. "I was watching Elijah."

"Zane went down." Jenkins pointed to Monitor #4.

"I saw that," said Bert. "But what happened?"

"No clue," Jenkins said.

Morrison pulled out his phone. "Is he hurt? Do we need to stop?"

"No," Bert said. "The boy's moving like nothing happened. Have Bill and Carol on alert, though. They may need to halt everything at a moment's notice."

CHAPTER 36

Zane felt a stinging near his shoulder blade and a little blood trickling down his back, but he'd been hit harder than that. What was Golly thinking? Could they have found a more dangerous way to give him tools for this challenge? At least the giant wrench that clattered to the floor had missed his head. He untied the ribbon, opened the tube, and read its paper scroll.

(Goat)
best

He had cracked it! More animals! Zane left the

wrench with the goat—it'd be there if he needed it—shoved the goat's scroll into his pocket, and sat on the hippo. One word at a time. He'd already gotten "seal" from "unsealed." Nothing in "letter." "Debatable"? Why would news be debatable? Because there was a bat!

Next long word. "Scattered." Nothing. Or not nothing. He was going too fast. "Scat." No. "Scatter." Not an animal. "Catter"? "Cat"! Next longer word. "Sightseeing." He went through the tedious process. Nothing there.

But still, he'd found half the animals. He'd grab their tubes and free his mind for the last five.

Zane dismounted the hippo and ran against the merry-go-round's movement to see the animals head-on. There! Bat! He climbed the pole, but before he untied the ribbon, he checked to make sure there were no hammers or screwdrivers waiting to attack him. It was clean. He freed the paper from the tube, but didn't read it. He'd wait until he had all ten. And there! Seal! Now just rat and cat. Rat and cat. He was at the hippo again. Staircase up. And there, one behind the other, the cat was chasing the rat.

He now had five pieces in his pocket. Just five more, and then he'd yell and be champion. Back to the puzzle.

An unsealed letter with debatable news
was scattered at sea on a sightseeing cruise
by a brat with a goatee and bowl-styled hair
who first cowardly hid it—"No reason to share."
But a kayaking girl brought ten pieces she found
and gave them to beasts on this merry-go-round.
Go! Find them yourself, yell the message out loud.
If you do this the fastest, you'll be doggone proud.

It was like two answers popped right out—in "cowardly" and "doggone."

He remembered the cow was on two, and the dog was on the bottom tier near the stairs. He ran to collect their pieces. Just three more.

He held on to the nonmoving pole between the dog and an owl and went back to the poem, back to the longer words. "Reason." No animal. "Kayaking." That had to have something. "Kay." No. "Aya." "Ayak." "Ayakin." "Yak." "Yaki." Wait.

Yak! What did a yak look like? The shaggy thing on the top tier?

He ran up, steadied a hand on its back, put a foot on its saddle, grasped the pole to hoist himself up, and pulled the pole from its socket. Zane tumbled to the floor. Maybe he was supposed to use that wrench.

In
THE EXECUTIVE VIEWING AREA

"You have to stop the Games, Bert!" said Morrison. "We can't take any more risk."

"He's right," Tawkler said. "(A) I don't want to kill a kid. And (B) This could be a public relations nightmare."

Jenkins jumped up. "Stop! There's blood on the kid's shirt. Had to be that wrench."

"We're not stopping," Bert said. "Look."

CHAPTER 37

Zane bolted up. Where had he left the wrench? With which animal?

Zane's stomach dropped. It didn't matter where the wrench was. Fireworks were shooting from Elijah's side of the wall.

Bill came up from behind Zane. "You almost did it."

"I did."

"No screaming? No crying? No shouting? No tears? Go ahead; the cameras won't show a thing."

Zane shook his head. "Too numb to react."

"Wait, you're bleeding." Bill called for a medic.

"Happens on the field all the time. But what were you thinking with the wrench? It nearly brained me. I was heading to get it when the fire-works went off."

"What wrench?" said Bill. He put on his headset, then stepped aside to let the medic tend to Zane.

In
THE EXECUTIVE VIEWING AREA

Danny pulled Bert aside. "That was Bill on the headset. He was asking about a wrench that fell on Zane."

"A wrench?"

"That's what he said."

"Get Security," Bert whispered.

Danny slipped out the door.

CHAPTER 38

Zane looked over the wall that separated his area from the celebration. There was Elijah, sitting inside the dog whose **body** had sprouted a hot-air balloon and was now rising above his merry-go-round.

The little dude soared around the top of their crazy warehouse world, looking so small and so large at the same time.

The medic finished up. "Are you okay, son?"

"I'm fine."

"Are you really?" Bill said.

"Just some scrapes."

"That's not what I meant."

"I know," Zane said. "I'll be fine." He shrugged. "You know, there was a point, really early, when I thought I had it. I'd cracked the code, I survived the wrench attack, and I was about to fix the yak. And I didn't know how Elijah would be able to get those ribbons down."

Bill walked him to the staircase. Leaning against the wall was a long scissors contraption.

Zane nodded and pointed to Elijah, rising to the domed ceiling. "I told him you'd give him everything he needed."

Bill smiled. "Word for word, that's what he shouted when he found it. 'Zane said you'd give us everything we'd need.'"

"Little dude learns fast. He was too hard to beat. Wish I could ride around with him, though."

"I can arrange that." Again, Bill whispered into his headset.

In
THE EXECUTIVE VIEWING AREA

Danny returned to the area with three men. One stood at the door, and the other two flanked Jenkins.

"Excuse me?" she said.

Bert brought his face three inches from her. "Who are you working for?"

She stepped back, and Security moved with her. "Bert, you're . . . What are you talking about? I work for you, for Golly."

Bert took a deep breath. "How'd you know about the wrench?"

"It fell from above the goat," she said. "Look for yourself, Monitor Four."

"Danny," said Bert, "have them run that feedback again."

Danny nodded. "I'm ahead of you."

The footage played. For half a moment, a piece of a blur was visible behind Zane's shoulder. Even in frame-by-frame stop-motion, it was indistinguishable as a wrench.

"Take her out of here," said Bert.

CHAPTER 39

A Spider-Man guy rushed toward Zane, opened the dog's saddle, and strapped Zane inside with a mess of cables. In rushed another guy, and a third to double- and triple-check it all.

The merry-go-round's top peeled back, and within a minute, the inflating balloon was lifting him up and up and up. When it lifted high enough, and both dogs had turned and were facing each other, Zane could only do one thing, the same thing he'd do for any teammate. He pumped his fist in the air. "You go, Elijah!"

Zane sat back on his dog, soaring. It should have been exciting, but losing sucked—in spitting contests, in football, in the Games, and now in this bet with Elijah.

Their dogs landed on one of the patios from the bridge challenge. The Spider-Man guys unhooked them and trotted off. One turned before he was completely out of sight. "Carol and Bill and your families will be here in two minutes. Have a seat."

Have a seat? Elijah had to be too wound up to sit. Zane picked up Elijah and spun him around. "You deserved it, buddy! Best competitor ever!"

Elijah laughed. "I doubt that, but I'll take it!"

Zane spun him a couple times more, hoping the thrill of victory, plus a good dose of dizziness, would have Elijah forgetting the bet. Either that, or Carol and Bill and the families would run in before Elijah could collect.

Zane let Elijah down and twirled him around one more time. The little guy wobbled, then flopped into one of the big recliners from the moving room. Zane spun that a few times.

Elijah kept laughing. "Stop! You'll make me vomit!"

Zane gave the chair one last push and let it wind down.

"Besides," said Elijah, "quit your stalling; it's con-fession time." He lifted his face toward the ceiling. "And if you're listening, Bill and Carol, give us five minutes."

Zane laughed. What else could he do? He took a muffin and a bottle of water from the table next to them, then sat in the other chair. "How'd you guess my strategy?"

"You know me by now. I learn fast. So answer my question. But what?"

"Huh?"

"Our conversation went something like this." Elijah looked straight at him. "You said, 'I'm a football player. I've always dreamed I'd play for my Tigers, then get drafted by the NFL.' Then I said 'But what?' Then you said—"

Zane waved him off. Put the muffin down. "Okay. Fine."

He shook his head, stared down, but there was no trapdoor to save him. Zane looked up, looked directly at Elijah. "I'll just say this. Can you get your genius brain to invent a better football helmet? I'd pay huge money."

"Oh." That's all Elijah said, but his eyes said more.

"You put two and two together?"

"Concussion?"

"Two of them. One mild, one not. I'm out of football this year. Maybe forever."

"Why?"

"I thought you were smart."

"So you can't play foot—"

"It's not just that." The little dude deserved to hear it all. "My whole world is football. All my friends are in football. We practice together, we work out together, we eat lunch together, have our inside jokes. It's what we do. And maybe I've been a football snob, and I don't do it on purpose, but that's the way it is. And now I might as well go into exile."

"Why?"

"Didn't you hear what I said?"

"I heard exactly what you said. 'All my friends are in football. We practice together, we work out together, we eat—'"

"So you heard me, but what's so hard to understand?"

"I don't understand why you have to give up football."

Zane closed his eyes and took a deep breath.

"No, really," said Elijah. "Hear me out."

"Fine."

"You love football. You're really smart, too. Right?"

"Sure."

"You were the person, I heard, who made your team competitive when you should have lost by a mile. You were the one who helped us kill that four-person stadium challenge with your strategy. You were the one who taught me that Golly would give me everything I needed. You were the one on that highlight reel who gave that pep talk to your team after you lost. I've never heard anything like it. You, Zane, are a coach."

Zane felt all the adrenaline rush to his face. He looked away.

"Not only are you a coach, you may end up being the best coach to ever walk onto a football field." Elijah paused. "Even so, when you're in college, major in engineering. In case you change your mind. Please."

Zane nodded, spun halfway around in his chair, and gave himself ten seconds to cry.

Then he took a shaky breath.

Bill and Carol had already given them more than five minutes, and Zane was grateful. He needed to pull himself together. And yet, suddenly, it felt like he'd won more than a million dollars. Elijah had given him his life again.

Zane grabbed a napkin from the table and blew his nose. He should have taken a gulp of water to clear the lump from this throat, then splashed some on his eyes, but it seemed like too much trouble. What he really wanted to do was crawl into a ball and sleep for about three days, then wake up to tell Coach and the JZs about his new plan.

First, he needed to find a way to thank Elijah.

Zane swiveled his chair back to face the little dude.

Elijah was picking at a poppy-seed muffin with his fingers. "Did you ever wonder how many seeds you eat in a year? Poppy seeds, sesame seeds, tomato seeds, cucumber seeds, the occasional accidental watermelon seed?"

Zane laughed. "Can't say that I did."

"I'm sorry."

"That I don't think about seeds?"

"No. That I'm eleven. And maybe too smart and absolutely awkward. But I'm sorry for what I said. I know you want to *play* football. Coaching is—"

"Elijah. Stop. You misunderstood. Coaching is . . ." Zane shook his head and looked up to keep the tears back in their ducts. "It's practically perfect. You deserve the million dollars just for that."

"Really?

"I've never meant anything more in my life."

Two Days After
THE GAMES

Bert Golliwop was practically skipping around his office. The panel of independent judges had finally returned with their ruling. The sabotage to Merry-Go-Wow had not affected the outcome of the Games. Elijah had already freed his sixth slip of paper before Zane had found his first. The Muscle could never have overtaken the Brain.

The third Gollywhopper Games was officially over. No need to call back contestants or camera crews or judges or anybody to run a new final challenge. They'd pulled off the Games with barely a hiccup. And they'd caught Ratso. The only problem was, she wouldn't admit which company—McSwell,

United GameCo, or Rinky Brothers—had paid her, probably handsomely, to sabotage the Games. That company would certainly try again if he decided to hold another Games, so he'd already set his investigators on the case. They'd crack it. Or maybe she'd crack in jail. Not that Jenkins was there yet. And why wasn't she?

His executive team and Danny were on their way to his office.

Bert barely let them get a foot in the door before he walked up to Morrison from Legal. "Why haven't they locked her up yet?"

"Nice to see you, too, Bert."

"Sorry, but you know me. I want things done."

"Then, like I said, you need to file a complaint. You need to press charges."

"She spied on us. She sold secrets to our enemy."

"This isn't like nation-to-nation warfare. It might feel like it to you," said Morrison, "but we are not the government. Her crimes aren't considered treason."

"She caused our generator to explode at the stadium last year. She rigged it so some poor girl tripped over an electrical cord. She rustled up rats in Kansas, and she hurt the Muscle; could have killed the Brain if he'd been on that side."

"I know," said Morrison, "but she's tricky. Like I've told you, the police already investigated the issues from last year, and there's still no direct evidence. No fingerprints, no nothing. No proof that Jenkins was involved, and she still swears she wasn't. Meanwhile, we have two choices. We can make sure she is a corporate outcast; make it tough for her to get a job. Her own bad name will follow her everywhere."

"One of those rat-fink companies seems to love her."

"Until they stop trusting her," said Morrison. "Or we can have her arrested. Consider, though, what happened the last time we had someone arrested."

"This time we have proof. How else would she know about the wrench?"

"I'm sure she'll claim she never said it or that you misunderstood her."

Bert Golliwop shook his head. "I can't believe I'm about to say this, but let him in."

Morrison opened the office door for Gil Goodson.

It wasn't only Gil, though. Gil's dad was right behind him.

"What's he doing here? Wouldn't sell me KidZillionaire. Would've made us a fortune."

"Still might from what I understand," said Charles Goodson. "You're poised to own Flummox, right?"

"Yes." Bert Golliwop smiled. "And your contract is with them."

"For better or for worse," said Charles Goodson. "But exactly why are we here?"

Bert related the goings-on with Jenkins. "And now I need to decide whether or not to press charges against her."

"Then decide," said Charles Goodson.

Bert shook his head. "She has kids, too."

"Since when are you this nice?" said Charles.

"I'm not." He looked directly at Gil. "How bad was it for you?"

"Pretty bad," Gil said. "But mostly because we knew my dad was innocent and no one would believe us. If he'd been guilty, losing my respect for him would have been worse, but I'd've understood why you had him arrested."

Charles Goodson clamped Gil's shoulder. "How sure are you that she's guilty, Bert?"

"Something she said. A couple of us heard—"

"It's not perfect evidence, but it was fairly condemning," said Morrison. "I have a criminal attorney heading over who can tell us if we have enough to move forward."

"The same one you had for me?" asked Charles.

"He's a good man. He just had bad information from us last time."

"I still want to know what you think, Gil," said Bert Golliwop.

"That's a lot of pressure to put on a kid," said Charles Goodson.

"It's okay, Dad." Gil turned to Bert. "If she's guilty, she should pay somehow. Just make sure this time."

"No worries," said Bert Golliwop. "I don't make the same mistake twice."

CHAPTER 40

Zane's team had just scored a touchdown, and they finally led by four points. But with twenty-four seconds left, the other team's receiver could still take the next ball all the way to the end zone. For the fourth time.

Zane took Jamaal aside.

"How many polyesters?" Jamaal said.

Zane smiled at the inside joke, but needed Jamaal to focus. "Later," he said. "Right now, number eighty-seven is going to try and beat you to the outside again. So here's what you do. Stand toe to toe with him, then move two inches toward the sideline." Zane showed him two inches with his thumb and forefinger. "When he finds there's no room around you, he'll curl inside, and you'll be ready. Just watch his eyes."

He pushed Jamaal toward the rest of the defense and glanced over at Elijah, who'd persuaded his parents to bring him here to see helmets in action. Zane tried to convince him there was better football than this—Elijah lived down the street from Northwestern University, where he'd already been accepted starting next fall, and he was a short drive from Soldier Field and the Chicago Bears—but Elijah insisted that for his first live game, he needed to see Zane as a coaching assistant.

"Two inches?" said Elijah. "How do you know that?"

"How do you know your physics stuff?"

"Just do."

"Exactly," said Zane, "but I see it as geometry. You know, the shortest distance between two points. Watch it that way."

Elijah held up the helmet he'd been carrying all game. "If I combine his geometry with my physics . . ." He turned to Jerome, who had to sit out today's game with a sprained shoulder. Zane had assigned Jerome to be Elijah's bodyguard. He didn't need the little guy to forget about the on-field action and get smashed by a play that drifted toward the sidelines. "What do you think, Jerome?"

"I don't know exactly what you're saying, little man, but you're cool, anyway."

Zane smiled at two of his worlds coming together until that jerk of a jealous seventh grader in the stands ruined the moment. "Hey, Braycott, you wimp. You won't even dress out to help us win this game. And second in the Gollywhopper Games? You loser."

"Shut your trap," said Daryl, whose garage band had performed at halftime.

"Yeah! Shut your trap!" Kelly, who still giggled at Zane, wasn't echoing only Daryl. "Shut your trap," the line Elijah used to tell off Berk, had gone viral.

Kelly, in fact, had been first, even before the JZs, to congratulate him on his second-place finish. He gave her a smile, but didn't bother to give the jerk the satisfaction of a dirty stare. If he only knew that the million dollars didn't really matter, that Zane was happier here on the middle school field than he'd been the whole time in Orchard Heights—

Who was he kidding? That guy would still be a jerk.

Instead, Zane focused on his parents' voices. For the fourth straight game, they sat side by side. They were cheering on Zoe, who'd become the first girl in school history to make the team. And she'd won the starting kicker position by a mile. Maybe she'd be the first Braycott to have a full career in the NFL.

She teed up the ball, took seven steps back and three steps sideways, and did what she'd been doing all season. She booted it high and long. The receiver fielded it on the fifteen-yard line but only advanced it to the twenty-two. Eighteen seconds left.

Zane grabbed Jamaal's arm before he went onto the field. "Remember. Two inches. And his eyes." He gave him a push toward the huddle. No question, they'd throw to 87 this time. "C'mon, Jamaal!"

Jamaal moved two inches to the outside. He brought his head up and looked, it appeared, into number 87's eyes. Eighty-seven discovered he couldn't beat Jamaal to the outside, curled in a little.

Jamaal kept his head up. Watched 87 watch the ball. Adjusted. Soared sideways, in slow motion, Zane swore, and intercepted the pass.

Zane jumped so high. "He did it! You did it!" Zane ran to Jamaal and leaped on his back.

Jerome rushed to them. "Man! That was a thing of beauty!"

It was. It was. Just let the clock run out, and they'd win. Zane could breathe. He'd done it. His idea. He sensed a pair of eyes staring at him. He turned. Looked down.

Elijah looked him straight on. "That felt almost as good as doing it yourself, didn't it?"

"Yeah, buddy. Almost."

And for that moment, almost was enough.